BIG SCREAM
IN A
WEE VILLAGE

BIG SCREAM IN A WEE VILLAGE

THE NIC KNUCKLES COLLECTION

NIC KNUCKLES

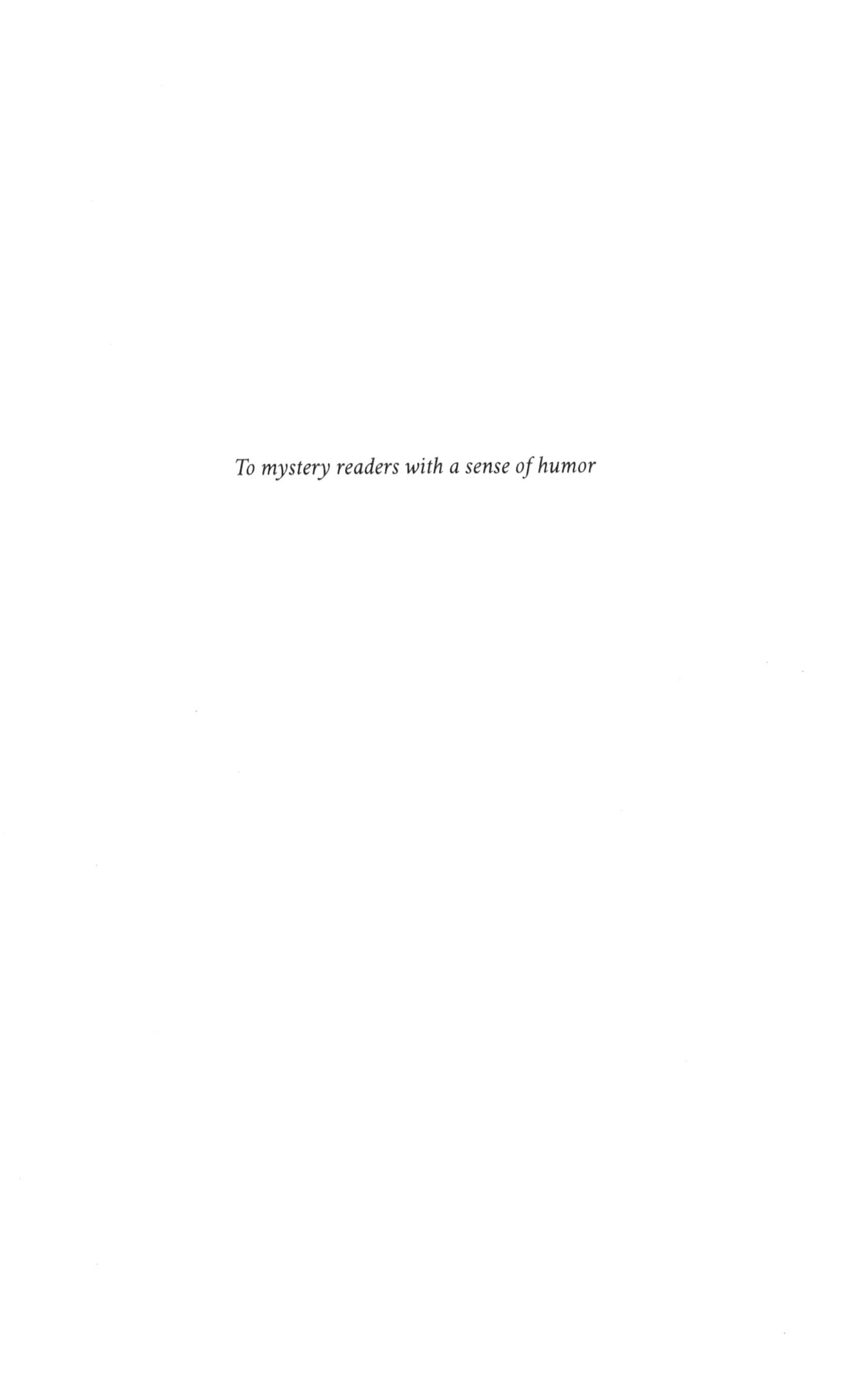

To mystery readers with a sense of humor

What Others Have Said About Nic Knuckles

"Not since Sherlock Holmes badgered the criminally-inclined of London has England seen a more audacious and dogged private investigator."—Sir Arthur Conan Doyle, as channeled at Mitzie Rosenberg's Bat Mitzvah party by **Miss Wisteria the Psychic**

"While Nic Knuckles may not be a household name, he's a clever creation with a growing fanbase—especially among readers who enjoy a blend of mystery and wit. Want a taste of Nic's style or a peek into the book's plot? I'd be happy to dive deeper."—**Robbie**, the AI Bot working for Microsoft

"I'm utterly amazed by this book. I didn't think he had it in him, not after watching him fumble through life for the past forty years."—**The author's mother-in-law**

Chapter One

It was the kind of August that New Yorkers dreaded. Living under a relentless heat dome that encapsulated all the poisonous fumes and toxic attitudes of eight million city dwellers and their modes of transportation. Some swore the girders on the Brooklyn Bridge had gone spongy, and the asphalt on 5th Avenue smelled like burnt licorice. Even the criminals, shape-shifting bond dealers or sticky-fingered pickpockets, took a break from indulging their immoral inclinations. Any private eye with half their wits retired to the dark, dank corners of their favorite speakeasy to sip something 80-proof while reminiscing about heartbreak with a woman named Sally.

Not Nic Knuckles, however. I was at Saigon Suzie's Emporium getting a pedicure. Surviving the horrid heat of a New York City summer often required wearing flip-flops; otherwise, fungus would populate my toes and make chasing the criminally disposed more difficult. Little did I know at the time that in three days, I'd be in a quaint village in the English countryside, tangling with a family that owned a dark history of unexplained deaths and disappearances.

It all started with a knock on the door, as most private eye stories do. It was a woman of uncertain antiquity, with jittery eyes, who spoke before I could say hello.

"Excuse me, sir, are you Nic Knuckles?" she asked, her slight nasal twang and flat annunciation suggesting she wasn't a local, but it sounded familiar nonetheless.

"Yes, I am. Why don't you come in and take a load off."

The woman shuffled forward as if her shoes were too tight, and I thought about sharing tips on toes and proper air circulation, but I resisted. A taut row of eyebrows across her forehead suggested she wanted to talk business, and she wanted to do it now.

"My name is Harriette Butterfield, and I require your services."

"What do you need done?" I said, adding a dramatic growl to my voice. Nic Knuckles knew potential clients felt they'd get their money's worth if the PI had an abundance of masculinity. I didn't know what my testosterone levels were. It wasn't like you could pull out a dipstick and check, so I deepened my voice just to be sure.

"I need you to determine what happened to my eldest sister, Gloria."

I liked a succinct introduction and leaned closer. "Why don't you give me a little more information," I said, "so I can see if I have the time to take you on as a client."

Butterfield pulled the dark tan leather purse resting in her hands closer to her bosom, suggesting she'd heard a few slanderous stories about New Yorkers. I drew back into my chair to give her space, and the woman relaxed.

"It was early summer in 1976, and Gloria was starting her third year of college. Even though I was only six, we were still very close."

"That's a big age difference."

Butterfield blushed as a gentle chuckle slipped from her mouth. "Yes, I was one of those *surprise* babies."

I could relate because I was one of those surprise babies myself. When I was a toddler, my mother would put me out at night like an unneutered cat, and when she opened the apartment door the next morning, acted surprised I was still there. But why slow-roll a potential client's backstory with my own? I returned to the woman sitting in front of me. "Go on," I said. "Tell me more."

"Gloria was accepted at a university in England for her year abroad. I was pretty heartbroken when I heard the news, but she was very excited. Gloria always had this fascination with British high culture and all that upper class rigmarole."

Butterfield continued, explaining how her sister left in June of 1976 and started orientation a week after arriving. Gloria frequently wrote home about her adventures and seemingly was having the time of her life.

"The family was stunned," Butterfield said, "when not more than a few months after she'd left home, Gloria wrote to announce she'd fallen in love with a rich man's son."

I felt my eyebrows shimmy up my forehead. Nic Knuckles knew what it was like to fall in love with someone with more money, greater status, and a father who called her Princess. It was amazing at first, then six months later, when her daddy lost his job, went broke, and asked you to pay his gambling debt, it all went to hell.

"Gloria planned to convince this rich boyfriend to marry her, and then she'd become a member of the British aristocracy. It was crazy."

"Was that out of character for your sister?"

The woman shook her head. "Not really. My parents always said Gloria was headstrong and determined once she set her sights on something."

"I get the feeling this love affair thing didn't work out," I said.

The skin on Butterfield's face took on a shimmer of emotion. "No," she whispered, raising the back of her left hand to dab her eye. "It didn't work out at all. We got Gloria's last letter early in January of 1977. She sounded upset with this boyfriend, but wrote that she was determined to make it work. After that, there was no more written correspondence, no phone calls, nothing. It was as if Gloria had fallen off the face of the earth."

"I assume your parents investigated your sister's disappearance."

Butterfield sniffed and spun off the rest of her story. "My folks didn't have any money to hire a private investigator, so we depended on others. Her American school was little help, and the British university claimed Gloria withdrew during the Christmas to New Year's break. The State Department eventually sent someone to investigate, and he supposedly talked to the university officials, as well as people at the manor where she stayed. It seemed Gloria and this boyfriend had broken up, and witnesses saw her taking her belongings from her dorm room and departing the school."

I was intrigued enough by Butterfield's account that I pulled a fresh notebook and pencil from my desk drawer. If Nic Knuckles was committing to a serious pursuit of justice, I needed a serious notebook to record clues, insights, conjectures, and lottery numbers that came to me in a dream.

"What was the name of the British university?" I asked.

"The University of Essex."

"Essex, huh? It probably sends the wrong message to parents when your kid's college has sex in its name."

Butterfield's lips tightened into a thin red slash. I guess she didn't find that comment informative. I quickly recovered by asking her opinion on what happened to Gloria. The woman didn't hold back.

"I think she was murdered, and I believe that rich British boyfriend had a hand in it."

I scribbled her comment into my notebook, laid the pencil on the desk, and intersected my fingers. "I have to tell you, Miss Butterfield, solving an almost fifty-year-old missing person's case, in a foreign country with their strange customs and food, is a mighty big challenge."

"I suspect so," she said.

"It won't be quick, and it'll require me spending weeks, maybe months, snooping around Merry Old England."

Butterfield's head bobbed.

"Which means, it will cost you dollars, lots and lots of dollars."

The woman sucked in a rattling breath and opened her purse. She pulled out two envelopes and placed them both on my desk. One was bursting with content, while the second looked empty. Butterfield patted the fat one and said, "This envelope contains all the letters Gloria wrote to my parents while abroad. I believe you'll find them informative and useful."

I calmly nodded, but inside my chest, my heart started thumping. Nic Knuckles sensed there were some juicy clues in those letters. It'd be a welcome challenge to apply my analytical powers as I discover clues buried among the adjectives and pronouns.

"This second envelope contains a cashier's check made out to you for twenty-five thousand dollars. It should be enough to get you across the Atlantic Ocean and settled in Village-In-Thistles, the small farming community nearest to Rockingham Manor."

"And why is this Rockingham Manor so important?"

"Because, Mister Knuckles, Gloria's former beau, the man who I believe knows what happened to my sister, lives at Rockingham Manor. His name is Myles Bethard."

I steepled my fingertips against my chin and fell deep into thought. Twenty-five grand was a pretty nice chunk of change, and having that pile of old letters would be a real time saver. My language skills were serviceable for Great Britain, what with me always talking English my whole life. It'd be nice to get away from the city's heat and humidity and spend time in the cool countryside. I also heard that the Brits made some of the best cheddar cheese in the world.

"Okay, Miss Butterfield, we have a deal."

The woman heaved a sigh, and a smile pulled at the corner of her mouth. "Excellent, Mister Knuckles, excellent."

I pulled out a contract from my desk drawer and handed it to her. She carefully read it and signed on the dotted line. I outlined my approach for communicating my progress with her, and what she could expect at the end. It took less than thirty minutes, and old Nic Knuckles was back working a private eye gig. I'd waited four months for a new murder case, and underneath my desk, I wiggled my toes in excitement.

As Butterfield and I stood and walked to the office door, I tried to satisfy my curiosity by asking, "Where are you from, Miss Butterfield?"

The woman grasped the door handle, paused, and turned back to me. "I'm from Indiana."

I snapped my fingers. "I *thought* that accent sounded familiar. I was in that part of the country about a year ago, working the big scream in a small-town murder case. I found the culprit who'd avoided justice for fifteen years and got her sent off to the big house for the rest of her life."

Butterfield's eyes glistened, and she sucked hard against dulled teeth. "I know," she said. "That criminal was my cousin, Sandi Fliminsky."

"Wow, I remember Sandi. What a small world, huh?"

"Smaller than you think," she said. "Sandi actually recommended I hire you."

I braced a hand against the door frame. "You're pulling my leg, right?"

Butterfield's shoulders gently rose. "No, I'm not. As much as Sandi resented you for solving the case and upending her life, she did admire your sleuthing skills."

I felt my chest press tight against my shirt. It wasn't too often that someone I helped send to the slammer gave me a compliment. Usually, their last words were hot with threats to my anatomy. I guessed Hoosiers, even the bad ones, couldn't help but be affable. Hopefully, I'd find that same sort of ah shucks friendliness in rural England.

Chapter Two

A long-ago failed relationship with a TSA agent named Bubbles caused me trouble getting through England's Heathrow Airport. The British Customs Official was a short, red-headed woman who exuded all the warmth of a cane toad. She'd pulled me from the line, stripped me nearly naked, and held me off to the side while a hundred other passengers were cleared. Every mother's admonishment about always wearing clean underwear rattled around in my head as the adults side-eyed me with shame and their kids pointed and snickered.

"Bubbles sends her regards," the British Customs official said with a sneer as I was finally sent through the checkpoint. I guessed my theory of an international cabal of disgruntled airport workers had some validity. I added investigating those people to my bucket list, along with busting the underground network of diner waitresses who tracked lousy tippers around the country. I had a busy retirement planned when the time came.

As a born and bred New Yorker, I did not need a car in the US, so the idea of Nic Knuckles motoring around England was never a consideration. I intended to ride the famous British Rail system to get to Village-In-Thistles. But first, I needed to escape the maw of Heathrow Airport and locate the appropriate train station. Fortunately, my cellphone had an app called What Ya Say? that translated the British gibberish of the airport personnel into American English with a Bronx accent. I quickly identified the correct train and soon departed from the Essex Road station for a two-hour ride, eating crisps and biscuits as the train moved my weary bones to East Essex in southeast England.

A regional bus took me from the Witham Railway station and dropped me a quarter-mile walk from my destination, Village-In-Thistles. It was after seven in the evening when I entered the village proper and wandered up a cobblestone street, exhausted and hungry. Just as I was about to despair, the travel gods shined their grace on me. I spotted a sign in the window of the Village Launderette, offering a room to let. That's where I met its proprietor, a smiling, ruddy-faced woman who went by the name of Gram Edwards.

"Just call me, Gram," she said. "Me wee bairn couldn't handle more than one syllable, so they call me Gram, instead of Granmama, like I preferred. They're dullards like their bloody father, they are."

Gram led me upstairs to a decent-sized room with a Murphy Bed, a private bathroom, and a reasonable weekly charge unless I miscalculated the dollar-to-pound conversion. She assured me that I'd get used to the bleach smell wafting up from the laundry below, and she claimed previous boarders found the sound of the rumbling clothes dryers therapeutic. I was so exhausted from travel that I skipped haggling for a better price. The New Yorker in me cringed at my laxness, but I was too wiped to care.

Once Gram Edwards closed the door on me, I collapsed onto the bed and fell into a deep sleep. I had strange dreams of being smothered by a lumpy pancake, but I suspected the Murphy Bed might've closed up with me in it once during the night. Nonetheless, I woke at about eight the next day, took a cold shower, and dressed, feeling completely refreshed. Nic Knuckles was ready to get out and solve yet another crime of the century.

"Morning, dearie," was the greeting I heard as I trundled down the stairs from my third-floor room. Gram Edwards, as perky as she appeared the night before, stood in the kitchen just off the stairs leading down to the launderette. She handed me a cup of tea and waved me into the kitchen. "Sit down here at the wee table and explain what an American is doin' here in our village."

"I'm Nic Knuckles, world-famous private eye," I said, "perhaps you've heard of me."

Gram slipped a plate with three biscuits on the table and shook her head.

"No, can't say I've heard of Nic Knuckles. I know of a Nuc Pickles who works a fair-sized farm over on the other side of the river, but no Nic Knuckles."

Maybe my jet lag was worse than I'd admit, because I wanted to snap back at her, crying, "You'll know who Nic Knuckles is by the time I get through with this little burg," but I didn't. Those villages can be tight-knit, and I couldn't afford to alienate anyone before I knew who was who in Village-In-Thistles.

"So, you gonna tell me why a foreigner who isn't a tourist has leased me spare room?"

"I've been hired to investigate the disappearance of a young American woman nearly fifty years ago. She was involved in a torrid love affair with one of your illustrious community leaders."

A cheetah wearing a jet pack couldn't move any quicker than Gram throwing her tush onto the chair across from me. "You don't say."

"Did you ever meet a young American woman named Gloria Butterfield?" I asked. "She was visiting the village in late 1976."

Gram shook her head. "Sorry, dearie, I didn't move here until 1978, so I missed her."

"That's too bad. What can you tell me about a man named Myles Bethard?" I asked.

The fingertips of Gram's right hand rose to her mouth as her eyes clouded over in thought. "Oh my, not much, sadly. I've never properly met the man, but his reputation is a wee bit dodgy. In fact, dearie, his whole family is known to be more than a bit dodgy."

While flying over from America, I'd read all of Gloria Butterfield's letters to her parents, so I had a list of the characters making up the Bethard family. If she knew nothing of Myles, maybe Gram knew something about one of the others.

"How about Colonel Jeremy Bethard, the patriarch of the clan. Is he still alive?"

"Oh no, dearie. He came to a sticky end probably ten years ago, perhaps longer."

"A sticky end, huh?" I pulled my notebook and pencil from my jacket and scratched down a line about glue, honey, or some other adhesive apparently responsible for the Colonel's death. I'm not even in England twenty-four hours and the British ways are already proving to be weird. No wonder Sherlock Holmes was on morphine, dealing with such criminal darkness.

"Now his wife, old Rosemond, is still takin' up space," Gram said. "That coffin dodger gotta be almost ninety, although I've never seen her out in public since the Colonel died."

"How about Myles's sister, Cissy. Is she still around here?"

A rumble of a chuckle worked its way up from deep inside Gram's chest before bubbling out of her mouth. "Oh, dearie, we only know Cissy as the Yellow Widow."

That comment made me cringe. "Is that more British slang that I'm failing to decipher?"

"No, she's known as the Yellow Widow because she's been married four times and widowed three. She wears bright yellow dresses to her husband's funerals, and the village thinks she's quite mental."

I recorded that comment and several others that Gram shared with me, like Cissy and her fourth husband lived at Rockingham Manor, along with Myles's wife, the Reverend Amethyst Bethard, an Anglican priest. There was also a daughter from Cissy and an earlier, unlucky husband's marriage, but Gram had no name.

"Well," I said, "I guess I'm going have to get to that Rockingham Manor and do me a look-see. How far is the place from here, Gram?"

"Oh, a little shy of two kilometers. You go up the dirt path behind the pub called Pissin' Pints and continue past the sheep dip tank. You can't miss the Manor because it's a whopper of a building."

Two kilometers, I thought to myself. How much was that? Two can't be that many, right? I could easily walk two of anything.

"Thanks for the information, Gram. I think I'll finish my tea and head on out."

The woman reached into an opened package of biscuits and added a few more to my plate. "You know, Nic, those Manor folks will clam up around a stranger like you. Now, since the locals are generally pissed off with the dandies living in Rockingham Manor, you might learn more from them, you know what I'm sayin'?"

Of course, I knew what Gram meant. One basic rule of sleuthing is to use the eyes, ears, and mouths of everyone and anyone. High or low, educated or ignorant, people see, hear, and smell things that might help you solve the case.

"I'll be sure to reach out to the friendly folks here in the village."

Gram patted my hand. "You know something else, Nic? Your missin' American lass isn't the first person to meet an unhappy end with the Bethards. You better be careful."

"That's also good to know, Gram," I said, closing my notebook and returning it to my sports coat pocket. "I appreciate you sharing your village wisdom."

"Of course, dearie. Is there anything else I can do for you before you go?"

The woman must've read my mind because I did have another question: "Do you have some cheddar cheese to go along with these biscuits?"

Chapter Three

I stepped away from Gram Edwards' kitchen, the flavor of a well-aged cheddar cheese still on my tongue. As much as I valued Gram's opinion that the chatty local folks would be a more fruitful conversation than what I'd get at Rockingham Manor, I was determined to make my first official call to the Bethard family.

Slipping down the stairs and through the launderette, I passed a bleary-eyed backpacker washing his clothes. Outside, I turned left and back onto the single street and main drag of Village-In-Thistles. Across the way was an apothecary, and next to it, a pub called the Pinecone and Wizard. Adjacent to the pub was a white stone building with a small bronze plaque attached to the red-painted front door, stating that Dr. Watson Johnson took patients there.

It was a chilly morning, which my toes appreciated, as they would now be confined to shoes for the duration of my visit. I continued up the busy street, and as the villagers scurried past me, I felt their eyes scanning my body and face. When their gaze hardened and the corners of their mouths turned down, I knew they were judging me. Being from New York City, where you never made eye contact with strangers, I felt uncomfortable. But if those villagers thought they could intimidate Nic Knuckles with a disapproving stare, they didn't know about my Nana. That woman once froze a rabid Pekingese in its tracks with nothing but her flinty glower.

Further up the street and to my left was another pub. This one had a giant wooden fist holding a red-painted dagger above the entrance, with Wasted Swan inscribed below it in dark green lettering. Back home, most taverns

Nic Knuckles visited might have a flickering electric sign that spelled out B-A-R, but that was it as far as artwork. I had to give the Brits credit; they worked hard at their beer-joint branding.

I took another fifteen steps and was drawn to a storefront with Warford's What Nots stenciled on the large, plate-glass window. I walked over to look inside to see what, whatnot, might be offered. It looked like a combination hardware store, bodega, and thrift shop, all rolled into one. I didn't think I'd ever seen a store with a more appropriate name. I'd check it out later to see if they sold those famous fish and chips that everyone talked about.

I passed several small cottages and their tiny, well-tended gardens on both sides of the street before arriving at the Pissin' Pints. From the outside, it looked much like the other two pubs in the village. If Gram Edwards was correct and I'd eventually have to tap into the heads of the locals to learn the secrets of the Bethard family, I'd probably spend a lot of time in here. I wasn't happy with that prospect, not with my tiny bladder and tendency to fall asleep after a few beers. Hopefully, my well-honed skills as an interrogator would work magic with the sober folks at The Rock, and I wouldn't have to pub crawl to find out what happened to Gloria Butterfield.

I stepped behind the Pissin' Pints and found the gravel path Gram had spoken of. I stumbled a hundred steps along the way as my eyes watered from an awful smell coming from beyond the big fence to my right. It was some structure that looked like a narrow swimming pool filled with dark brown water. I guessed that was the sheep dip Gram talked about. Knowing nothing about farm animals and their hygienic needs, the thing reminded me of my childhood Saturday night bath when mom made me use the same water that my three sisters used to scrub off their weekly grit and grime. Only that water smelled slightly better than what the poor sheep had to bathe in.

The farm landscape of plowed fields and stone fences was soon replaced by thick woods on both sides of the path and all those woodland animals you couldn't see, but you heard. And don't get me started on the trolls, fairies, or other underworld critters sneaking around in the weeds. I knew the British Isles were teeming with such unnatural creatures. Give me old-fashioned concrete and asphalt, squirrels, and pigeons any day.

Finally, the woods cleared, and about a hundred yards ahead, I saw a big old house like nothing I'd seen before. It was made out of stone blocks stacked three stories high, and topped off with a steep blue-green slate roof. Windows peeped out from beneath the English Ivy, covering the structure's front and sides. As I got closer, I noticed weeds had broken through the grout of the brick walkway, and the fencing alongside a field sagged heavily. I'd never owned a house, but Nic Knuckles had more than a few wealthy clients who lived beyond their means, and the care of their homes were the first thing to go.

I hoofed it up to the big wooden door and lifted the heavy iron knocker, dropping it three times. A clanging of a deadbolt being thrown open was followed by the sound of rusty hinges being worked against their will. Peeking through the space between the door frame and the door was an older woman with watery blue eyes. Strands of almost white hair hung limply from underneath some unhip durag.

"Yullo," she said.

"Good morning, madam; I'm Nic Knuckles, and may I ask with whom I'm speaking?"

The woman's eyes narrowed as the door opened wider, and she took a closer look at me. "I'm Melba, and I'm the cook and housekeeper. What do you want?"

"I'm here to speak with Myles Bethard. Is he available?"

Melba, who looked well north of seventy years old, rolled her eyes at me again. "Do you have an appointment?"

"I do not, but I've come from the good old US of A, so I hope Mister Bethard will give me a break and meet with me."

Melba grunted and said, "Hang on, as I'll check." The door closed, and I heard the deadbolt slide into place. I turned around and took in the property. About a hundred feet away was an outbuilding with missing roof tile and a rusted tractor parked in front of it. The fields further away were overgrown with scrub and small trees, and it was weirdly quiet. I mean, I wasn't a farm boy by anyone's imagination, but I still expected more animal noises.

No mooing cows or bleating sheep could be heard, although the sound of clucking chickens indicated some fowl were being kept somewhere. I couldn't see any pigs, but I could smell them.

I recalled Gloria's letters to her folks mentioning a struggling farm owned by the Bethard family. She thought she and Myles could someday make it profitable. It was one of their many shared dreams of a life together.

Judging from the unkempt property, it looked like Myles could never accomplish that feat alone. Thriving agriculture wasn't being practiced at Rockingham Manor.

The clank of the deadbolt lock on the other side of the door signaled Melba's return. Her expression wasn't any more welcoming than when I first saw her.

"What's the purpose of your visit?" she asked.

"I'd like to talk with Mister Bethard about an acquaintance of his who went missing back in the late seventies."

I swore I saw a minute flaring of Melba's nostrils. "And, whom might that be?" she asked.

"Her name was Gloria, Gloria Butterfield. She was romantically involved with Myles, perhaps even engaged to be married."

The muscles around Melba's eyes tightened, making her look like a naked mole rat who was also a mobster's defense attorney. "Mister Bethard has no time for you," she said, "good day, sir."

With one quick maneuver, Melba slammed the door, bolted the lock, and left me stunned.

"If you think Nic Knuckles is giving up, you have another think coming, Melba," I said. I don't know why I was shouting at a big wooden door that was probably two hundred years old and had seen many a fool turned away. But it felt good and, to my surprise, my tantrum paid off.

"What can I help you with, mate?"

Standing behind me was a man in his mid-fifties, balding in the undisciplined way most men in their mid-fifties go.

"Well, I'd like to meet with Myles Bethard, the owner of this broken-down mansion."

The man smiled. "Mister Myles is a difficult bloke to get to a sit-down," he said. He then introduced himself as Rufford, no last name, and apologized for Melba's rudeness. "Me mum can be quite protective of the Bethard family. She's been their housekeeper since before I was born."

Rufford continued sharing his story, telling me how he'd grown up on the estate, him and his mother living in the servants' quarters. He attended the village school until he was fifteen and then worked on the surrounding farms until ten years ago, when a cow kicked him in the head. Apparently, that blow to the old noggin created a rare auditory capability where he could understand the squealing of pigs, but only the Gloucester Old Spot variety. He'd get so anxious around the early winter slaughter when the pigs asked him if they were *really* going on a field trip to the Victoria and Albert Museum. Now, the man kept close to the manor, running errands for his mother or other members of the Bethard family.

"Any chance you saw a young American woman here in the late seventies?"

Rufford nodded. "Are you talking about Miss Gloria?"

Oh, baby, Nic Knuckles might've just struck the information motherlode. Rufford was not only a talker but also had a long history with the estate. I lifted my notebook and pencil from my inside coat pocket.

"Yes, I am, my peculiar friend," I said. "What can you tell me about her?"

Rufford folded his beefy arms across his chest as his eyes went dreamy. "I was ten years old when Mister Myles brought her to Rockingham Manor. Miss Gloria, as me mum instructed me to address her, was beautiful. She was almost as tall as Mister Myles, and she had beautiful red hair and a laugh that made you want to be around her."

"How did Myles's parents feel about Gloria?" I asked, hoping to confirm their hostility as noted by Gloria in her letters.

"The Colonel never approved, for sure. It's not that he disliked the girl, but he thought she was distracting Mister Myles from his schoolwork. Or, at least, that was what me mum always told me. She always knew who was doing what around the Manor, she did."

I found that odd. I once watched this PBS series about British aristocracy called The Rich and the Wretched, and someone like a housekeeper would never talk with the big boss of the manor, especially about personal matters.

"Was your mother tight with the Colonel?" I asked.

The side of Rufford's mouth hitched up. "Ah, no, mate, mum knew her place. She was always afraid she'd get fired, and me and her would be on the outside. But living in a house for almost fifty years, you hear and see a lot, you know what I mean?"

"How did Myles' mother feel about Gloria?"

"Oh my, Miss Rosemond was absolutely gutted over Miss Gloria. She hated foreigners unless they had some lineage to offer, and even then, she looked down on them. The idea Miss Gloria might marry Miss Rosemond's precious Myles was too much for her. Even now, as a grown bloke, I steer clear of Miss Rosemond."

I scratched in my notebook a summary of Rufford's observations of Miss Rosemond and her snooty attitude before asking, "What can you tell me about the Yellow Widow?"

Rufford cocked his head to one side, seemingly surprised I knew Cissy's moniker. That's how Nic Knuckles liked to operate, keeping people off guard so they never knew what might come out of my mouth. I didn't, so why should they have an advantage?

Cissy and her multiple spouses lived in an apartment within Rockingham Manor, and Rufford had seen and heard about everything regarding the woman and the troubling men in her life. It didn't take much encouragement for him to spill some details.

"Miss Cissy was nineteen when Miss Gloria showed up. Mum said Miss Cissy liked Miss Gloria only because the woman made Mister Myles look bad in the eyes of the Colonel and Miss Rosemond."

Nic Knuckles had three sisters, and he knew how much joy female siblings got from tormenting the family boy. My sisters were like a pack of hyenas circling an innocent baby gazelle, laughing and snarling. But I didn't have time to relive those horrors, not with Rufford rattling on about Cissy.

"Miss Cissy married her first husband, Baron Monteque when she was twenty-one, and it was a marriage with lots of fightin'. It ended about six years later when the man died."

"How'd the Baron catch the A Train to the afterlife?"

Rufford shrugged. "I dunno, but probably the ol' heart gave out. I don't know for sure, but he wasn't an old bloke when he passed, maybe fifty."

I quickly created a separate page in my notebook for Cissy Bethard. I had a feeling Rufford was going to give me more dope than my poor brain could keep organized.

"She then married Count Blix-Vixen when she was about thirty, making her a ledge in Miss Rosemond's eyes. They had a daughter they named Turquoise, who still lives in the Manor. And, trust me, mate, as the Colonel and Miss Rosemond's only grandchild, she is a spoiled scrounger."

Like Cissy's first husband, Rufford claimed the Count met an untimely death after seven years of a tempestuous marriage. When I pushed Rufford to explain why he thought the deaths were untimely, he gave me a snarky look. "Don't be a plonker, mate. Those men were years older than Miss Cissy, but the Baron and the Count weren't buffers. You know what I mean?"

I jotted down his comment and would later have Gram translate the slang. Rufford's excessive use of local jargon made me wonder if he was trying to pull a fast one on Nic Knuckles. If I later confronted him about his comments, he could always argue that I misunderstood him. One thing I'd learned solving crime all across America is that the more someone wanted to help me, the more likely they were trying to protect themselves from legal trouble.

"Miss Cissy recovered from the Count's death and married a nice bloke named Brice Johnson. Pricey Bricey, as the family called him, didn't have a title but was minted. It seemed he was just as much a shark as Miss Cissy, because, as a real estate developer, he had hopes of sub-dividing Rockingham Manor into housing. But the Colonel never allowed that to happen, and the marriage ended after eight years."

"I assume Mister Johnson eventually died from some undiagnosed ailment," I said.

Rufford slowly rolled his head side-to-side. "Naw, the poor bugger fell from the roof of the Manor and broke his neck."

"What the heck was he doing on the roof?"

Rufford's lips squiggled like a worm on a hot plate. "Another mystery, innit. Just another bloody mysterious death for the Yellow Widow."

"According to my count, that's three husbands for Cissy. I'd heard there were four."

Rufford pushed his hands into the pockets of his slacks and bowed his head. "Miss Cissy married a widower about ten years ago. His name is Alexander Wilton Dinwiddie, and everyone figures the bloke is a perfect match for Cissy."

"Why's that?"

"Dinwiddie has been married five times and buried three wives, so he knows his way around a matrimonial cage match. But I'm still betting on Miss Cissy to outlive him."

Before turning to a new subject, I finished scribbling my notes on Cissy Bethard, Baron Monteque, Count Blix-Vixen, builder Johnson, and multiple widower Dinwiddie.

"You said your mother has worked at The Rock for fifty years."

"More like sixty years," Rufford corrected. "She was but sixteen when Miss Rosemond hired her on."

"When I mentioned Gloria's name to your mother, she seemed upset. Do you have any reason to explain why?"

Rufford did offer an opinion on Melba's hostile reaction to the mention of Miss Butterfield. It seemed whenever Gloria visited Rockingham Manor, she'd complain about the American conveniences she missed, like peanut butter, Mexican food, or ice cubes. The woman would whine to Myles, who'd turn on Melba and demand that she gin up a substitute.

"Mum felt Mister Myles would do anything to make things right for Gloria. Me mum was raising a child of her own, and working full time as the housekeeper and cook, so she had no patience for Miss Gloria and her demands."

I finished recording Rufford's comments and closed the notebook. "Sounds like to me, other than Myles and you, no one was very fond of Gloria Butterfield back then."

Rufford's eyebrows pulled together as if he were squeezing a memory from the dry sponge of his mind. "I think Gloria got along well with Mister Bristol. I recall him trying to be her friend."

Who was Bristol? I didn't recall seeing that name mentioned in Gloria's letters.

"How was this Bristol connected to Rockingham Manor?" I asked.

"He's married to Miss Pauline."

"And who is Pauline?"

"She's the Colonel's daughter."

"I thought Cissy was his only daughter?"

Rufford smiled. "I'm being a bit loose-lipped here, but bloody hell, those Bethards have a few secrets, don't they?"

Chapter Four

I returned directly to the Village Launderette after my encounter with Rufford. He'd given me a good start on understanding the Butterfield-Bethard dynamics from 1976 but left me hanging when he introduced a daughter and son-in-law I'd never heard of.

I had to admit an uncomfortable connection with him, a man well into adulthood with an unhealthy relationship with his mother. Not that I lived with my mom like he did. My mother always insisted I leave the nest and survive on my own. Sure, Child Protective Services kept bringing me back, telling her that an eight-year-old kid was not ready to live on the streets of New York City, but I was never a momma's boy.

"So, how was your first mornin' walking among the pleasant folks of our wee village?" Gram Edwards called out as she stood by an industrial-sized dryer, pinching lint from a screen. "What did you learn, Mister Knuckles?"

"I found my way to The Rock and got a frosty greeting from the Bethard housekeeper, Melba," I said. "Then I met her boy, Rufford, and found him to be as chatty as a happy squirrel with a bag of nuts."

"Let me make you a cuppa," Gram said, waving me over. "And you can tell me all about it."

The woman stepped to a rumbling clothes dryer with a teapot atop it, wisps of steam drifting from its spout. "Does that dryer run hot enough to boil water?" I asked.

Gram smiled as she lifted the kettle and poured the steaming water into two teacups. "They say a legitimate Englishman can't be far from a cup of tea or they'll shrivel up and die, so I tap the heat from the dryer, and me customers can help themselves to a lovely cuppa whenever they desire. Pretty clever, init?"

I congratulated Gram on her customer service acumen and proceeded to dunk a tea bag into the hot water, like it was a suspected witch in 1693 Salem, Massachusetts. "Let me update you," I said. "My new best friend, Rufford, gave me a high-level overview of the Bethard family history. He said Jeremy, more famously known as the Colonel, didn't approve of Myles's relationship with Gloria because it threatened his son's academic performance. And, oh boy, that Rosemond was a total snob. That woman hated Gloria and her humble Yankee background."

Gram slurped her tea and nodded more vigorously with each revelation I shared. She seemed to be having a grand time.

"And I gotta say, Gram, you called it about the Yellow Widow. Cissy has been busy for decades burying husbands left and right. She's a gravedigger's best friend."

"That's all good and well, dearie, but I'd watch me self around that Rufford," Gram said, "and his mother even more. That woman may be simple downstairs staff, but she's dodgy, or so I hear."

Gram swallowed the contents of her teacup and lifted the kettle for a refill. I decided now was a good time to satisfy my curiosity about all things Gram Edwards. It was one thing to trust the woman to provide a clean room and another to use her as a primary source for information. I opened my notebook and created a page dedicated to her.

"What's your story, Gram?" I asked. "I'm guessing you're a transplanted lassie from Scotland, what with you dropping the wee this and wee that."

Gram blushed and blew air over the top of her cup. "There's no foolin' you, Mister Knuckles. Me and my Jimmy met in Glasgow. He was a sailor on leave, and I was a wee bairn just out of school. We hit it off straightaways and jumped the broomstick soon after, but there was no reason for us to stay in Glasgow, so we came here to this part of England where Jimmy had relatives."

Hearing Grams' story of young lovers pulling up stakes and taking a chance in the world reminded me of one of my first loves, Loose Limbs Libby. We, too, were an adventurous couple ready to make our way in the world, but unlike Gram and Jimmy, it wasn't meant to be.

I shut down my rising sentimentality and fell back into listening to Gram telling her story.

"It was 1978 when Jimmy brought me here, and we opened a pub and then this launderette. We called the pub, The Wash & Rinse, and yeah, I know, you think that'd be the laundry's name, but me Jimmy had a wicked sense of humor, he did. Sadly, Jimmy also didn't have an ounce of common sense, he liked a drop of the good stuff, you understand? And what wee profits we earned from the pub and the laundry, Lord forgive me, he pissed up the wall. Soon his liver collected on all that abuse and widowed me ten years ago. So yeah, me tale is one of woe, it is."

"I know what you mean, Gram," I said. The story of Jimmy's weaknesses reminded me of Loose Limb Libby's bad habit and how it eventually cost me dearly, as well. She ate Velveeta, and I was a gorgonzola man. I tried to wean her off the fake stuff but she was weak, and the taste for emulsifying salts was too strong. At least Gram ended up with a thriving business enterprise. All I got was a broken heart.

Pulling back from the tearful brink of sad recollections took me a few seconds, but I got my act together and resumed recording Gram's backstory.

"By the time Jimmy went toes up, I'd become part of the village and had no reason to move back to Scotland," she said. "Village-In-Thistles is me home, now."

"Being the center of commerce here in the village must've given you an opportunity to meet and know the locals."

"Aye it, did, laddie. I also got to know me fellow merchants, a gossipy gaggle if there ever was one. I know as much about this wee village, even if half of it isn't true."

"You're an investigator's Godsend, Gram," I said, as sincerely as anything I'd say that day. Hopefully, her extensive village knowledge would be able to help me learn more about the people on my suspect list, as well as any new ones I might meet along the way.

I flipped my notebook to my scribblings taken after my visit to The Rock and quickly found the note of interest I wanted.

"Rufford mentioned a woman named Pauline, and a man called Bristol, who were Bethard family relatives, but didn't live at the big house. And he was especially coy when talking about them, giving me little more than a wink. What can you tell me about those two?"

"Oh, everyone in the village knows Pauline and Bristol Warford. She's the Colonel's daughter from his first marriage. Other than gossip, no one knows who did what to whom to get her expelled from the Bethard estate, but I'd wager that Rosemond had a hand in it."

"Do you have any idea where Pauline and Bristol live now? I'd love to meet them."

Gram chuckled into her teacup. "If you wanna see them in the flesh, they operate a shop not far from me door, you know?"

"Warford's What Nots," I said, snapping my finger. "I was just there this morning looking into their window."

After quickly adding Gram's revelation about Pauline and Bristol in my notebook, I paged back to my list of useful sources earlier gleaned from Gloria's letters to her parents.

"Miss Butterfield mentioned a woman in her last letter home. It was the only time I saw her referenced. Did you ever hear of someone called Aunt Jane, no last name?"

Gram sputtered and sent a spray of tea out her mouth. "Oh, my, so your lass knew Aunt Jane. That's no surprise, I guess. Of course, Jane, that old busybody, would have stuck her nose into the business of a missing woman."

Without any probing on my part, Gram described the now-deceased older woman known throughout Village-In-Thistles as Aunt Jane, the amateur sleuth who'd put away dozens of East Sussex criminals and malcontents.

"Some folks confuse her with her doppelganger, who operated in the village, St. Mary Mead, northwest of here, but our Aunt Jane was smarter, more meddlesome, and feared, not beloved. She had the bloody talent for sniffing out your worst days, no matter how many years ago it might've happened. Yes, she did, that woman."

"Too bad for me she's deceased," I said. "I'd love to match wits with her and learn what she thought about the mysterious disappearance of Gloria Butterfield."

Gram poured more hot water in her cup and continued dipping the tea bag until the liquid achieved the desired copper color.

"You're in luck, Mister Knuckles. Aunt Jane had a niece who lived with her for many years. She has a reputation for solving criminal cases that rivals her auntie."

I poised my pencil over the page. "And her name might be?"

"Lizabeth, Lizabeth West. She lives down the lane, just off the gravel path that edges the meadow."

I thanked Gram for the information before asking whether she had any of that excellent cheddar cheese she'd served me earlier. The woman bounced from her chair and scurried up the stairs from the launderette to her kitchen. Alone, with nothing more than the rumbling dryers, my thoughts shifted to Lizabeth West. The prospect of going up against an amateur private eye, especially someone whose only skill was being a nosey Nancy, concerned me. True private investigators were hard-boiled, and you didn't get that way by solving murder cases while running a neighborhood bake sale. You had to get knocked around, have a .38 pointed in your face, taste blood in your mouth after taking a knuckle sandwich. Those busybodies with their supernatural observational powers were a different sort of sleuth. I'd have to be on my toes whenever I interacted with her.

But first, I'd have to find what the Brits called the WC. Less than a cup of Earl Grey and I was crossing my knees to keep from embarrassing myself. Gram, however, kept pounding down teacup after teacup. I tried to calculate the size of the woman's bladder based on her height, weight, and the amount of tea she consumed in front of me. From what I'd observed, her bladder had to be half her body weight.

Chapter Five

Unlike my hometown of New York City, where public transportation was critical, I could quickly get around Village-In-Thistles on foot. After leaving Gram Edwards and her perpetual tea brewing laundry, my first target was the shop operated by Myles Bethard's half-sister, Pauline. Maybe I couldn't breach the walls of Rockingham Manor, but Pauline might help me learn what had gone on inside there decades ago. A little bell triggered when I opened the door, and a woman materialized from behind a curtain. She didn't seem delighted to see me, but judging from the deep lines around her eyes and mouth, joy wasn't something she experienced much at all.

"Hello," I said. "I'm looking for Pauline Warford."

The gleam in the woman's eye cooled further. "I'm Pauline Warford. Who are you?"

I slipped my card on top of the glass counter. "I'm Nic Knuckles, private investigator. I've been hired to discover what happened to a young American girl visiting this part of England in late 1976."

The woman didn't pick up my card, keeping her focus on my hands as if she expected me to do something dangerous, like pull a gun. I hated when people made that assumption after hearing my New York City accent.

"Her name was Gloria Butterfield, and she was romantically involved with your relative, Myles Bethard. Perhaps you met her back then."

"I met her once," Pauline said, "She came in, and we spoke briefly."

"A lot can be said briefly."

"She told me she was Myles' friend, and I said I couldn't care less, and she left. Why don't you speak with Myles if you want to know about this Gloria woman?"

"I intend to do that. But right now, I'm working my way up the food chain, talking to the minnows before going after the whales. It's a proven private eye approach to gathering information."

The woman nodded as she chewed the inside of her mouth, apparently unimpressed with my sharing of effective investigative techniques.

"So, you had no curiosity about a young woman rumored to be the paramour of your brother, Myles?"

"Half-brother," she said, and then whispered, "and the great disappointment for our father."

"Come again."

A tremor along the edge of Pauline's lower lip suggested a suppressed smile. "The only thing I found interesting about this American girlfriend was how the Colonel and his wife were probably angry over Myles' choice. Yes, I was pretty chuffed thinking about that."

A notebook and pencil appeared in my hands and I started scribbling. Now we're making progress, I thought. Nic Knuckles might've found the disgruntled relative that all private eyes hope to find during their investigations. There's no more potent incentive to be transparent than family bitterness toward each other.

"What can you tell me about Myles and his relationship with his parents?"

"Myles was a pompous Little Lord Fauntleroy who was bullied by his father and manipulated by his mother."

"Do you now have many interactions with Myles?"

Pauline grunted and related how Myles had always treated her as the pathetic half-sister. "He's no better than our father. I can't stand to be in the same space with him or Rosemond. I never could, and I never will."

I felt a presence fill the air behind me and turned to see a large, older man coming around me and joining Pauline behind the counter. He looked about the same age as the woman, reinforcing my suspicion that Village-In-Thistles was a final gathering place for British Baby Boomers.

"Cheers, mate, I'm Bristol Warford." The man gently caressed Pauline's shoulder. "I heard you asking about Gloria Butterfield."

Pauline's eyes shifted from me toward her husband. "I have things to do."

Bristol grinned and stepped aside to let Pauline move and leave the shop through the curtained back entry. He then pointed toward a pair of chairs near the store's front.

"Let's sit and talk. Would you like some tea?"

I passed on the flavorless brown hot water and soon had Bristol yammering about his personal history. The man was a local lad who met Pauline Bethard in 1974, or about then, as best he could remember. He knew he was lucky that Paulie, as he called her, agreed to become his wife, with her being of Bethard blood and him being the local son of a farmer. According to Bristol, however, the Colonel and Rosemond supported the marriage.

"The Colonel helped me, and Paulie set up a cottage in the village and gave us a start to get inventory for the shop. As you might think, based on what my wife said, she was more than happy to get away from the Colonel, his wife, and her brother and sister. She claimed they'd always treated her poorly, although I never had problems with either the Colonel or Miss Rosemond."

Bristol glanced behind us before pulling closer to me. "This is our secret, mate, but we'd never make it without Miss Rosemond buying up much of our inventory. I appreciate her being a loyal customer, but me Paulie sees it as charity and despises the woman."

Rosemond Bethard, wicked stepmother or generous benefactor, who knew?

I recorded that thought and twice underlined it.

"Tell me everything you remember about Gloria," I said.

"It was December and very cold when I first saw her. I'd arrived at the Manor to make a delivery, you know, sausages, tins of biscuits, toothpicks, stuff needed to operate a manor. I see a young woman standing in the garden. She looked knackered. I didn't know who she was or why she'd be on the grounds, so I left the delivery in my van and walked over to check her out."

Bristol reclined deeper into the chair and continued. "I introduced myself. She said she was Gloria Butterfield and that she was a guest of Myles. Once she heard that the Colonel and Miss Rosemond were my in-laws, she asked all manner of questions about them. The poor thing couldn't understand why Myles' parents were so unfriendly toward her. She swore Rosemond was particularly cold."

My brain whirled like a slide projector carousel, flashing the images of Gloria's letters to her family. She'd written several times that Myles' folks were frosty at best and intent on destroying her relationship with Myles at worst.

"Did Miss Butterfield have a legit concern about the Colonel and his wife?" I asked.

Bristol's chest rose with a low rumble of laughter. "I told her if your bloodline was of a higher status than Miss Rosemond's ancestry, then you were golden. But if you were common, there'd be a steep hill to climb to get into the family graces."

"How'd you escape unscathed, knowing how judgmental Rosemond was about where people came from."

Bristol confided that since Pauline wasn't Rosemond's child, she wasn't bothered by him, a local farm boy, marrying her stepdaughter. In fact, after first meeting him, she'd deemed Bristol a suitable husband and actively promoted the idea with the Colonel.

"I wasn't fooled," Bristol said. "I knew she liked me because I was a way to get Paulie out of the Manor. That's why I think me and Gloria hit it off because we were kindred spirits, of sorts. Now I had a different opinion of Cissy, however. Gloria thought the girl was just the dog's bollocks, but I knew Cissy, and I warned Gloria not to trust her."

I looked up from my notebook and laid an insight on the man. "I imagine the Yellow Widow showed her devious tendencies early."

A smirk slowly crawled across Bristol's face. "Cissy seemed to have the bad luck of having people falling in love with her and then dying before their time."

"Was it just bad luck?" I asked. "Did the local law enforcement ever investigate those deaths?"

Bristol drank from his teacup, smacked his lips, and answered. "It wasn't like this all happened over one year, mate. Maybe then the authorities might've called on her, but it happen every eight, nine, or ten years, so not likely they'd investigate."

"Was anyone in the Bethard family suspicious?"

Bristol snickered and again leaned in. "Each of Cissy's dead husbands had life insurance policies that paid out some major quid, and I suspect it all went into a common pot. So, no, no one cared. But still, it made you wonder how contagious her vibes might be. Some people do have bad luck hoverin' over them like a storm cloud."

I immediately thought of a client I had who was a New York City cab driver with the inability to avoid accidents that killed his passengers. His cab company tried to dismiss him, and the City wanted to revoke his taxi medallion, so he hired me to collect evidence proving it wasn't his fault. Unfortunately, I had to drop him as a client when he rolled his taxi taking a turn on 6th Avenue during the Macy's Thanksgiving Day Parade and took out the St. Eammon's Dancing Leprechauns. No luck of the Irish that day.

"Did the family have big money problems?"

"Oh, blimey, did they. The Colonel made bad investments after bad investments right up until he died. Myles inherited the estate with debt up to his eyeballs and had to sell off bits and pieces of the property over the years to keep afloat."

The financial background info on the Bethards was interesting, but I wasn't hired to do an audit. I asked Bristol about Gloria Butterfield. "Did you see much of Gloria while she was at Rockingham Manor? Did you attend any of the family dinners and holiday parties?"

Bristol slowly rolled his head back and forth. "Naw, me and Paulie weren't part of that crowd celebrating up there at the Manor. Yeah, sure, I might've seen Gloria when I made deliveries, but nothin' I recall as memorable, you know."

The man and I parlayed for another ten minutes, me with the questions, him with no recollections, before I gave up and closed my notebook.

"I appreciate you sharing what you knew about Gloria," I said. "If something else comes to mind, I'd appreciate a call."

"Sure, mate, any time."

I lifted myself from the chair and turned to Bristol. "What do you think happened to Gloria Butterfield?"

The man didn't hesitate. "Oh, I think she went back to America."

"Why are you so certain of that happening?"

"Because I was the last to see her when I drove her back to the dormitory. She didn't say much, other than wondering if there was a bus to London on a holiday. So, it was obvious to me she wasn't stayin' around to finish school."

"Or marry Myles?"

"Right, mate, or marry Myles."

Chapter Six

I left Bristol Warford and his opinion that Gloria had actually returned home, wondering if the man was a worthwhile source. Sure, he had a lifetime of connections with the Bethard clan, and had interacted with Gloria, but why did he think she left England? The man only knew for certain that he dropped off Gloria at the university dorm; everything else he believed was based on speculation. I'd note his tendency to jump to conclusions in my notebook on the Bristol Warford page.

I returned to the launderette looking for Gram. If the Warfords were biased and unreliable, and I couldn't get past Melba, the housekeeper, I would need to chat up the folk living in the village. Hopefully, my landlady would generate some names for me.

"So, you're takin' me suggestion to heart, are you, lad?"

"I humble myself before you, Gram. Which local citizen should I interview?"

"You should know, Mister Knuckles, Village-In-Thistles never had to bring in some American dick to find our killers. No, we had our own home-grown talent; we did. That'd be Lizabeth West and her aunt, Jane. Yes, those two were native-born crime solvers; they were."

Gram couldn't resist, however, inserting a less flattering view of the two local celebrity sleuths.

"Miss Lizabeth and Aunt Jane were good at what they did, but it shouldn't be surprising when they had nothing better to do than stick their noses into everyone's business, especially when they've made a pig's ear of it."

"Even up there at Rockingham Manor?"

"Oh, yes, dearie. Aunt Jane had a tight relationship with Miss Rosemond, or so they said. But she's been in the ground maybe twenty years, so I don't know if Lizabeth works for Miss Rosemond like her aunt did."

"Where might I find this Lizabeth West?"

Gram rolled her bottom lip. "Aye, Lizabeth West lives in a cottage just three hundred meters from me front door."

Wow. I now knew of two amateur sleuths with deep connections to the community who knew the hiding places for all the skeletons, literally and figuratively. Hopefully, Lizabeth West would ignore any jurisdictional conflicts and be willing to serve as a source for my Gloria Butterfield inquiry. If I were lucky, Aunt Jane would have kept extensive written notes of the community happenings from back in the day. Perhaps Aunt Jane could provide old Nic Knuckles with an assist from the grave.

I thanked Gram for her guidance and headed out, hoping to introduce myself to Lizabeth West. Crossing the street, I saw parked in front of the building housing Doctor Watson Johnson's medical office, the biggest automobile I'd seen since arriving in England. A man in a uniform was vigorously wiping the windshield.

"Whoa, man, that's some vehicle you got there," I said. The man continued polishing the glass, avoiding eye contact and saying nothing.

"Is it a Rolls-Royce?"

I knew nothing about cars and guessed my ignorance was enough to set the man off. He huffed and muttered. "This is a classic Bentley T-Series, you dolt. It's superior to a Rolls-Royce."

"I apologize for hurting your feelings and those of your car," I said. "My ride back in New York City is a subway train, and I'm happy just to get a seat."

The man sniffed and stepped to the front of the car to wipe the headlights. I put two and two together and figured he was a chauffeur, and his boss might be visiting the doctor. I also suspected that only those who could afford a uniformed Uber driver lived at Rockingham Manor.

"Do you work for the Bethard family?" I asked.

To avoid answering me, the man ducked to clean the insect splatter off the car's bumper. I feared he'd crawl under the vehicle if I pressed him, so I left.

I walked on, looking for the cottage that Gram had told me belonged to Lizabeth West. I assumed it'd have a thick thatched roof, like I saw in tourist guides, with ceramic gnomes patrolling a well-tended garden. But it wasn't meant to be. West's cottage was a little beige-colored bungalow with two windows and a steep metal roof. At least there was a garden, and as I stepped through the wooden gate, I was surprised by a kneeling woman of about sixty calling out from behind a blind of thick blooms.

"Cheers, Mister Knuckles," she said. "How might I help you?"

This prescient villager had to be Lizabeth West. If her reputation for knowing all things great and small about Village-In-Thistles had any merit, then she already knew who I was a few minutes after I stepped off that bus two days ago.

"As you might know, Miss West, I'm from America," I said. "I've been hired by a distressed Midwesterner looking to determine the long-ago fate of her sister, Gloria Butterfield."

West rose from her knees with a purpose belying her age. "What are you, a member of Private Eyes without Borders?"

I chuckled before delivering my favorite retort. "No, I'm nothing but a big city private eye with a boatload of heartbreak, traversing the universe in pursuit of justice for the little guy. And, in this case, that little guy has brought me to your fine village."

"Is that so," West said, pulling a soiled glove from her right hand and reaching to shake mine. "You know, you remind me of an American tourist who came here in the aughts', lookin' to turn the village into a resort, and the meadow into an eighteen-hole golf course. A few days later, they found him at the bottom of the well, upside down. The constable swore the poor Yank must've gotten properly pissed and fell into the well and drown. But my auntie, Jane, knew right from the start it was murder. She pointed out that the Yank's hands were tied behind his back, and embedded in his skull was a meat cleaver."

"Amazing powers of observation, your Aunt Jane had."

"Yes, the woman was a legend."

"I understand that you yourself are pretty sharp at solving mysteries."

West smiled as a pink tint pooled under her eyes. "Aye, I know a thing or two about identifying the good and evil of life, and everything in between."

"Judging from the age of the village's inhabitants, I doubt there's too many crimes of passion committed here."

The woman pulled the other glove from her hand and moved toward the entrance of her cottage. "One thing I learned from my Aunt Jane was that people of weak morals are of every age, and the residents of our village are no exception. For example, I once assisted Aunt Jane in solving a case of a local wealthy man found shot dead in a nearby vicary. Can you imagine that, murder in the house of a man of the cloth?"

"Dead man in the vicary, huh," I said, feeling the competitive spirit rising inside me. "I had a case involving religious people and their mayhem, as well. A mysterious woman dressed in brown hired me to track down a runaway girl. Now, that was the case for the ages. I finally trapped her in the back room of a sleazy Bowery tavern. She was small and wiry but turned vicious, ready to stick a knife between my ribs."

West puffed the air from her mouth. "In our case, there were so many suspects that I couldn't guess who did the deed, but it was not a problem for Aunt Jane. She'd get this twinkle in her blue eyes and announce she knew who was the culprit, but only needed time to put all the pieces together. She eventually identified the killers, a cheating wife and her younger lover. They're both still rotting in prison."

I huffed right back at West. "In my case, only when the woman who'd hired me showed up and announced she was the Mother Superior of a convent did I learn that my target was a poor overworked nun teaching third graders at a local Catholic school."

West stopped and turned to me. "Well, Aunt Jane's rich man shot in the vicary case involved a murderer, not some whining schoolmarm who skipped out on her responsibilities." West turned away and entered the cottage. "We do serious crime here in our village, Mister Knuckles, or we don't do it at all."

Just as I feared, the local amateur PI had a professional sense of self-worth.

I'd tread carefully around West so as not to let her steal my thunder when I finally solved Gloria Butterfield's mysterious disappearance. That's why I never liked reading The Hardy Boys as a kid. You work off your butt, defying the skeptics, dodging possible injury, and your buddy gets most of the credit because he's better looking. Give me solo practitioners like Nancy Drew any day.

"Why don't you come inside, Mister Knuckles, and I'll make you a cuppa." West peeked over her shoulder and added, "I understand you have a peculiar taste for a nice slice of cheddar with your tea."

I followed the woman into her cottage and sat in a wooden chair in the room off of the kitchen. Once I got comfortable, I started my questioning. "I have on good authority that your Aunt Jane knew Miss Butterfield back when the girl was visiting in 1976. Do you have any knowledge of their interactions?"

"I lived with my father then in Manchester, so I don't know. I moved in with my Aunt Jane when I was twenty. It was 1980, and she was getting up there in years and needed some assistance."

Hearing about West's generous nature, I wondered if any of my sister's kids would take care of old Uncle Nic when his time came. I had three sisters who sired a half-dozen children, so the odds sounded good that one of them would be there to usher me through my dotage. Unfortunately, my nieces and nephews had the nature of rabid wolverines, and I wouldn't turn my back on any of them. Forget about being around them after the cogs in my brain started slipping.

"But I tell you what, Mister Knuckles. Carrying for my Aunt Jane for over twenty-five years before she died helped me master the private investigator's craft. As time passed, I did more of the work finding killers among the British upper class, while Aunt Jane knitted tea cozies. If I say so myself, my skills might now supersede the old girl's."

"That's all interesting, Miss West, but either you're dodging my question, or you're auditioning to be my assistant."

"Not quite correct, sir," she said, narrowing her eyes in a way that intensified their blue color. "You are, after all, a visiting investigator who is greatly deficient in the knowledge of local culture and ways. While I'd consider the opportunity to work with you, I'd never do so as a mere deputy."

The woman nailed my weaknesses, and I couldn't argue with her. "Okay, I get you. We'll be partners in solving Gloria Butterfield's disappearance."

"Thank you, Mister Knuckles." West's face gave up a slight smile, and she tacked on another demand. "I live on a tiny inheritance from my father, a mystery writer, and it's a struggle to make ends meet. Therefore, I must be paid for any work I perform for you."

I wanted to tell her that a mystery writer who earned enough to leave an inheritance sounded awful fishy, but I kept mum. Maybe the writing class was well compensated in the land of Jane Austen. Nonetheless, Nic Knuckles never used a partner to solve any of his cases, let alone pay someone. But I was at a profound disadvantage working here in the land of tea and crumpets and had to reconsider.

"Okay, Miss West. I'll give you a daily stipend of fifty dollars."

West grunted. "I know today's exchange rate, Mister Knuckles, and that fifty American isn't worth forty quid. Do I look as if I came 'up' on the 'down' train?"

Holy Provolone, Lizabeth West was as quick as a mongoose wearing silk pajamas. We haggled back and forth for twenty minutes before settling the terms of our relationship. She'd serve as my local specialist, drawing upon her knowledge of the village and Rockingham Manor to keep my investigation on a proper track. If we solved the mystery, I'd pay her a daily stipend of forty-five quid and share equal credit. I'd also give her fifty percent of any true crime follow-on revenue, including TV, podcasts, and t-shirt sales.

"Now that we have our terms settled," I said, "Please answer my question. Are there any records of Aunt Jane meeting Gloria Butterfield in late 1976?"

"If Aunt Jane had any conversation with Gloria Butterfield, I'm sure she wrote about it. The woman took meticulous notes all her life, and I've kept every last scribble."

I felt my toes wiggling inside my shoes. What a break for my investigation. Aunt Jane was an obsessive note-taker, and Lizabeth West had hoarder tendencies. Aunt Jane may be bones and a dusty hunk of white hair now, but she and I were going to connect through the written word. Hooray for literacy!

"May I have access to Aunt Jane's daily diary?" I asked. "I'm primarily interested in the last few months of 1976 and early 1977."

West sighed and stood, asking me to follow her into the next room. The space was cluttered with books and clothing, and the window shade was down. West stopped before three large wooden chests and lifted their lids to reveal that each was filled to the top with loose paper. I could make out sheets of stationery, three-hole loose-leaf, paper napkins, pieces of cardboard, and luncheon menus, all jumbled together.

"This is Aunt Jane's collection of notes, almost a century's worth of observations and commentary. Unfortunately, as you can see, the woman had zero organizational skills."

My sense of disappointment almost dropped me to my knees. I could grab a handful of paper from one of the chests and read stuff from any month, year, or decade starting before World War Two. Lizabeth West must've smelled by desperation.

"Not to despair, Mister Knuckles," she said. "For an additional ten quid a day, I'll do all your data mining, so to speak."

Miss West and I left Aunt Jane's archival disaster and settled at her kitchen table, a cup of tea in front of each of us and a plate of cheese and biscuits in the middle. I'd agreed to pay her a fee for digging through Aunt Jane's papers, but it was eight quid per hour above her retainer, and she had to produce results within twenty-four hours.

"Mister Knuckles, why don't you give me some details on this Gloria Butterfield, and I can get started researching my aunt's collection?"

"First of all, we need to drop this British formality, if we're going to work together," I said. "You can call me Nic, and I'll address you as Liz."

West's response was immediate and non-negotiable. "I'm far more comfortable as Lizabeth."

"Okay, three syllables instead of one won't wear out my vocal cords. I'm ready to start our partnership, Lizabeth."

I pulled out my notebook and found the pages where I wrote my notes from my meeting with Gloria Butterfield's sister in my Queen's office. With my molars grinding a biscuit, I shared what I learned from that encounter.

"According to my client, Gloria was twenty years old and an undergraduate at a small, Midwestern college when she came to England for a year's study at a university not far from Village-In-Thistles. Apparently, she intended to study the effects of medieval English cuisine on the writings of Chaucer."

Lizabeth inserted her right index finger through the teacup handle and raised the steamy liquid toward her lips. "Blimey, another American English major destined to become a warehouse supervisor."

I shook my head, pleased to have the opportunity to put my new partner in her place. "Well, Lizabeth, Gloria gave up her liberal arts dreams not because they were impractical but because she met a man who could make better ones come true."

"Of course," Lizabeth said, a dismissive grunt squeezed through her thin lips. "Those American girls always expect to find their prince when they visit England."

Lizabeth's brittle voice suggested that perhaps she had a history of romantic disappointment. Most good criminal investigators did; otherwise, if we had happy marriages, we'd be too busy driving our kids to play dates to solve any crime.

"Based on what I was told and my readings of Gloria's letters to her parents, soon after arriving in July of 1976, she met a handsome young graduate student and teaching assistant named Myles Bethard."

Lizabeth's right eyebrow tipped upward, but she remained silent.

"The young couple immediately took to each other, and a heated affair began. By November, Myles wanted to introduce Gloria to his family. At that time, the young American wrote her folks that 'she'd been swept off her feet and believed she'd found the man of her dreams.'"

Lizabeth's eyelids dropped, and her lips disappeared into a slit of a smile. "How nice for her."

I continued summarizing my initial insights, telling my new partner how Myles introduced Gloria to his family in mid-November of that year. Gloria wrote that his parents, the Colonel and Miss Rosemond, were friendly yet distant. She assumed they were being typical Brits and didn't take offense. However, she hit it off with Myles' younger sister, Cissy.

At the mention of Cissy Bethard, West whispered. "Ah, the Butterscotch Widow."

"Excuse me, I believe she's known as the Yellow Widow among the village folk."

Lizabeth waved my words away like they were a swarm of annoying gnats. "If those locals had a discerning level of observational skills, they'd know the color of Cissy's mourning gown is a butterscotch shade of yellow."

Oh boy, I thought, Lizabeth noticed the tiny differences in things that often broke a tough case. That skill could be invaluable, yet problematic if she used it against me. I decided I might want to know Lizabeth better before sharing too much. As the woman had earlier pointed out, I was a visiting investigator greatly deficient in knowledge of local culture and ways.

"That's about all I have," I said. "If you could dig through that mountain of paper and find anything where Aunt Jane mentions Gloria Butterfield, I'd appreciate it."

"That's three mountains of paper, Nic. I'll start as soon as you leave."

So that's what I did. I left feeling a mix of trepidation and hope that my new partnership would be money well spent. It concerned me that my feeling of hope was the weaker of the two.

Chapter Seven

It was good that I'd wrapped up my call on Lizabeth West when I did. The cheese she served me was delicious but inadequate in quantity, and I was starving. Fortunately, the Pissin' Pints was only a hundred steps from Miss West's cozy domicile, and I entered the pub. Inside, there was a well-stained bar seemingly requiring a dozen men leaning against it to keep it from falling. Or, maybe it was the bar holding the men in place. The windows were frosted, which allowed enough light to distinguish daytime from night, but not much else. A dozen tables with chairs filled the rest of the space. I fell into one of those chairs, and ordered a steak and chips. Before they arrived at my table, two dangerously large tankards of beer appeared in front of me, along with my Rockingham Manor buddy, Rufford.

"Here you go, mate," he said as he sat down. "Nothin' better than a pint with your meal."

The man was correct. The grub was tasty, while the beer refreshed a throat raw from drinking the incessant tea, I did to be polite to Gram and Lizabeth. I then put a grin on Rufford's face when I asked the waitstaff to deliver another pint to my table companion. I suspected he wanted to talk, and I thought that more alcohol might loosen his tongue.

"You grew up there on The Rock, Rufford," I said. "Would you give me the deep skinny on the Bethards? I'm barely scratching the surface of understanding that family."

"Course, mate. You might want to scribble this down because it quickly becomes a bit of a mish-mash."

I did as Rufford suggested, pulling out my notebook and pencil. His narrative came fast and furious, starting with Colonel Jeremy Bethard's father, Colonel Martin "Pepper" Bethard. The grandfather of Myles served in Her Majesty's Royal Marines and was part of an English diplomatic station somewhere in the Austro-Hungarian Empire. That was where he met Eva Von Swizlelback, daughter of an Austrian Duke and Duchess.

"I have to say, Rufford, you have an impressive amount of knowledge of a family that isn't your own."

Rufford emptied his glass and burped. "Believe me, mate, I heard the Bethard history repeated over and over again growin' up at the Manor. And since I didn't know who me own daddy was, I guessed it kinda soaked in."

I signaled the waitress to refill Rufford's glass, and he continued his storytelling. Before WWI, and everything went to hell between the Brits and the Germanic tribes, Duke Von Swizlelback purchased the Rockingham Manor estate as a wedding gift for Martin and Eva. A decent-sized trust was also attached, which kept the estate operating while Martin eventually fought against his father-in-law in The Great War.

"It's always smart to marry money," I said. I'd dated the entire financial spectrum of women, from those who'd never seen a W-2 to those who cleaned those people's toilets, and the rich ones tended to keep me around longer because I never dressed better than them. Nonetheless, only wearing a fedora on my head and black Oxfords on my feet soon got on their nerves, and the relationship fell apart.

Rufford sipped his beer and wiped the foam from his lips. "Martin and Eva had a boy, Jeremy, and that boy grew up to be the man I knew as the Colonel. He had two sisters, Brunhilda and Margaret. Brunhilda went to school in Germany and married a high-ranking Nazi assigned to the Eastern Front early in WW Two. Margaret married poorly and eventually died in an asylum."

It seemed the British Royal family's association with Nazis and insane asylums filtered down to the outer branches of the aristocracy as well. Not that Nic Knuckles didn't have some kooks in his lineage. Don't get me started on my father's second cousin, Bruce the Klan Wizard, who sold bedding out of his apartment in Hoboken. The white sheets move quickly, with the members of his Klavern buying most of his stock. Bruce eventually went out of business when he over-ordered lavender-colored sheets and pillowcases. Those never sold.

"Jeremy, like his daddy, served in the Royal Marines and became a Colonel, like his daddy," Rufford said. "However, people called him Little Pepper so not to confuse him with his daddy, who they called Big Pepper."

"I bet Jeremy hated being called Little Pepper."

Rufford snorted. "Oh, he'd do his nut, if someone called him Lil' Pepper. The Colonel inherited that hard Bethard temper, let me tell you. You never wanted him flippin' his lid on you, believe me, mate."

After a deep swallow of his ale, my chatty drinking companion described, in slurring words, how the younger Colonel returned to England after the Second World War and discovered that Big Pepper had squandered the trust. Rockingham Manor was within the taxman's grasp, and everything looked dire.

"So that was the start of the financial problems, huh?"

Rufford giggled. "Yesh, and the tradition of them marryin' minted other halves to keep the Manor open."

I could pick out enough of Rufford's coherently spoken words to create the rest of the story. The younger Colonel took matters in hand and canvassed the English countryside, looking for a rich woman willing to marry him. He found one in Queen Victoria Jones-Raleigh, and they quickly married. Within a year, a daughter, Pauline, was born.

Thinking about how many spouses Cissy Bethard had buried, I asked the next question with a sense of trepidation. "What became of the Colonel's first wife?"

Rufford moved closer, his hoppy breath climbing up my nostrils. "The Colonel soon learned that his wife's family was not as posh as he thought, and a lot of hidden debt was coming due. According to me mum, the Colonel moved quickly, again cruising the local estates for eligible women, until he met Rosemond Bittersweet, heiress to the lug nut fortune."

Ah, I thought. Now I see why Pauline might hate her father and stepmother. I pushed my notebook to a new page and prepared for more juicy data.

"What happened next?"

Rufford dropped his head and snickered. "Now, here's the goss that'll curl your ears. The Colonel and Miss Rosemond fooled around, and she got pregnant with Mister Myles. Big Pepper arranged a quickie divorce for his son from Queen Victoria and an even quicker marriage to Miss Rosemond. Old Queen Victoria and Miss Pauline soon left Rockingham Manor and disappeared."

Wowzer, now we're talking money, infidelity, sex, and abandonment. The spirit of Henry VIII was still strong in England.

"Pauline didn't stay gone forever," I said. "Because I met her and her hubby in their shop. When did she return to the Manor?"

"It was before Miss Gloria showed up, maybe two years. I don't know for sure; I was only five at the time." Rufford waved his finger in my face. "No, wait, mate, I was eight, yeah, eight, I think."

I stopped writing and tried to rub out the cramp crippling my right hand as my furious notetaking took a toll. Most investigators couldn't continue with such an injury, and Nic Knuckles was no different. However, I had a secret talent that allowed me to move forward. I switched the pencil to my left hand. Not that I was ambidextrous and could record legible text, but I had this odd ability to draw stick figures as a leftie. With a picture worth a thousand words, it was a very efficient way of recording information.

"Tell me what you recall from the time Gloria arrived."

"Oh, I know a lot, I do." Rufford raised the glass to his mouth, drowning his words in the ale. "Me mum always said me ears were too big for me own good. If she only knew what I'd seen and heard as a lad back then, she'd throw a strop, she would."

Rufford emptied his glass, smiled as his head wobbled, and then face-planted on the table.

"He'll be okay, mate," the waitress said. "He'll be awake and talkin' nonsense in a few hours."

I had no interest in sitting in a chair looking at the top of Rufford's head, so I paid what I owed and left. My suspicion of Rufford stayed with me, however. The man carried some seriously weird vibes, and I couldn't exactly nail down what bothered me. He was eager to tell tales out of school, but why? Was Rufford just a gossip, or was he on a mission? He seemed to have a drinking problem. He garbled his words after two glasses and the passed out after three. Not a big drinker, I'd say, but then I didn't test his blood alcohol levels when he came in.

At least I now understood why Pauline hated her father and the family he sired. The Bethard inclination to marry wealth explained why Gloria Butterfield never stood a chance. I felt a deep unease in my gut, and it wasn't the chips. Did the easy disposal of inconvenient Bethard spouses apply to girlfriends, particularly a working-class girl from Indiana?

Chapter Eight

The following day, Gram Edwards cornered me in the kitchen as I came down the stairs from my room. She had a cup of tea in one hand and a plate loaded with cheddar cheese in the other.

"Where you be rushing off to, Mister Knuckles?" she asked. "Sit down here at my wee table and indulge my curiosity."

I had little interest in chatting up Gram when I was anxious to get back to Lizabeth West's cottage, as she had promised to search thoroughly, Aunt Jane's pile of notes for anything written when Gloria Butterfield was at Rockingham Manor. Unfortunately for me, the old laundry woman was darn clever and knew if I didn't want the tea, I'd be unable to resist the cheese. I ended up sitting in one of her kitchen chairs.

"I met with Lizabeth West yesterday," I said as the bite of a wonderfully aged cheddar jostled my taste buds awake. "And I have to say, the woman was very intuitive."

Gram drank deeply from her cup of Earl Grey. "That's one way to describe the ol' lassie, intuitive."

I told her how Lizabeth and I agreed to partner in pursuing justice for Gloria Butterfield. Gram didn't look happy. "Watch yourself around that woman," she said. "She's just a younger version of her aunt, what with their supernatural ability to sniff out other people's troubles. She'll turn it on ya, if she can."

I nodded and briefly mentioned sharing a pint with Rufford at the pub. Her opinion of him wasn't stellar either.

"I first met that Rufford when I came to Village-In-Thistles, and he was a young fella of little ambition," she said, her jaw tight against what had to be mail-order dentures. "He was a sneaky scally back then, always poppin' up when you least expected it. He might've been a natural born peeper, he was, with all his hiding in the shadows, watching folks."

I had to agree with her. "I believe you're correct on that one, Gram. He did seem to know what was going on up at the Manor, even as a young boy."

Gram tried to refill my teacup but stopped when I covered it with my hand. "I gotta run," I said. "I still need someone to make me an introduction to Myles Bethard and the lot up there on The Rock. Hopefully, Lizabeth has some connections."

"I can't help you there, Mister Knuckles. The Bethards don't bring their laundry here to be washed and dried. Oh no, me struggling to make ends meet, and the rich ones up on the hill can't send me any business."

I was tempted to tell Gram that, based on how shabby Rockingham Manor appeared on the outside, I wasn't so sure there was much money to be made. I reassured Gram I'd only have my dirty clothes cleansed at Village Launderette, which made her smile.

"You're a decent lad, for an inquisitive American, you are."

Gram wished me a good day doing my snooping and excused herself. I slipped the leftover chunk of cheddar into my coat pocket and left the kitchen. I arrived at Lizabeth West's door within ten minutes of departing the launderette.

"Good morning, Nic. Can I make you a cuppa?"

"I'm good."

'You sure?" she said. "I can't make it through my morning without a continuous flow of nice hot tea."

"You Brits must have extra-large bladders or spend half your life in the loo. What did you find for me?"

I sat on the small sofa across from a rocking chair that Lizabeth commandeered. Both pieces of furniture had seen better days, well, actually better decades, but they were spotless, as was the rest of the interior of the cottage.

"I spent much of last evening after you left," she said, "digging through the first chest of Aunt Jane's material. It was exhausting, but I found something

I think will help you."

Lizabeth straightened her posture and assumed the look of a no-nonsense teacher about to lecture a thick-headed student. Her mannerisms triggered a memory of me and my fifth-grade teacher, Miss Thudberry, aka The Paddler. She acquired that nickname not because she recreated in a canoe on the Hudson River. As Lizabeth cleared her throat and started speaking, I felt my butt cheeks tighten as if I was about to get spanked.

"This was written on the back of a laundry list from sometime in early 1974. Aunt Jane wrote that she called on Rosemond Bethard that morning. The lady of Rockingham Manor had requested a visit to discuss a private matter. According to Aunt Jane's note, Rosemond wanted her to find the Colonel's long-estranged daughter, Pauline."

Lizabeth's gaze slipped down her slim nose and triumphantly swirled around me. "Don't you wonder why she did that?"

I pulled both my notebook and the breakfast cheese from my coat pocket. I opened the notebook to the Rufford page and lodged the cheddar into my left cheek.

"According to my source," I said. "Rosemond had a good reason to locate Pauline. After all, her dalliance with Colonel Bethard and eventual pregnancy broke up the girl's childhood and sent her mother into oblivion. Rosemond's guilty conscience probably motivated her to use Aunt Jane to find Pauline."

Lizabeth sat back and steepled her fingers. Behind those dusty blue eyes, I knew she was upset that I easily topped her research findings with even better stuff. The match between two world-class private investigators was on, and Nic Knuckles was ahead on points.

"That's salacious and probably irrelevant," Lizabeth said, puffing the last syllable through pursed lips. "I believe this meeting between Rosemond and Aunt Jane was the continuation of a decades-long relationship built upon my aunt's ability to keep all kinds of Bethard family matters confidential."

The possible collusion between the two women was very interesting, and Lizabeth must've felt excited because the corners of her mouth rose slightly in a smug, self-congratulatory way. She lifted an old yellow legal pad so I could see the faded ink of a full page of scribbling.

"This was an undated entry, but it looks far older. From what I could make out, it appears that Aunt Jane investigated Colonel Bethard's rumored indiscretions on Rosemond's behalf." Lizabeth's smile stretched tighter, and her cheeks colored. "Based on my review of my aunt's bookkeeping for that period, it seemed she would report to Rosemond that there was nothing to be concerned about and collect her fee."

"Wowzer, Aunt Jane was a crafty tart, wasn't she?"

Lizabeth blushed. "I also found entries for payments from the Colonel about the same dates. It seemed my aunt was enjoying the benefit of Rosemond's friendship while collecting a fee from Jeremy Bethard to mislead his wife."

I chuckled. "Now that, my English muffin, is a juicy bit of background. But how is it relevant to Gloria Butterfield's disappearance?"

The hurt look on Lizabeth's face quickly changed to one of anger. "Well, bloody hell, Nic, I spent hours pulling apart garbage to find this. Show some appreciation."

I apologized and was pleased to hear she had additional important material. I hoped she was right. I hated paying her forty quid to learn about her Aunt Jane's duplicitous behavior and the unethical people she took advantage of.

"This next piece was dated June 18, 1977. An investigator from the US Embassy arrived in Village-In-Thistles, asking about Gloria Butterfield. He interviewed the Bethard family and got nothing. They all stuck to their story that Gloria dropped out of school and left the country."

"How did Aunt Jane know about the embassy investigation?" I asked.

"I'm not sure, but knowing Aunt Jane, she probably knew the man was in the village and why he was there within an hour of his arrival. She must've ambushed him before he left to return to London because, according to this note, she gave him testimony."

"What? Now that's important. Did she record what she told him?"

"Calm yourself, Nic. I have it right here." Lizabeth lifted a small notebook to her eyes. "It's not dated, but she mentioned meeting the embassy official and telling him that she went up to the Manor and queried Rosemond about

Miss Butterfield's sudden disappearance. Rosemond was very cool to the questioning and suggested Aunt Jane stay out of it to allow Myles the privacy to get over his heartbreak."

"Okay, now we're cookin'. So, Aunt Jane knew Gloria, and well enough, that she felt compelled to go up to The Rock."

Lizabeth shook the paper at me. "There's more, Nic. Aunt Jane told the official that she also confronted the Colonel, who strongly suggested she stay out of it. He wanted to protect Myles's feelings and the family's reputation."

I jumped to my feet. 'Wowzer, what did he mean about protecting the family's reputation? I mean, no one cared about my family rep when some woman dumped me. What's the big deal?"

"You never had the wealth or title, Nic, that Myles had. He probably had never felt the sting of rejection. You, on the other hand, could swim through a sea of stinging jellyfish and not feel it."

I could've gone low and pointed out that at least I was out there mingling with members of the opposite sex, but Lizabeth and I had more important things to do than fight over who had the worst love life.

"It looked like the Colonel and Rosemond were selling the same story," I said. "It sounds practiced to me."

Lizabeth stood up and went into the kitchen to add hot water to her cup. As she dunked her teabag, she turned and said, "My aunt seemingly agreed because she wrote a line in the margin about feeling that the Colonel and Rosemond were covering up something."

"Did she go after them? How could she resist if she was the obsessive investigator that everyone makes her out to have been?"

Lizabeth and her teacup returned to the room. "No, sadly, Aunt Jane got distracted by some murder in an estate north of Village-In-Thistles. I think it was a young hotel dancer who ended up dead in some Lord or Duke's library. Strangest thing how bodies show up in the most peculiar places here in this part of Britain."

Lizabeth sipped her tea and continued explaining. "After she solved that case, there was another, and then I arrived after Aunt Jane hurt herself crawling through a neighbor's pet door while gathering clues on the disappearance of a beloved bulldog. The broken bones she suffered from that incident impaired her mobility and kept her homebound." Lizabeth gently sighed and took another swallow from her cup. "She never mentioned Gloria Butterfield to me, and if she had, we were too busy solving new mysteries to pursue it."

"That's too bad," I said. I was thinking otherwise because if Aunt Jane *had* solved the mystery years ago, I'd never been hired, and right now, I'd be walking in ninety-degree heat on Queens Boulevard wearing flip flops, sucking on Italian ice."

"It must've been a great experience being tutored by a talented sleuth," I said. "I bet you learned a trick or two from her."

Lizabeth, a faraway look in her eyes, sighed and said, "Yes, she taught me well, and we were very close. It was a sad day in 2002 when she died."

Nic Knuckles, always sensitive to a distressed damsel, quickly asked, "Do you miss her?"

The woman inhaled deeply before answering. "No, not really. I could never relax when she was around, what with her always seeing something suspicious in everything anyone did. I could never have friends over without her making them confess to the most minor indiscretions."

Wow, and I thought my mother was a horror. Could being around the unrelenting suspicious glare of influential adults have made us both natural investigators? Maybe, after I retire from the private eye business, I'll become a child development specialist and get the answers to that question.

"And it wasn't just my friends that Aunt Jane drove away," Lizabeth said. "Soon after I arrived in the village, I met a man who was deeply attracted to me, and I to him. I guessed Aunt Jane feared I'd leave her alone because she conspired with others to break us up. After that, I never loved again."

Hop on my back and ride me in the Kentucky Derby; Lizabeth's sudden revelation stunned me. She and Aunt Jane might've been close, maybe so close it stunted her life. Lizabeth sat there silent and lost, unable or unwilling to go deeper into her heartbreak. As a survivor of many romantic, flaming Hindenburgs, I recognized the deep sadness taking control of Lizabeth West. I closed my notebook and slipped out of her cottage, leaving Lizabeth, her memories, and a cooling cup of tea.

Chapter Nine

After leaving Lizabeth in a state of crippling melancholy, I found myself at the Pissin' Pints, sitting in a corner looking over my notes on what I'd learned to date about Gloria Butterfield's time in England. It wasn't much. Gloria had definitely met Aunt Jane and was befriended by Bristol Warford, although Pauline was not interested in her. A young Rufford had a major crush on Gloria, while his mother disliked her immensely. But then again, Melba seemed to dislike everyone immensely.

"Mornin', love." It was the waitress speaking to me, and she looked unhappy doing it. "The breakfast is closing up in fifteen minutes if you're gonna order it. Otherwise, buy a pint and cover the table you're sittin' at."

"I could use something to eat," I said. "What do you suggest?"

"You can't go wrong with a traditional full English breakfast." She pointed at a man two tables over. "That chap is enjoyin' it. It's bloody good."

The meal the waitress was encouraging me to order was a heaping pile of fried meats and vegetables. Back in New York City, at my favorite deli, they had a name for a similar offering: The Gut Buster. I never took it on because I had too much respect for my internal organs to risk busting any of them. However, I was a guest in a foreign land, so what could I do but order this British monstrosity?

The traditional English breakfast arrived at my table, and as I cautiously tasted the Black Pudding, Rufford appeared and welcomed himself to my table.

"Cheers, mate," he said. "I see you indulging in one of our favorite creations, eh?"

"Yes, my friendly Englishman, I hope to enjoy this spread of interestingly prepared proteins and carbohydrates."

"Yep, lovely grub, init?"

I nodded in agreement and hoped my response would satisfy Rufford's need for conversation and send him on his way. I didn't feel comfortable with someone looking at me while I ate. It went back to my infancy when my mother watched me as I suckled the wet nurse who lived in a cardboard box behind our apartment building. If I went beyond the agreed-upon ten minutes of nursing, Ma would jerk me away, screaming. "I ain't payin' to make you a fat baby."

Rufford ordered up a pint and seemed ready to settle in for the duration of my dining experience. I figured if he were going to be my table companion, I'd use the opportunity to learn more about the Bethard family. First, however, I needed to satisfy my curiosity about why Rufford seemingly had nothing to do but shadow me.

"Looks like you're not too busy at The Rock."

He shook his head as he scratched the freckled skin of his neck. "Naw, me mum sent me out this morning to collect the eggs from her hens, and then things got all barmy when they wanted to know what I would do with their eggs. I had to go somewhere where no one would bother me with questions like that."

I stopped mid-way, inserting a spoonful of pudding into my mouth because the man now had my full attention. "Come again," I said. "Are you saying the hens wanted to know what you intended to do with their eggs?"

"Yeah. The Sussex birds aren't as curious, but there are a couple of Dorkings who won't let me leave the hutch without answering their bloody questions. It's too much sometimes, you know, being responsible for explaining to the animals how we humans feel about them."

From our first conversation, I knew Rufford had suffered a kick to the head that gave him the ability to translate pig squeals into English, but I didn't know other barnyard animals could communicate with him.

"I just have to stay away from the Manor," Rufford said, "until after the sun goes down and the Dorkings go to roost."

Now, most private eyes would ignore someone like Rufford and drop some loose change into his cup. But not Nic Knuckles. One thing I've learned in my years solving the unsolvable was a crazy source was better than no source. And Rufford was probably a normal lad when he knew Gloria Butterfield, back before he took the hoof to the noggin.

"Rufford, my buddy. Tell me what you remembered about the time soon after Gloria disappeared. What was going on up there at The Rock?"

Rufford sucked down half of his pint, and his mouth took off. "Oi, it was all tight at the Manor that year after Miss Gloria went away. The Colonel was dead worried Myles might spend all his time cryin' and babblin' like a baby, and he had good reason to think that. I remember Myles acting all mental at times."

The spoon in my hand was quickly replaced with a pencil, and I had my notebook in front of me. Rufford was on a roll, and I didn't want to miss a thing. "How long did Myles suffer with his heartbreak?"

"Oh, I don't know, but he dropped out of Uni and never went back. Mum said at the time that the Colonel should give his son a kick up the arse, and that'd get him over the heartbreak."

It seemed old Melba had the sentimental instincts of a slaughterhouse stun gun operator, even back then.

"But I remember me mum getting worried when the Colonel threatened to let Roland, the chauffeur, go. She feared we'd be next because the Colonel had bet wrong on some investment and burnt through Rosemond's money. But the Colonel fooled her. He turned on his adult children and demanded they do more."

"What kind of jobs did Myles and Cissy get?"

Rufford choked on the mouthful of stout he'd just drank. "Ha, that's a joke. They never got their hands dirty doing real work. They married the poshest blokes and birds they could find."

Rufford described how Cissy first stepped up to her father's assignment by marrying a baron. I was unable to understand why the man's inability to bear children was important, so I just listened. Rufford said the man was a dandy whose father built a small fortune from running a circus.

"The bloke lived off the hard work of clowns and sideshow freaks, he did," Rufford said, his words dripping in condemnation. "Me mum never liked Baron Monteque, and neither did I."

Whatever the opinion of Rufford and his mother, Cissy and her family seemed to like the Baron. According to Rufford, the Bethards all proved adept at weaseling money from the poor sucker, which helped stabilize Rockingham Manor. The relationship went well for almost eight years, and then the Baron grew a spine and demanded partial ownership of the estate.

"I'm guessing that didn't happen."

Rufford slowly bobbed his head. "Righto, the poor bloke died in his sleep before he got close to getting his hands on Rockingham Manor."

"With the Baron no longer around to tap," I said, "I'm guessing the money circus left town."

"No, Miss Cissy was the brainy one in that family." Rufford explained how the Baron went lights out a week and a half after Cissy had gotten him to take out a bigger life insurance policy. The new widow got a large enough payout from the Baron's death to survive and assist the family until she got over her grief and found her second husband.

"I have to meet this Cissy," I said. "She sounds like a cold operator."

"Me mum used to say she knew money was getting short at Rockingham Manor when one of Cissy's husbands died. She'd hold her breath until the insurance man showed up with a check, and we'd be okay for another few years until the Colonel did something a bit stupid."

I made a mental note to ask Lizabeth if her Aunt Jane had any records of investigating the Baron's demise. Indeed, Aunt Jane's instinct for picking up on criminality would've perked up if she'd heard about the man's very convenient death. Even if I weren't getting paid to investigate Cissy's departed husbands, I'd like to know how high I should place her on my suspect list.

"What about Myles? Did he contribute anything toward saving the Manor?"

Rufford swallowed the last of his pint and, thankfully, covered his belch. "Sorry, mate," he said, "Mister Myles laid about all burnt a good two years after Miss Gloria disappeared. He supposedly started goin' out and met a nice bird, but she wasn't posh enough, and Miss Rosemond snuffed out the flames before it had time to catch on. The Colonel also rowed with Myles and threatened to boot him off the estate."

"I imagine Cissy was unhappy carrying the load," I said, "knowing from sad personal experiences how vindictive sisters can be."

"Oh, yeah, Cissy was pretty angry pullin' the weight. Miss Rosemond pushed the Colonel to find a gentle girl for Mister Myles to marry."

According to Rufford, the Colonel found a young woman named Amethyst Perkins, a sweet young thing with a sizeable trust fund. Her parents were anxious to get her married off because her sweetness was matched by her strong-headedness.

A fresh page in my notebook was titled Amethyst, and I prepared to record every word Rufford gave up on the woman. I waved at the barkeep, and another pint was dropped in front of my friend. He drew deeply from the golden liquid before describing how the future Missus Bethard had trained to be a member of the clergy, and only agreed to marry Myles if his family built a chapel at Rockingham Manor. She and Myles wed once the final pew was installed in the new chapel.

"Reverend Amethyst, as she called herself, stood up at the pulpit the following Sunday mornin' after they were married and led services, and she's been leading the service ever since."

Rufford described how he and his mother attended most Sundays, more to ensure Melba kept her job than for spiritual subsistence. Myles showed up if he'd gotten in trouble with his wife and needed to return to her good side. Rosemond and Cissy occasionally came, as well as Bristol Warford. Sometimes, a hired farm hand sat in the back.

"But it didn't matter if the pews were full or empty, the Reverend Amethyst gave her all, singin', preachin', and prayin.'"

"Reverend Amy sounds like she could hold her own against the Bethards."

Rufford agreed but added that she had her challenges. "The Colonel expected Mister Myles to tap up Reverend Amethyst's for the dosh to help keep Rockingham Manor goin', and she fought back. As I remember,

Reverend Amethyst and Mister Myles were always arguin' about it."

"I'm guessing that the Colonel worried Myles would never properly run an estate as big and as broke as Rockingham Manor."

"You got that right, mate, and the Colonel was proven correct. Old Rockingham Manor is a ragged shell of what I remember it being when the old man was still alive."

Rufford emptied his glass and pushed his chair from our table. "Even though the Colonel was eighty-five when he died, me mum thinks him always getting' in a row with Mister Myles finally did him in. Yeah, that Bethard temper caused them all a bucket full of grief."

Rufford thanked me for his drinks and excused himself, claiming the Dorkings were huddled in their coop after a hawk flying overhead spooked them. They wanted him back at The Rock to chase the predator away.

"Cheerio, Mister Knuckles," Rufford said as he stepped away. "Don't believe everything Lizzy West tells you, mate."

Although my mouth hung open, I couldn't speak. Rufford had befuddled me beyond repair with that comment. How'd he know I was meeting with Lizabeth West? Something was definitely going on inside that man's head besides conversations with chickens and pigs, and I had to find out what.

Most confounding was how he stuck me with his pub tab.

Chapter Ten

I paid my breakfast bill and for Rufford's morning beer consumption and left the Pissin' Pints determined to gain an audience with some member of the Bethard family. I'd been in Village-In-Thistles for three days, and everything I'd heard was from second or third-hand sources. A private eye working the mean streets couldn't do it from the comfort of their living room. You had to get close to people, smell their breath, and marvel at their nose hairs to find out what they were really thinking.

After hiking past the stink of the sheep dip and clearing the haunted woods, I arrived back at The Rock. I pounded the heavy front door until my fist went numb. The cranky housekeeper appeared and snarled. "What do you want?"

"I demand to speak with Myles Bethard. I have very important business to discuss with him."

"He's not available."

I pushed on the door, and Melba demonstrated surprising strength by preventing any forward progress on my part.

"Then I insist on talking with Cissy," I said, with as much of a Nic Knuckles basso as I could muster. It failed to move Melba. "Missus Dinwiddie is busy," she said, snapping back with a guttural response of her own. "Now git out of here, you arse."

I had zero intention of going away. Melba didn't realize that Nic Knuckles had multiple tools to secure entry into any residence, and it was just a matter of choosing the appropriate one. I could strong-arm it, break and enter it, disguise my way in, or, as I preferred, turn on the buttery charm.

"I must say, Melba, you have the most interesting face. Were you caught in a hailstorm recently?"

I was caught off guard when Melba shut the door and loudly engaged the deadbolt. I'd blown that one, I had to admit. Maybe she wasn't used to a smooth-talking man telling her she had an interesting face. I guess if you're boiling cabbage and potatoes all day, you give up thinking that you might be intriguing.

The sound of a sports car's rumbling engine caught my attention. Turning around, I saw a dark green Aston Martin pull through the entrance and around the back of the house. I sprinted into the spiraling cloud of dust and stopped just as the youngest-looking person I'd yet seen since my arrival, step into view.

"Hello, there, ma'am. Sorry to bother you, but I'm Nic Knuckles, and I've been trying to get a meeting with Myles Bethard or his sister, Cissy."

The woman looked to be in her mid-thirties. She had brown hair cut short and a ready smile of bright, white teeth. "Yullo, Mister Knuckles," she said. "I'm Turquoise."

I offered her my right hand, and she gave me a loose set of fingers in return. "Why do you need to speak with my mother and uncle?"

I knew Cissy had one child, but I'd forgotten whether the girl was a Monteque, Blix-Vixen, Johnson, or Dinwiddie. It didn't matter. I was just happy she appeared willing to talk with me.

"Almost fifty years ago, a young American woman named Gloria Butterfield was romantically involved with Myles Bethard. She never returned home, and her family wants me to determine if she ever left England."

"How dreadful." Turquoise's lips narrowed into a smile. "Uncle Myles was a bad boy, was he? I always suspected something was up with the way Grandfather and Granmama coddled him."

"Would you mind giving me a little more detail?" I asked, my notebook and pencil now in hand. "I've been hearing nothing but second-hand reports and rumors about your uncle."

Turquoise folded her arms and settled against the hood of the car. "I have no recollection of a woman from America. By the time I was born, Uncle

Myles was long married to his current wife, Amethyst."

"Could you share your earliest memories of Myles?"

"They aren't very pleasant, I must say. I was six and a half years old when my father died, and I can still recall him and Uncle Myles never getting along. It always seemed to be about money."

The woman dipped her head and sighed. "Then again, it was always about money with Uncle Myles. Even with my first stepfather, Brice, and now, with my new stepfather, Alexander, money seems to be forever the topic of dinner time conversation."

"I imagine running a big old mansion like The Rock sucked up a lot of cash."

Turquoise shifted her head slowly back and forth. "I don't know why mother stayed here at the Manor when my father, huh, actually, all my stepfathers hated it. None of them were happy, but mother insisted they live here."

With that comment, Turquoise left me with too big of an opening not to step through. "Why do you still live here?" I asked. "You seem bright and well-adjusted."

The woman's eyes twinkled. "Oh, I may be intelligent, kind sir, but well-adjusted, I'm not so sure."

How could I not be charmed by Turquoise's humor and sensual accent? She reminded me of one of my favorite girlfriends, Dolly the Ventriloquist from Biloxi, Mississippi, whose dummy recited limericks. No one could ever cut through her syrup-thick accent to understand the humor, but she stuck with her act. I always admired her pluck.

"I'd also like to talk with your grandmother, Rosemond. Do you think you could make an introduction?"

"Oh, my dear Granmama is not in enough good health to greet strangers. She's confined to her bed and is surviving on tea and Turkish soap operas." Turquoise sniffed back the start of a teardrop. "It is so sad to see a once vigorous woman reduced to nothing more than a puddle of false teeth and snowy white hair."

"You seem very fond of her."

Turquoise took in a deep breath. "Yes, Rosemond has always been good to me. I could not have asked for a more loving grandmother."

That was another positive comment about Rosemond Bethard. Maybe she truly was a decent woman whose only fault was being particular about who'd marry her boy? Perhaps she wasn't the mean-spirited witch Gloria had suggested in her letters. A sharp bite of envy sank its teeth into my heart. My mother never cared what kind of woman I dated. She'd push anyone on me. Her only regret was that they'd hadn't taken me away decades earlier and freed her from the hard work of raising me from a feral state.

"If I might, could I ask you a question about your mother?"

Turquoise left the dreamy reminiscence of her kind grandmother, and her eyes turned hard. I suspected she'd rather not discuss Cissy, but since she didn't refuse me outright, I dove right in, "How does it feel to have a mother known as the Yellow Widow?"

Turquoise's facial expression strongly suggested she didn't appreciate my question. Her words, however, left no doubt. "Sod off, you wanker."

"I'm sorry, Miss Turquoise," I shouted as she turned on her heels and walked toward a door leading into the house. "If you want to swap stories about terrible mothers, I have a few of my own that'll curl your toes."

My offer to commiserate failed to slow Turquoise's departure, and I was left again, standing at a loss with a closed door in my face.

Actually, I reconsidered that thought. The young woman *did* confirm Rufford's statement that the estate was always on the edge of insolvency. And my sense that a malicious and manipulative family dynamic was operating behind those walls was strengthened. Turquoise also added a layer of humanity to Rosemond's persona and confirmed that Myles was a bit of a scoundrel.

My understanding of the Bethard family was taking shape, but I still had some gaps. Maybe my crime-fighting partner, Lizabeth, had recovered from her bout of sad romantic memories from this morning and could help me. Even better, she might offer some of that excellent cheddar cheese.

Chapter Eleven

The late afternoon breeze that always seemed to come blowing in from the east pushed the summer mustiness from the air. I walked by Lizabeth West's cottage and found her again, head down, digging in her garden. Next to drinking tea, those Brits seemed to love dirt and the things that grow in it. I called out. "Good afternoon, partner. How are those petunias doing?"

Without looking up, she tossed a correction. "Those lovelies are Peachleaf Bellflowers, my ignorant friend, and they look brilliant, I must say."

I shrugged. What'd I know? Most New Yorkers only saw an abundance of flowers at a Catholic funeral.

"How was your foray up at the Rockingham Manor?" she asked as she stood and removed her gloves.

"How'd you know I was just there?"

I winced as Lizabeth's imperial smile sliced across her face. The despondent woman I left this morning had been replaced by the old, brassy Lizabeth I'd first met days ago. "I can smell the odor on your coat that you picked up, twice passing the sheep dip. I also see a coating of gravel dust on your shoes, and the only driving surface in this area covered in that type of gravel is at the Manor."

"Okay, smarty pants, you're correct. But which family member did I actually talk with while I was there?"

Lizabeth's right index finger tapped her chin, and her eyes rolled over me from my fedora to my shoes. "It was Cissy's daughter, Turquoise Blix-Vixen."

"Dang, how'd you do that?"

The woman chuckled in a way that I suspected I'd be hearing a lot of and finding it progressively annoying. "I saw her speeding by in her sports car. She blew through the village as if it were her private roadway. That child was raised without discipline, and my aunt never understood why Rosemond allowed it."

Lizabeth may have thought she'd humbled me, what with her impressive display of observational skill and deductive reasoning, but she'd be wrong. Nic Knuckles swam in the ocean of humility all my life, and I kept washing ashore, drying off, and renewing my pursuit of a full life as America's premier private eye.

"Take a break from your flowers, and let me share what Turquoise told me," I said. "And maybe you can offer me a cuppa and some cheese."

Lizabeth and I went inside, and I sat as she served up the Earl Grey and two slices of Jarlsberg, which I gobbled down. I asked her whether Aunt Jane had ever investigated the death of Turquoise's father or any of the other deaths that occurred up at The Rock. She walked to a wall shelf and pulled a thick, stained leather book.

"I'd been living with Aunt Jane for about five years, and she'd totally frustrated me regarding her terrible record-keeping. To keep my sanity, I kept a log of what she was doing and then, later, what we were doing as private investigators. I thought such a record might be useful if I ever decided to follow in my father's footsteps and write murder mysteries."

I wasn't sure writing mysteries paid much better than solving them, but I kept my mouth shut. I asked this instead. "So, did Aunt Jane or you investigate the Baron's death?"

Lizabeth ran a finger down a page and stopped. "There's an entry about the sudden death of Baron Monteque on October 27, 1985. I wrote that the official diagnosis was a heart attack, but in parentheses, I added the word unexpected and underlined it twice."

"Sounds like you and your aunt had your doubts."

"As I recall, I had doubts, but Aunt Jane waved me off. She thought I didn't know the village's families well enough to cast suspicion."

Lizabeth returned to her log. "There was a family-only funeral within two days of the death, and the new widow went to the Lake District to recover from the shock. That's all I have on the Baron."

"Is there anything on Blix-Vixen's death in there?"

"There should be." Lizabeth pushed through the pages of the log and stopped halfway in. "Count Fredrick Blix-Vixen was found dead the morning of February 9, 1995. The coroner reported that the man, fifty-four years old, appeared to have had a heart attack and died in his sleep."

"Was there no reported analysis of his blood or tissue to see if he'd been poisoned?"

Lizabeth sniffed. "He was only Cissy's second husband to die prematurely. Colonel Bethard's high social status in this county would've made pursuing a more aggressive inquiry impolite."

"Based on the scuttlebutt I've heard about your dear Aunt Jane being the village super sleuth, I can't believe she didn't pursue her own investigation. A woman twice widowed by suspicious early deaths had to be too enticing to ignore."

Lizabeth stared at me, slowly blinking her eyelids to convey her exasperation, before flipping to the next page of the document she held in her hands. "I didn't say my aunt ignored a potential murder," she said. "I said that there was no official inquiry. Please be patient and let me continue."

True to her reputation, Aunt Jane *had* dug into the goings-on at Rockingham Manor that month when Count Blix-Vixen died. Lizabeth recorded Aunt Jane telling her that Rosemond confided that the Count had gotten into a loud argument with Myles at the dinner hour. Aunt Jane failed to learn the details of the disagreement, but she did notice that Melba, the housekeeper, was particularly rattled by the death.

"Rufford told me that his mother knew the estate was in financial trouble when one of Cissy's husbands died. Maybe that had some connection with the death."

"You can't trust that man, Rufford," Lizabeth said. "He's mental when he's when sober and worse as a drunkard."

I thanked Lizabeth for her candid comments about my primary informant and asked her to read on. Hopefully, Aunt Jane had more to say. I was right.

"Aunt Jane told me that Cissy woke about two in the morning," Lizabeth read, "and noticed an offensive odor emanating from the bed where her husband slept."

"Sounded like the dead man's sphincters cut loose and created a mess," I said.

Lizabeth's nose crunched against her face, and she spat out her words. "That's disgusting. What's wrong with you?"

I didn't feel I had to defend myself. Any true detective who'd surveyed a murder scene or two knew that the smell was something you never forgot.

"Anyway," Lizabeth said, "the odor coming from the Count's side of the bedroom was a bowl of cold cabbage soup that her husband was eating. According to Rosemond, Cissy demanded to know why her husband was consuming the soup in bed late at night. The man replied that his dinner-time argument with Myles ruined his appetite and now he was hungry."

"I can relate," I said. "When Nic Knuckles misses his supper, I might as well not bother to put my jams on, because I cannot sleep. Thank God, New York City has a million all-night diners."

"Do you mind, Nic?" Lizabeth said, rolling her baby blues into her head. "Let's stay on topic."

I apologized and pulled out my notebook and pencil to take notes. If my hands were busy, I wouldn't have thought how empty they felt without holding something like a piece of cheese.

"It was five hours later, according to what Rosemond shared with Aunt Jane, that Cissy had gotten up, dressed, and eaten her breakfast when she wondered why her husband hadn't come down. She became alarmed and asked her brother to check on him."

"That's odd, don't you think?" I said. 'Why not open the bedroom door and pull back the covers?"

Lizabeth mulled the question for a handful of seconds. "Maybe the situation reminded her of her first husband, the Baron Monteque's sudden death. Perhaps she was unnerved by the circumstances."

I shrugged. That was a pretty good explanation. "Then was it Myles who found the body of Count Blix-Vixen?"

Lizabeth was suddenly intrigued by something in the notes she'd recorded decades ago. "Oh, my Lord," she murmured. "Bristol discovered the corpse, not Myles or Cissy."

"That doesn't make sense. I thought Bristol and Pauline were never residents at the Manor after they married?"

Lizabeth nodded but pointed out that Bristol was the family's errand boy. "If anything was messy," she said, "it seemed Bristol was called to handle it."

"Taking the pulse of a dead man is one heck of an errand. I wonder why they didn't call a doctor or the local police. Why'd they wait until Bristol came from the village before checking on the Count?"

The slim dark eyebrow over West's right eye arced. "If Cissy had a reason to suspect something fatal had happened to her husband, calling a doctor would've been a waste of his time."

Nic Knuckles appreciated the efficient use of people's time, but Lizabeth's comment sent a shiver through me. The woman had a cold, calculating side to her.

"Did you write anything else?" I asked.

The woman shook her head. "Other than being officially recorded as a heart attack, that's all I wrote. I assume Aunt Jane thought it was a natural death and convinced me that two husbands dying in very similar ways was just a terrible coincidence."

"I dunno, Lizabeth. I don't like coincidences, especially terrible ones."

I scribbled a few lines in my notebook that I didn't share with Lizabeth. Why did Melba have the jitters over the Count's death? Rufford had said his mother always worried the Manor was about to go under when one of Cissy's husbands croaked. But what if this time she was anxious because someone might think it was bad cabbage soup that had caused Count Blix-Vixen's death? Could that've been the reason Cissy didn't call a doctor?

If Nic Knuckles thought those things, why hadn't Aunt Jane? And why hadn't Lizabeth? She'd been in the sleuth business for a few years by then. I was starting to better understand Lizabeth West, and I wasn't sure I liked it.

Chapter Twelve

I t was a rainy morning and the drops quickly puddled and topped the cobblestone streets in front of Gram's launderette. I decided to spend the time sitting in my room reviewing my notes. Of all the discussions Lizabeth West and I had, our conversation about the deaths of Cissy's husbands bothered me the most. How could she and Aunt Jane write them both off as accidental? While I had to cut her some slack for not investigating Cissy's third husband's convenient plunge off the Manor roof, it was the same year Aunt Jane passed. Nonetheless, I still wondered why she thought taking a dive off a three-story building was a conventional way to die.

Maybe memories of my mom demanding I sign a Do Not Resuscitate form before she'd take me to the emergency room when my red-hot appendix was about to burst might've made me more sensitive to how people died.

My curiosity was soon overridden by the rumbling of my empty stomach. It had to be getting close to Noon, and it was time for me to explore the wonderfully drab world of English cuisine. The rain had stopped, and the sun was out as I stepped into the street and the village.

As I walked past Warford's What Nots, I recalled seeing a good-sized cooler in the corner of the main room that offered pies and sandwiches for sale. If Bristol happened to be working the counter, I could kill two birds with one stone by stopping in. I'd fill my stomach, chat up Bristol, and maybe figure out why killing birds with stones ever became okay. Nic Knuckles was from New York City, and I knew birds. Pigeons everywhere, doing pigeon stuff all over everything, yet we didn't go about stoning them to death.

Another mystery to solve once I retired from this private eye gig.

I entered the Warford establishment and was greeted by the grinning countenance of Bristol, backed up by Pauline's frowning mug.

"Hello Mister Knuckles. What can I do for you?" Bristol asked.

I mentioned my hankering for some quick and easy British lunch fare, and Pauline pointed to the cooler in the corner. I asked her what was good, and she answered with an extra dose of inscrutable accent, something to the effect that it was all tasty.

I purchased a sandwich called the Ploughman's Cheese. If a ploughman liked it, and it had cheese in it, I figured I couldn't go wrong. Pauline accepted my payment, and unlike our first encounter, she smiled as she gave me my change.

"Thank you, kind storekeeper," I said. "By the way, Pauline, I met your niece this morning, Turquoise Blix-Vixen."

If I expected Pauline to act at least mildly curious, she disappointed me. She only stared and said nothing. Since I had my sandwich, I risked little by pushing her with more questions.

"Do you see her much? She seemed like a nice enough young lady."

Pauline edged forward so her mouth was six inches from my face. "Turquoise has never stepped foot into this store, and I expect she never will. And since I have no reason to attend any family functions at the Manor, I doubt our paths have crossed more than a few times since she was born. To answer your question, I don't see her much at all."

Bristol must've sensed that his wife was about to lift off because he stepped next to her and encouraged me to go and enjoy my sandwich.

"How about you join me while I eat?" I said. "I need answers to some questions about Gloria Butterfield." I looked at his wife. "And you're welcome to contribute as well."

The skin around Pauline's throat turned pink, and, shaking her head, she walked out of the room without saying a word. Bristol let loose a big thunder of a laugh. "Blimey, mate, you know how to press all my wife's buttons."

"Sorry about that, but maybe it's a good thing Pauline left the room. You'll probably feel more comfortable answering my questions about Gloria."

"I pretty much told you all I remember the first time we talked," he said.

I halfway closed my eyelids and grunted. "Come on, Bristol, I know there's more to your story."

Bristol threw back his head in laughter. "If you're playing Sherlock Holmes, then you have to work harder at getting me to talk, because I don't know what you want me to say."

"Fair enough," I said, always flattered to be compared to Sherlock Holmes. "I understand you were the man the Bethards called when a peculiar job needed to be done, like checking whether Cissy's husbands were dead."

Bristol smiled. "Those Bethards have tender feelings, so yes, I did that once or twice over the years."

"So now you'll understand why I can't shake the feeling that your talents for handling distasteful tasks might also involve ridding the family of an annoying American woman. After all, you told me you dropped her off at the dorm on New Year's Day, the last time she was ever seen."

The smile on Bristol's face went flat. He pointed toward two chairs near the store's front window, the same seats we sat in when I first talked with him. I went over and sat, unwrapped my sandwich, and bit off a chunk of bread and cheese the size of a ferret's head.

"Listen, I liked Gloria, I really did," Bristol said, his words coming fast. "I was looking out for her, mate, seriously."

"Why don't you start from the beginning?" I said. 'When did you first meet her?"

"It must've been early November 1976. I'd heard Myles was back at the Manor with a woman friend, which was surprising, with his schooling going on. Apparently, the bloke was so in love with this American that he wanted the Colonel and Miss Rosemond to meet her. For whatever reason, the woman came into the village and found her way into the shop, where she met Paulie and me."

I stuck the quarter-eaten sandwich under my armpit and retrieved my notebook and pencil. Bristol seemed to be picking up steam, and I had to get everything he said written down, my hunger be damned. "How'd Pauline react to Gloria's surprise visit?"

"My wife was polite but distant, and since I didn't have the history with the Bethard family as she did, I treated Gloria friendly. I even suggested she and Myles come into the village and join me and Paulie for a pint at the pub."

"That was mighty bold of you."

Bristol sighed and swept the back of his hand under his nose. "I thought it'd be good for us to get to know the American and her to know the part of the family not livin' up at the Manor. Gloria liked the idea, but it never happened."

"Let me guess," I said. "Pauline shot down your idea like it was a Messerschmidt during the Blitz."

I hope I'd score some cultural points with my World War Two reference about the relentless German bombing of London, even though Bristol's likely knowledge was from his primary schooling because he hadn't been born yet. Nonetheless, the metaphor seemed to work.

"Me Paulie was not happy, sure enough," he said, "but I heard it was Myles firing the anti-aircraft gun to shoot down my proposal."

"Who told you that?"

Bristol leaned back in the chair and scanned the ceiling. "Let me give that a bit of a think."

I looked down at my hands, holding my notebook and pencil, and felt weak in my gizzard. The professional PI in me wanted to keep writing whatever information I could squeeze out of Bristol. The primitive homo sapiens version of Nic Knuckles, however, wanted to use my incisors to rip off the remaining plastic wrap and sink them into that sandwich.

"It was Gloria. Yeah, she told me."

With my mouth cavity stuffed with bread, cheese, and whatever else a ploughman would eat, I forced out this question. "When did Gloria share that information with you?"

Bristol folded his arms across his chest, an upper body thick with muscles long turned to fat. He took on a serious expression and again lowered his voice.

"I saw Gloria a few days later at the Manor when I was making a delivery. I asked her whether we was going to get together for a social, but she said Myles had gone off on her for making her introduction. Gloria apologized, and I told her no harm. I knew Myles and Paulie didn't like sharing the same space, and I suspected Gloria's lover boy didn't care for me much either."

"What's the history with Myles and Pauline? How come they despised each other?"

Bristol failed to keep the grin from taking his face hostage. "There's a bit of a tale to that, mate," he said, barely holding back a cackle. "Let's just say the Colonel and Miss Rosemond acted a little more common when they were young, more than she'd ever admit now."

I hadn't forgotten Rufford's smoking gossip about the Colonel getting Rosemond pregnant while still married to Pauline's mother, so I dropped what I already knew into Bristol's lap. He sat straight up, his mouth wide open.

"Whoa, mate. You're the Billy big bollocks entcha? How'd you work that out?"

I smiled. "I'm Nic Knuckles, and that tells you all you need to know."

Bristol needed a minute to process his newfound respect for me and probably had to gauge how far he could try and fool me.

"Okay, mate, here's the answer to why Paulie and Myles don't like each other. Myles was seventeen years old and about to go off to the university when Miss Rosemond had the village's snoop investigate the whereabouts of the Colonel's ex-wife and his daughter, Pauline."

"The village snoop we're talking about is the legendary Aunt Jane, right?" I asked.

"That's the one."

Bristol shared that Aunt Jane located Pauline and found that the child's mother had died two years before, leaving the girl in a bit of a struggle. Rosemond insisted that Pauline come live at the Manor until she found someone to marry.

"Even though Myles was about to leave the Manor for Uni," Bristol said, "he wasn't happy sharing his place of privilege or his parents. He feared that after he left, they might hand off part of his inheritance to the girl. Cissy was none too happy either, suddenly having an older sister. Me poor Paulie, as a child growing up in Manchester, had acquired an attitude by then, and was willing to tell Myles and Cissy to shut their gob. It was never a happy time for none of them."

I turned a few pages back until I found notes from my first interview with Bristol. "You told me that the Colonel and Rosemond supported you marrying Pauline. What's the details on that story?"

Bristol smiled. "Me and Paulie had gone to the pub a few times, and she liked me enough to give us a snog after a few pints, but I wasn't in no mood to settle down. But one day, the Colonel called me up to the Manor and gave me a proposition."

It was my turn to chuckle. "Let me guess," I said. "You were about to do your first side job for the Colonel by asking Pauline to marry you."

"Now, that sounds so cold, mate. I had feelings for Pauline and probably would've gotten around to asking her to marry me. But the Colonel gave me such an incentive to move quickly, I took him up on it."

I'd seen and heard enough to know that Bristol marrying Pauline got him a shop of his own, a lifetime customer in Rosemond, and occasional side work from the Colonel. Not bad for a farm kid with no prospects.

"Since you were indebted to the Colonel, did he ask you to keep an eye on Gloria when she showed up at The Rock and around the village?"

A grin returned to Bristol's face. "Oh yeah, I didn't mind doing that," he said. "Gloria was great fun, and I liked to torque off Myles by befriending his woman. Paulie did not enjoy hearing what I was doing, but the extra quid the Colonel gave me helped us have a nice Christmas."

"Was taking Gloria to the dorms on New Year's Day of 1977 another odd job the Colonel asked of you?"

Bristol again folded his arms and leaned back. He didn't look happy. "Like I told you, mate, Gloria came to me askin' for a ride."

"Did you tell the Colonel about that?"

Bristol nodded.

"Did you tell Myles as well?"

"The Colonel told me he'd handle him, and to keep me mouth shut about any of this Gloria business."

I didn't respond. Not that I didn't want to ask Bristol a follow-up question, but the rest of that Ploughman's Cheese sandwich had found its way into my mouth. All I could do was mumble and shake my head. I'd done myself no favor because Pauline came back into the room, and her eyes were all small and smoldering, like two radioactive buttons on a Chernobyl janitor's coverall.

"Well, Nic," Bristol said as he stood. "I gotta say cheerio and spend some time with me Paulie. Let yourself out the door, if you will."

I wanted to thank Bristol for our conversation and express hope to meet again, but it'd be another two minutes before I cleared my mouth of food to speak. By then, Bristol and Pauline had left the room. I wondered what angered Pauline enough that she needed to get Bristol out of his chair. Did she overhear what her husband was saying to me and wanted to issue him a reprimand?

While those questions bothered me, I was more concerned by Bristol's memory of multiple conversations with Gloria, yet Gloria never mentioned him in her letters home. Could I believe Bristol's stories? Was he telling me the truth, or was talking to me just another odd job for the Bethard family?

Chapter Thirteen

With a full stomach and multiple filled pages in my notebook, I left Warford's What Nots for Lizabeth's cottage to do a data dump. Hopefully, she'd corroborate enough of Bristol's stories that I could consider him a reliable source. Otherwise, I was afraid he was playing me.

The sun had climbed higher in the sky, and it was growing warmer as I knocked on the door of Lizabeth's cottage. She didn't appear annoyed this time and welcomed me in. The Earl Grey tea she offered was appreciated, as it might help me digest that Ploughman's Cheese. I pulled out my notebook and settled into sharing time mode.

"My friend, Bristol Warford, admitted knowing Gloria from when she first arrived," I said. "The Colonel paid him to keep track of her and report on her behavior."

"Sit tight, Nic, because I have some excellent backup to what you said." Lizabeth quickly thumbed through a pile of loose papers. "Here," she said, pulling what appeared to be a cut piece of butcher's paper. "I found this note of Aunt Jane's from late December of 1976."

"I'm sitting tight. What do you have?"

"Aunt Jane wrote that she and Gloria had met in the village, and Gloria told her that Bristol came to the Manor daily and had always taken the time to speak with her."

"It didn't sound like she suspected his true mission, did it?"

I sipped my tea and discovered the blasted liquid was hotter than a West Texan chili pepper. Lizabeth took advantage of my burnt tongue by hogging the floor, excited to share more of her discoveries. "Here is another entry on the back where Aunt Jane wrote that Gloria confided her concerns that Rosemond hated her and was determined to break up her relationship with Myles."

Lizabeth raised her hand. "Then she wrote that Gloria said Bristol told her that if you're not aristocratic blood, Rosemond frowned upon your very existence."

"Okay, that's good. At least Bristol was truthful about befriending Gloria."

Lizabeth smiled and picked up her teacup. "I gave myself a bloody headache by going through Aunt Jane's mess of an archive, page by page. It was only that first chest, but at least I found something of use to you."

I hated bursting Lizabeth's happy bubble of success, but I was only mildly impressed with what she'd found.

"Yes, you've confirmed Gloria and Bristol knew each other, which gives some credence to what Bristol tells me. But I also know the man was paid to do the Colonel's bidding. How do I know he's still not collecting a dime from the family?"

"You don't, Nic. You must assume that everyone from that family works to keep you in the dark."

"I must get inside The Rock and see Myles and his mother. I know if I talk to them face-to-face, one of them will break and spill secrets."

If Nic Knuckles had one talent, and trust me, my crime-solving talents were legendary in quantity and quality, it was getting people to talk.

"If you feel that strongly about it, why don't you try going in the chapel door?" Lizabeth said. "That might be a smart way to start."

"Say what?"

"Myles' wife, the Reverend Amethyst, leads services every Sunday morning at the Rockingham Manor chapel. I doubt she'd turn you away, considering how few people fill the pews."

"That's not a bad idea, Lizabeth. What can you tell me about her?"

I intended to bounce what Bristol and Rufford said about Reverend Amy with what Lizabeth told me. I was taking to heart her warning that everyone associated with the Bethards was working to keep me in the dark, including the woman of God.

Moving her chair closer, Lizabeth started her story by describing how poor, heartbroken Myles took almost two years to start socializing again. Rosemond was more patient than her husband with their son's recovery, but she might not have known how quickly Baron Monteque's money evaporated.

"According to Aunt Jane, the Colonel went to Cissy and asked his daughter to squeeze the Baron for ten thousand pounds to help cover the Colonel's latest bad investments. Cissy must've thought her lifestyle had suffered enough because she refused."

Lizabeth covered her mouth, attempting to keep a snicker from growing into a guffaw.

"My aunt loved telling me how she heard that Cissy told her father, 'It's about time Myles pulled his head out of his arse and contributed to the welfare of Rockingham Manor.'"

I opened my notebook and wrote that maybe Cissy had nothing to do with the Baron's death. Perhaps her father was the mastermind behind the Baron's demise and the other husbands, as well. If the man was prone to murder, maybe his enthusiasm for the sport started with Gloria Butterfield.

"Excuse me, Nic, are you listening?"

I looked up and found an exasperated Lizabeth West. "I'm sorry," I said, quickly marking my last entry with a bold letter x. "You were saying?"

"I was telling you about when the Colonel put out the word across the countryside that he was looking for a wife for his son. Eventually, he learned about Amethyst Perkins, who lived in the county over."

"How'd the young woman feel about an arranged engagement?" I asked. "Was Myles considered a catch back then?"

"Yes, actually, he was rather a good-looking young man."

"How'd Myles feel about being auctioned off by his father? Didn't you say he was starting to socialize with the ladies again?"

Lizabeth wobbled her head as if several answers were rolling inside her mind like lottery ping pong balls. "Uh, he had actually met a woman on his own. Sadly, she didn't have the wealth needed to help save Rockingham

Manor, so Rosemond killed the relationship before it could blossom."

"I guess Rosemond wouldn't let him create another Gloria Butterfield situation."

"Right, absolutely not."

I scrawled some lines in my notebook while Lizabeth quietly sipped her tea.

"Was it one of those old-fashioned arrangements where the two patriarchs got together and forced the kids on each other?" I asked.

"Actually, that wasn't exactly the case with Amethyst Perkins. She agreed to marry Myles but negotiated her own arrangement. She'd always wanted to be a vicar and, since women were not ordained by the Church then, she insisted that Bethards build a chapel on the grounds for her use."

Okay, old Rufford gets a pat on the head for being right.

"The first women to be ordained didn't happen until the mid-1990s," Lizabeth said, "so poor Amethyst had to pretend being a vicar for the first fifteen years of her marriage."

"Fake it until you make it, huh?"

Lizabeth tilted her head to the side and was poised to ask me to explain. She seemingly concluded it wasn't worth the effort and continued talking. "No one knows for sure if she ever was ordained, but she never missed holding a service at her chapel, even if only a farm hand, or Rufford and his mother, sat in her service."

"That sounds sad. A shepherd without a flock, a coach without his ballers, a garbage can without raccoons. I feel for her," I said.

My mom had a mixed record as far as sending me to church. When I was about four, she'd drop me off at any church on Sunday morning she found opened and then would take my malevolent sisters shopping at a mall in Jersey. Her favorite house of worship was the Church of the Eternal Salvation over near the old Shea Stadium. Their dogma was of no interest to Mom, but she liked that the services went well past two o'clock in the afternoon and included food. She'd say how lucky I was that she could arrange for God to be my babysitter.

"Gimme the time when the service begins," I said, "and I'll be there in my

Sunday best."

Lizabeth was unsure when Amethyst's service began and suggested I arrive at sunrise just in case she started early. She waved off my idea of her joining me, saying that she was more comfortable with the village vicar's preaching style. More importantly, most of the village's populace attended that service, giving her the opportunity to pick up scuttlebutt.

"That's a sweet deal, Lizabeth. You can pry as you pray."

Lizabeth didn't appear flattered by my comment. She finished her tea and slumped in her chair. I think she was tired of talking about the Gloria Butterfield case, so I took the hint and wrapped things up.

"This has been a good work session, Lizabeth," I said. "What do you think?"

"I'm delighted you're happy," she said, although with the corners of her mouth drooping, I didn't think delight was what she felt. She stood and took our teacups to the kitchen, dropping them into the sink. She then walked quickly to the front door and opened it.

"It's time for you to go, Nic," she said. "I've got hours of reading Aunt Jane's litter stored in the second chest."

I pocketed my notebook and stood up. "Hopefully, my visit to the chapel will pay dividends, and I'll have a good scoop to share with you."

"Cheers," Lizabeth said, gently but firmly pushing me outside.

I turned around to look at her before she shut the door. "This just occurred to me, Lizabeth. Assuming everyone associated with the Bethards was incentivized to keep family secrets, how can we trust anything Aunt Jane wrote? She was a confidant of Rosemond, right? How do we know she wasn't employed by her to watch Gloria as well?"

Lizabeth closed her eyes and sighed. "Aunt Jane didn't take obsessive notes because she planned to write a beloved BBC television series. She did so because she didn't trust the Bethards or anyone in Village-In-Thistles."

Nic Knuckles immediately understood what Lizabeth meant. When your profession revealed the worst in people, you never had friends, only acquaintances who feared you.

Chapter Fourteen

I was up and out of Gram Edwards's place at sunrise, hoping the early morning English country air would sweep the cobwebs from my eyes. I also made a mental note to ask Gram to get an exterminator to work their magic in my bedroom. I hated waking up with my head encased in a spider web. Those creatures have brains big enough to handle eight legs, they should be smart enough to stay outdoors where God intended them to be.

Speaking of The Almighty, I was unfamiliar with the nature of the God worshipped by the Church of England. Nic Knuckles was a god-fearing man, regardless of which deity one feared, so I'd show up, get on my knees, and see if I could learn anything new about the Bethard family.

I knew from Rufford and Lizabeth that a few years after Gloria Butterfield had disappeared, Jeremy Bethard, the Colonel, arranged a marriage between his son, Myles, and Amethyst Perkins. Myle's new wife was the honey with the money, and also seemed to have the moxie to go up against the Colonel and Rosemond. I was anxious to see Reverend Amy on the pulpit, and hopefully, meet her afterwards. I'd introduce myself and solicit her help in breaking through that protective Bethard family wall. Heck, who knows, maybe by attending a church service, Nic Knuckles might find some non-cheese, inner peace.

I arrived at Rockingham Manor and saw the chapel about a hundred feet away on the edge of the woods. It was built in the old English style with big stones, a square tower, and a tiled and sloping roof. Unsure when services started, I let myself into the chapel through the unlocked front door. There were four rows of wooden pews with wide aisles on either side, so sitting in the back still had me close to the front. I was hoping that Myles might need spiritual nourishment that morning and would attend. If so, being where I was, I could get in his face quickly.

The wood pew felt hard against my tush, but not uncomfortable enough to keep me from dozing off. I might've been slumbering for thirty minutes when the sharp grunt of a wild boar startled me awake. I soon realized it wasn't a forest animal, but the housekeeper, Melba, walking by me. Her man-child, Rufford, waved as he followed in behind her. They moved to the front pew, joining a man I recognized. The rows of buttons running up and down his suit jacket confirmed it was the chauffeur I'd seen a few days ago in the village. That must be Roland.

Two other men, one older by twenty years to the other, sat in the middle pews and, based on their attire, I figured they were field hands delaying the start of another day of labor.

That was it. Me and the few employees who kept The Rock operating. No Myles, no Cissy, no Rosemond, and no Turquoise. Not even Turquoise's stepdad, Mister Dinwiddie. Dang, just my luck. The Bethards might be pagans and never attend any church services.

There was a rustle at the front of the chapel, and a woman entered from a side door, all dressed up in priestly robes. That had to be Reverend Amethyst. She stood about five foot two and confidently walked to the front of the chapel, her hands clasped. She greeted us in a strong, warm voice before suddenly stopping. Her eyes lost their cordiality as she stared toward the back of the chapel. I turned to see Bristol standing, hat in hand. He quietly apologized and scurried into the seat across from me. We exchanged nods.

Reverend Amethyst regained her composure and spoke, her voice clear and strong. "Blessed be God, the Father, Son, and Holy Spirit. And blessed be his kingdom, now and forever. Amen."

The rest of us mumbled a collective ah-men, and Amethyst sang a hymn in a sweet melodic tone. I was immediately lost, however, when everyone opened a prayer book and flipped to the pages dictated by the Reverend. I finally located a copy of The Book of Common Prayer, but couldn't find the prayer they were reading, so I moved my lips and nodded with the best of them. I think I passed the challenge by the time the group praying stopped, and Amethyst ordered us to sit. She climbed into this little elevated booth and started her sermon.

"Greetings to all who come to taste the succulent peace that our God willingly grants us. All the Lord asks is that we humble ourselves and atone for our sins."

Reverend Amethyst continued, announcing that we could gain the Lord's grace, if we again humbled ourselves and atoned for our sins. Then came another admonishment, telling us to gain God's bounty by coming off our high horses and atoning. Even though her accent sometimes clouded the sounds of what she said, her annunciation of the word, atone was always clear.

I had to wonder, who in her meager audience had so much to apologize for? My first choice was that nasty woman, Melba. Her rudeness was epidemic and probably affected the whole household at Rockingham Manor. Any bad things Rufford did could be excused because of his unfortunate head injury. I only knew Roland as a rude man, and perhaps, the two field hands were guilty of sloth, but that hardly seemed to be outrageous enough to earn Reverend Amethyst's ire. That left Bristol as the possible target of her focus. I peeked over at him each time she encouraged the guilty to repent, and all I saw was a face with dull eyes and a mouth edged flat. He was no longer the cheerful proprietor I'd twice had conversations.

Holy Provolone, I swore the Reverend Amethyst and Bristol had some sort of competition going on. She was tossing wave after wave of innuendo at him, and he was letting them wash over him like the ocean against a big block of granite. I resisted the urge to pull out my notebook and record this observation, but I committed it to memory. It was obvious to me that Reverend Amethyst could be more than a conduit to Myles, but a source on the other characters involved in Gloria's disappearance.

The pastor at the pulpit wrapped up her sermon with a few more examples of the gifts God would grant the folks in her chapel, if only they lowered themselves and made amends. More singing and praying followed, and she raised her hands and intoned that we leave the service and sin no more. I mumbled that I would do my best. Melba, on the other hand, blew up any expectation of her avoiding sin by giving me the evil eye as she waddled by on her way out. Roland, Rufford, and the farmhands followed her through the door, leaving just me, Reverend Amethyst, and Bristol. I stepped from the pew, and Bristol looked at me. His eyes shifted back and forth between me and the Reverend, and when I started walking toward the front of the chapel, he aggressively pulled his hat on his head and left.

"Great sermon, Rev," I said. "I don't get to church too often, but if you were preaching, I'd be there every Sunday."

A small smile appeared and then widened across the woman's face. "Well, thank you."

"I like that your speech was light on the fire and brimstone," I said. "In my line of business, we like to coax a confession from the guilty, not bombard them with threats."

"What line of business are you in, mister...?"

"Knuckles, Nic Knuckles." I reached out to her, and we shook hands. Her fingers were soft, as if they mostly turned bible pages and clasped together in prayer. "I'm a private investigator."

"My, my, why would an American investigator be sitting in my chapel on a summer's Sunday morning?"

Bingo! That's the question I wanted her to ask. Maybe my prayers for access to the other Bethard family members would be answered, which seemed only fair, with me spending an hour kneeling. "I've been hired to look into the disappearance of a young American woman from a good forty-five years ago."

Reverend Amethyst's smile slipped into neutral, and her eyes struggled to hide her emotion. "I don't suppose you're talking about Gloria?"

Well, blow the heavenly trumpets and shout Hallelujah, Reverend Amethyst Bethard *had* heard of Gloria Butterfield.

"Yes, I am," I said. "The sister of Gloria hired me to determine why Miss Butterfield never returned home." Pointing at the front pew, I suggested we sit and chat. She joined me without hesitating.

The woman looked to be in her mid-sixties, at that stage in life where her vanity hadn't conceded to time, and she still colored her hair. Judging from how she operated the service, I knew she still had her spunk. Hopefully, this conversation might finally get me inside The Rock.

"As I understand it, Rev, you came upon the scene a few years after Gloria went missing."

The woman nodded. "Yes, that's true. And, consequently, I don't know much about her or her circumstances. My husband was uncomfortable talking about it, so we never did."

I took my notebook and pencil from my inside jacket pocket. "I understand that," I said. "Whatever you can tell me, however, would be greatly appreciated."

"There's not much to share. I had heard that my husband, Myles, had been involved with an American girl when he was young, but his father told me it was nothing more than what you Americans call a summer fling."

"Actually, while they met in early July, they were together through the end of that year. Hardly a summer fling, don't you think?"

"Oh, my, that's a bit of a clarification, I dare say."

"Did you know Myles had asked Gloria to marry him?"

Reverend Amethyst stiffened, and her right hand pulled at the wedding band on her left-hand ring finger. "I understood that she wanted him to marry her, but that he had absolutely no interest."

A silence fell over us, yet the Reverend maintained eye contact, as if she was bracing herself for one more uncomfortable question. I obliged. "Did you know your in-laws vehemently opposed their son's relationship with Gloria?"

"No, they never talked about it, and I didn't see it my place to probe."

"Did anyone talk about how Gloria disappeared under mysterious circumstances?"

"Like I said, she and her circumstances were never talked about among the family. At least not with me."

The fingers on my right hand slowly stroked my chin. Reverend Amethyst might've thought Nic Knuckles was deeply reflecting on his next question, but I was thinking my facial stubble might need some trimming. Hopefully, I'd packed an extra razor or two.

"Is there anything else, Mister Knuckles?"

I switched from my grooming concerns back to the woman in front of me.

"You sure you have nothing more to share about Gloria Butterfield and Myles?"

"Yes, Mister Knuckles, I have nothing else to tell you."

Or, nothing else you wanted to say, I thought. The woman, trained to administer to confessing sinners, surely had a sixth sense when a deeper truth was being hidden from her. How could she not have asked Myles for details about Gloria Butterfield?

My eyes lifted from the Reverend's face and scanned the chapel ceiling. "I understand Myles built this house of God so you could preach until your dream of being ordained came true. He sounds like he's a wonderfully generous man."

Reverend Amethyst slowly bowed before she spoke. "My husband was a generous man back before I married him. But his parsimonious way reared its ugly head soon after the nuptials."

I scribbled the comment in my notebook, taking an extra twenty seconds to phonetically sound out parsimonious. Wasn't that some kind of fruit? I'd check my dictionary for the meaning later tonight, but right now I felt this new line of inquiry was about to pay off. Boy, was I right.

"Soon after we married, Myles became very careful with money. He'd scrimp on the heat in winter by burning fallen tree limbs collected from the property. The temperature in the Manor was no warmer than fifteen degrees. I'd complain, but he'd argue that he was helping me build respiratory strength by living in such a frigid environment."

I was aware the Brits had a different way of measuring temperature, so I knew fifteen degrees wasn't fifteen degrees American. But it still sounded cold.

"Eventually, he closed off most of the Manor to save on heat and cleaning expenses, and started leasing out the ballroom for bar mitzvahs and weddings. The rich Russians were big customers, and they always paid in cash."

Even though I knew the answer, I asked the question anyway. You never realized when you might get a different take on what you thought you knew.

"Did you and Myles have children?"

Reverend Amethyst forced a smile to appear, but her glistening eyes hinted at some internal heat. "Early in our marriage, Myles claimed it'd be easier for me to preach and administer to my flock if I wasn't burden with babies. So, no, we never had children."

The woman stared off for a few seconds before shaking her head and forcing her lips into a cheerless smile. "But, otherwise, Myles has been a good husband."

Having a heart riddled by failed relationships, Nic Knuckles could easily translate the language of those with bruised souls. Reverend Amethyst carried a whole lot of hurt behind that priestly face.

"You know I'd really like to have a meeting with Myles. I'd wager that his recollections could move my investigation along. Do you think you can arrange that for me?"

The Reverend sighed and shook her head. "I don't know. My husband is a very private man who struggles with a multitude of personal issues."

"I'm sorry to hear that," I said. "I've spent more than a few hours on a shrink's couch; maybe he and I could exchange notes."

"I doubt he'd be willing to do that," Reverend Amethyst said. "Myles's father was a domineering man, so my husband has self-esteem issues. His mother is manipulative, and he's her favorite puppet. My poor husband suffers from migraines, his gout flares up at unpredictable times, and he deals with a severe form of misophonia. All in all, he's a miserable human being."

Reverend Amethyst might have to atone for trashing her husband, but what she said was juicy information and the best I'd gotten on the man. I scribbled in my notebook: Myles Bethard was cheap, selfish, and often in the sick bed.

"I must go," Reverend Amethyst said. "I'm late for my pastoral visit with my husband. It's one of the rare times he'll talk with me." She stood and thanked me for coming to her service. "If you ever need to talk about God and His role in your life, I'd be happy to meet with you."

With that comment, I stood and eagerly shook her hand. "Old Nic is far from home and could use some spiritual fine-tuning, Rev. Yeah, I'd like that very much."

"That would be wonderful," she said and turned to leave, but stopped. "And maybe you can tell me more about that Butterfield woman. I've always felt Myles never got over his love for her."

Chapter Fifteen

Nothing says Sunday to a New Yorker than brunch with lox and bagels. While I had little hope of finding a Jewish deli in Village-In-Thistles, I headed into town after Reverend Amethyst's service, both hungry and open to alternative sources of food. I barely stepped within the village limits when Bristol Warford appeared by my side.

"Hey mate, fancy seein' you at the chapel," he said.

"I must say I found your attendance a bit surprising, as well. I never saw you as a church-going man."

Bristol shook his head. "You might be unfair, labeling me as a heathen." Then he slapped me on the shoulder and said, "But you wouldn't be too wrong."

The man explained that, as his and Pauline's most reliable customers, he felt it important that one of them should support a Bethard family project. Having him sit in Reverend Amethyst's Sunday service was easy, and the least he could do. "The sermon is boring, but sitting there gives me time to think about how I could upsell Miss Rosemond the next time she orders pork bangers."

"I actually enjoyed hearing The Rev delivering her sermon. She gave me a lot to think about," I said.

"I hate to ruin the party, but if you come next Sunday, you'll hear the same sermon or thereabouts. Reverend Amethyst sings one tune, and one tune only."

I ignored Bristol's criticism, suspecting he had nothing good to say about the Reverend. My attention was focused on finding some Sunday dining fare outside of the Pissin' Pints, or a sandwich from Warford's. I kept walking, hoping to discover a food-oriented establishment that I'd not noticed before. Unfortunately, Bristol kept pace, yattering on about the wife of Myles Bethard. "The old Reverend basically has one bloody message, you know. Always on about the confession and remorse. Those religious types can't seem to enjoy life. That's true, innit?"

I stood outside a pub called the Wasted Swan, and while it served breakfast, I worried I'd violate some community standards by eating and drinking in another establishment. I could check with Bristol, but he was too busy running his mouth. "Because Paulie and me business depends upon keeping Miss Rosemond and Myles happy, and Paulie won't step a foot onto Rockingham Manor property, so, I go. You know, if Reverend Amethyst is happy, then so is Myles. You understand, don't you, Nic? You have to keep your paying punters happy, right?"

Maybe the man thought that Nic Knuckle's brain slowed to a crawl when I was hungry and felt he had to repeat himself. I thought differently. As a seasoned investigator, I found the man's repetitive yakking as a sign he was anxious. What was bothering him? Maybe I should go on the attack and see what he gives up.

"I couldn't help but notice the crackling look The Rev sent your way when you came into the chapel," I said. "What was that all about?"

The smile on Bristol's face flipped off, then back on. "Uh, that was nothing. She doesn't like blokes coming in late, you know, she's a stickler for timeliness. It was nothing, really."

I withdrew my notebook from my coat pocket. I had a gut feeling Bristol wanted to tell me something. I might as well help him out by showing how one asks a question.

"The Rev told me her husband was tight with his money," I said. "Have you found that to be true?"

Bristol shrugged. "Miss Rosemond pays me, so I couldn't say."

"Can you verify that most of the Manor's rooms are closed off and unheated in the winter?"

"I usually don't go much beyond the kitchen, so I couldn't give you an answer," Bristol said, "but I heard that Myles is lookin' for someone to take the Bentley off his hands. He could probably buy a bloody Kia and still have enough left over to heat the house during the winter."

Ah, another sign that money was an issue at Rockingham Manor. I bet that snotty chauffeur, Roland, wouldn't act so superior driving a small car. I smiled, imagining him squeezed into the driver's seat like an ordinary working man.

"I understand that Myles is sickly and..." I tapped my forehead, "prone to emotional issues."

Bristol's shoulders again climb, but further up his neck. "I usually meet with Miss Rosemond and, sometimes, the housekeeper to get me instructions. I don't know much about Myles, since he doesn't come down from the upper quarters."

I paused talking so I could record Bristol's response. He stood silently waiting for me to finish, which seemed strange. Why was he hanging around? Did he want to tell me something, and was struggling to form the question?

"The Rev knew of Gloria Butterfield and that she was once a romantic interest of Myles. But the Colonel told her it was just a dalliance, nothing serious. From what you saw back then, was Myles as in love with Gloria as Gloria wrote in her letters? Or, was he toying with her emotions?"

The pink hue of Bristol's nose darkened, and he chuckled. "I dunno, mate. Like I told you, I just took orders from Miss Rosemond and made deliveries to the Manor." He shuffled his feet to turn away. He said he had to get home to make Pauline her breakfast. "She's never happy with me going off to chapel, and cop's a strop if I don't come right home."

"You do that, my friend. Happy wife, happy life, am I right?"

Bristol grimaced. "Yeah, that's right."

As the man walked away, I wondered if that old, happy wife, happy life cliché was based on any scientific research. What if the wife was only happy when she was abusing the spouse? If the wife was naturally jolly, would the husband have a happy life without any effort on his part? I'd never married, so I had zero first-hand knowledge of such an arrangement, and Mom was never happy as a wife. Ah, the mystery of relationships. Something you'd think a successful investigator and mystery solver would have a handle on.

The rumbling of my empty stomach brought me back to the here and now. I found the page in my notebook titled Bristol Warford and quickly jotted down some bullet points.

- He's working hard to manage me
- He knows more Bethard dirt than he lets on
- The Rev and him don't like each other
- He acts like he has something to confess.

I couldn't yet tag Bristol Warford as a suspect in Gloria Butterfield's disappearance, but he was seriously auditioning for a spot.

Chapter Sixteen

It was Monday morning, and the rains had returned, confining me to the launderette. But not for long. Gram shooed me away from her kitchen table, claiming she had dryer lint to collect, but I think she'd grown tired of me eating her cheddar cheese while sharing little about my investigation. It was probably good she did because my mind was more on Reverend Amethyst and her invitation to return and chat about God and another cosmic mystery, Myles Bethard.

I knew Reverend Amethyst was now my best chance at accessing the Bethard family. If I couldn't get past Melba at the front door, I'd go back to the chapel and try that side door by the pulpit that Reverend Amethyst entered through on Sunday.

The rain had turned into a mist, so I left Gram's place without an umbrella. I didn't realize that my sports coat seemingly had the same properties as a sponge, and even though the air was a steady mist, I was soaked when I entered the chapel.

"Gee- zuz," I loudly grumbled as I shook the water off my fedora.

"Oh, hello, Mister Knuckles."

Yikes, it was Reverend Amethyst kneeling at the altar. "May I help you?" she asked.

"Greetings, Rev," I said. "First, let me say when I said gee zuz, I was referring to my buddy Jesus Cortez, not your man, Jesus."

The woman stood and walked toward me. "That is what I assumed," she said. "Is there a reason for coming to my chapel in this awful weather?"

"I wanted to take you up on your offer of some chit-chat."

"When I made that suggestion, I thought you might approach the house at the front door rather than sneaking in the chapel like a ferret."

I skipped dishing on Melba and her intransient nature and said something I never thought I'd say. "Any chance a man can get a cuppa? I'm chilled to the bone."

Reverend Amethyst tittered, which was another rarity in Nic Knuckles' experience. My mother growled, my three sisters cackled, my girlfriends snorted, chortled, barked, and howled. But I'd never heard a woman titter. It was endearing.

"Of course, Mister Knuckles. I was finished with my prayers and was about to return to my office to work on next Sunday's sermon." She pulled on a bright yellow slicker and told me to follow her. We left the chapel through the side door, stepping outside as the rain resumed pouring. Her rain gear repelled a few thousand raindrops as we walked fifty feet from the chapel to the Manor. My clothing absorbed an equivalent number of drops. We entered the Manor through a side door, and once we got to her office, the Reverend directed me to sit while she got the teapot heated.

Soon, a steaming cup of tea was in my hands. "Move over here by the electric heater, Mister Knuckles, and let me relieve you of your coat. It's absolutely soaked with rain."

As if the hot tea and kindness weren't enough, she uncovered a plate and offered me a biscuit. "You must be hungry. Please enjoy. Eat all you wish."

Reverend Amethyst sat across from me and sipped from her teacup, the steam misting her glasses. It was so warm and cozy that I immediately thought, what the hell was that woman's game?

Yeah, I know. Why would Nic Knuckles suspect The Rev was operating from the dark side of human nature? That's what happens when you're a premier private investigator. You can't trust the kindness of people, because they usually have some motive behind it. Most rookie gumshoes learn the hard way. I know I did. Her name was Peaches, and she wore size twelve clodhoppers. She'd hired me to snoop on her husband, an orthodontist named Chip. Peaches oozed kindness, and I fell for it. Only after Chip mysteriously died and my toothbrush was found parked next to his larynx did I realize I'd been played for a fool. Lucky for me, the police found size twelve shoe prints in the toothpaste smeared at the crime scene and tied them back to Peaches.

"So, Mister Knuckles, I'd like to apologize for some of the comments I made on Sunday when we conversed after the service. I unfairly painted an inaccurate picture of my husband."

My sport jacket, shirt, and pants had been drenched, but I had the foresight to place my notebook into a plastic baggie. I pulled it out and sat prepared to scribble the highlights of anything said by the Reverend.

"Myles might be overly concerned about expenses, but to be fair, Rockingham Manor is, and has always been, very expensive to maintain. He is actually quite creative in finding ways to keep us all housed and comfortable."

Never being one to beat around the bush, I said, "I'd love to meet the man."

Reverend Amethyst raised her teacup to her mouth. "As I mentioned yesterday, Myles is in ill health, making it difficult for him to meet people."

Unfortunately, my brain didn't register what the woman said. No, as it so often did, my mind wandered back to the idea of beating around the bush. What did that even mean? Why beat *around* the bush instead of beating the bush itself? What did the bush have to do with anything? Such mysteries of the American language.

"I don't need to give the man a physical exam, Rev. I just would like to ask him about the last days of Gloria Butterfield's stay at The Rock. I had all my vaccinations before I arrived, and I'd be happy to mask up if you're worried about me infecting him."

The Reverend shook her head. "Oh, it's not that."

"Then what is it?"

Reverend Amethyst lowered the teacup onto her lap. "Are you familiar with Charlotte Brontë, Mister Knuckles?"

"Wasn't she married to the American actor Charles Bronson? I believe he met her on the Revenge of the Forgiving movie set back in the eighties."

"No, Charlotte Brontë wrote a classic novel titled Jane Eyre. Perhaps you might've read it in your English literature class."

Nic Knuckles was a proud graduate of Bernie Madoff Secondary and usually landed in the top thirty percent of academic performance each grading period. Charlotte and her friend, Jane, however, I didn't know. When you're born to pursue criminals, your reading habits tend toward Hammett, Chandler, and Highsmith.

"In the story, Jane falls in love with a darkly handsome man named Edward Rochester, yet he can't marry her because he has a wife."

"Let me tell you, Rev, Nic Knuckles has investigated more than a few cheating husbands. There's nothing classy about that kind of behavior."

Reverend Amethyst hesitated as if she was trying to process what I'd said, which I appreciated. Most people just blow by me. She finally shook her head and continued her story: "Edward loves Jane, but he can't leave his wife, who suffers from a case of profound melancholy."

I couldn't be sure where the woman was going with this melancholy thing. I thought I'd help her along by offering a range of mental health issues I've dealt with over the years. "Are you saying Myles is a psychopath, a sociopath, or a borderline personality disorder?"

"Oh, my no," she answered. "He's cranky, and sometimes he explodes in anger, but it passes quickly."

"Exploding anger, huh?"

I once knew a NYC Bomb Squad specialist named Bits O'Brian, a heck of a guy. He had amazing self-control while on the job, less so when arguing with his wife. His Bomb Squad co-workers still remember the tragic day Bits and his dear spouse argued over a hand grenade she'd bought at a yard sale.

Reverend Amethyst's head slipped from side to side as she struggled to explain. "Well, perhaps to say he explodes might be a bit of an exaggeration, but certain things set him off."

I leaned closer, shrinking the space between us so nothing useful could slip by me. "Like what? Does the pressure of perpetual money problems set him off?"

The woman straightened her shoulders, and the pallor of her cheeks colored. I'd obviously touched a nerve.

"Well, I'd rather not say, Mister Knuckles."

I had enough conversations with Bristol, Rufford, and Lizabeth West to know Myles and Cissy Bethard 's primary mission on earth was to ensure Rockingham Manor stayed in the family. There were *always* money problems for the Bethards.

"How about issues living with Rosemond? I know from experience how challenging it is for an adult son to share space with his mother."

"Rosemond can be cold toward people, but she's very protective of Myles."

"Would she meet with me?"

Reverend Amethyst shook her head. "As I said, she's very protective of her son."

I laid down my notebook, picking up my cup of Earl Grey. "I gotta think that Momma Bear wouldn't have to protect her cub if the cub has nothing to hide. Are you suggesting that she needs to shield him from consequences?"

"I'm not sure how to answer that question."

I felt bad watching my host squirm. She'd said enough last Sunday and today to convince me she was almost as befuddled by Myles and his family as I was, and she lived with them.

"What about Cissy and her current husband?" I said, shifting hopefully to a more fruitful line of inquiry. "I've met Turquoise, a young woman who speaks her own mind."

"I don't know Turquoise well, I must say. Cissy and her family occupy the back half of the Manor, and I only see them at the Sunday evening dinner."

"How do you get along with Cissy?"

"We have a cordial relationship."

"Cordial, huh?"

Reverend Amethyst nodded. "Yes, but we're not each other's confidante if that's what you hope to hear."

Yeah, that was what I was hoping to hear. I retrieved my notebook and recorded what I'd heard about The Rev's relationship with her in-laws. I felt frustrated. Six days on the job, and I had few notebook pages with much of value. My hope of gaining access to the Bethards' emotional vault through Myles's wife looked like a dead end. Those Bethards were more than living up to the reputed English stiff upper lip. The top lip, bottom lip, and everything in between were immovable.

To salvage something useful from the visit, I was about to ask my host if she happened to have any Gorgonzola available when she surprised me. "Tell me about Gloria."

"Okay," I said, taking my notebook in hand. "Let me rummage through my notes and see what I can tell you." I quickly located the page that listed the highlights of what I knew about Gloria. I figured I'd give The Rev all of it and monitor her reaction. Maybe I'd discover something, like her tell or personal hot buttons. Any successful PI has mastered reading a person's facial and body language. Otherwise, you'd be like a seagull in a fog off of Nantucket. Fluttering blind until you ran into the blade of a giant windmill.

"Here is relevant information from a letter to Gloria's family dated July 1976." I cleared my throat and read the first lines in a falsetto register. "Dear Ma and Pa. I arrived at the Uni, as the Brits call a university, and my dorm room was small but comfortable. Imagine the chicken coop with a bed in it, and you'll know what I mean."

"Excuse me, Mister Knuckles. Why are you reading in that high-pitched voice? It's disturbing."

"Uh, I just thought I could make it more authentic, like Gloria was talking to you."

"Please stop. It's annoying."

I bobbed my head to show I'd heard her request, but I wasn't happy. Reenactment was a proven technique for solving murder mysteries, and Nic Knuckles had great success with it. There was the Giuseppe the Toy Maker murder out on Long Island, where I used puppets to demonstrate that it was impossible for a two-hundred-pound, balding man with a thick grey mustache to suffocate from inhaling pixie dust.

That was The Rev's loss if she didn't want a dramatic rendering. I returned to reading my notes. "It was Gloria's twentieth birthday two days after she'd arrived, and her fellow students took her into Brighton to celebrate."

I looked at Reverend Amethyst. Her hands were clasped, and she was slightly bent at the waist, her eyes on me. I read the parts where Gloria met a handsome young graduate student and teaching assistant, Myles Bethard.

Gloria claimed they immediately took to each other, and a heated affair began.

I paused and studied the face of the woman sitting in front of me. That sad mist I'd seen in her eyes when she spoke of never having children had returned.

"I'll save us time by summarizing what Gloria wrote about her adventure in the autumn months," I said. "Apparently, your in-laws, the Colonel and Rosemond, reacted coldly to the budding relationship. That didn't deter Gloria and Myles. She wrote they returned to the university more in love than ever."

Reverend Amethyst whispered. "Yes, I suspect the Colonel and Miss Rosemond were not fond of the romance."

"The Colonel and Rosemond's disappointment only worsened when Myles said he'd asked her to marry him."

"Really?" The Reverend asked, the tone of her voice rising along with the arc of her right eyebrow. "Did he propose to her?"

"Yes, indeed. When he and Gloria returned to Rockingham Manor at the start of the winter break, Myles announced his intentions to marry Gloria."

Reverend Amethyst inhaled, then exhaled with a weary-sounding remark. "Oh my. I didn't know that."

"According to what Gloria wrote in the letter that followed the announcement, the Colonel said nothing, and Rosemond fainted. Myles tried to convince Gloria that his mother fainted from happiness, but she was hurt and then angry. But she decided to stay and give his parents the chance to know her better."

That earlier hankering for a taste of gorgonzola returned, so I did a quick summation. "Gloria spent time at Rockingham Manor with Myles, rode horses, surveyed the property, tried her hand at grouse hunting, and spent hours reading the family's history in the library. Oh yeah, Gloria and Cissy shared funny stories about Myles, apparently, much to his embarrassment."

"Cissy never shared funny stories about Myles with me," the Reverend said, her face sagging as if pulled down by the tiny hands of heartbreak. "I've heard no funny stories about my husband. None at all."

When first meeting me, most people think Nic Knuckles is without flaws. I wish that was true. It seems that when I'm hungry, I tend to miss the facial and verbal clues other people put out when they're distressed. As I said, the desire for gorgonzola was taking over my mind, so I didn't react to the sadness in The Rev's voice and pushed on with my report.

"Oh, here's a juicy part. Myles surprised Gloria on Christmas morning with a beautiful necklace that once belonged to his great-grandmother, the Great Gram Dame Swizlelback, a German heiress. She had willed it to Myles, with explicit instructions to pass it on to the love of his life."

I paused as a grin formed on my lips. "And when Rosemond saw it, she passed out and rolled under the Christmas tree."

I loved that image and looked up, expecting to see a smile on the Reverend's face. Instead, I saw a teary-eyed plum tomato of a woman barely holding her feelings together. "I never was given any necklace," she said.

Oy, the poor woman was melting before my eyes. I felt horrible missing how much the details I shared were hurting her. I supposed I could cheer her up by discussing my miserable love affair with Imogene the Executioner. I'd met her attending the hanging of the master criminal, Mister Boots, in Texas. Not that I had any reason to witness the execution. I had nothing to do with his capture and trial. I was at the state pen visiting a prisoner who'd hired me to prove his innocence. I'd gotten lost in the hallways, and before I knew it, I stood before the gallows, staring up at Imogene and a man with a hood over his head. Imogene was dressed like an avenging angel in black leather and four-inch heels. I caught her eye just as she yanked the release that opened the floor under Mister Boot's feet. The next time I saw her was when she was slapping my face. "I'd never had someone go unconscious faster than the man I was hanging," she said. "You okay there, handsome?"

We dated about a month before things got ugly, but that's all I'm gonna say because The Rev needed my attention.

"Maybe I should stop," I said. "You're upset."

The woman sucked in a breath, taking a nose full of mucus with it. Shaking her head, she whispered to me. "No, go on. I need to hear all of it."

With the green light to resume, I read more text, talking about the week between Christmas and New Year's, when Gloria attended luncheons and parties at various estates in the county. Once, she met a young man named James, who, in a drunken state, recounted witnessing Myle's explosive temper. He said he had no clue what set Myles off to beat some poor fellow so severely that he was hospitalized, but the Colonel was able to get the lad to drop any charges.

I peeked up from the paper to evaluate The Rev's face. She was lost looking into an empty teacup, so I continued reading.

"Gloria wrote that she brought the incident up to Myles, who pointed out the man's reputation for lying to besmirch his betters. 'Pitiful case of jealousy, that James,' Myles had said before admitting to the fight. 'I was all of sixteen, and it was nothing more than your typical schoolyard fisticuffs. My opponent's pride was far more bruised than his face.'"

I added that Gloria wrote that she laughed, finding it difficult to envision Myles losing his temper and actually getting his hands discolored. Reverend Amethyst's gaze lifted to match mine, but she said nothing, so I continued, sharing what Gloria had written about an upcoming New Year's Eve party and someone she hoped to see again.

"Here is where Gloria explicitly mentioned a woman called Aunt Jane," I said, "Did you ever meet Aunt Jane?"

The sad expression that had taken up residence on Reverend Amethyst's face lifted and was replaced with a pair of tight eyes and an equally snug sneer. "Of course, I know Aunt Jane," she said. "That old goss would try and get me to break confidences as if my ethical vows were nothing to take seriously."

The woman closed her eyes and slowly regained her pastoral vibe. "Please continue reading, Mister Knuckles."

My concern about the Reverend's emotional state prevented me from sharing the contents of Gloria's last letter, mailed on New Year's Day, 1977. I felt I'd given her the background on her husband's decades-old romance, and it'd be cruel to say any more. I didn't want to hurt her further; I only wanted her help meeting the family.

"All the rest I have is hearsay," I said. "I believe everything before Gloria's disappearance on New Year's Day was built on this developing Bethard family tension. That's why I need to talk to the people directly involved with Gloria during her visit."

"You mean Myles and Miss Rosemond and Cissy, I assume."

My head bobbed. "You got that right, Rev."

Reverend Amethyst pressed folded hands to her lips. "I'll see what I can do, Mister Knuckles."

Holy holiness, The Rev, the woman of God, was stepping up. She'd put aside a boatload of personal disappointment and help me get justice for a woman she'd never known. A woman who'd gotten from Myles much more than she had.

"You know, Rev," I said. "If I could nominate you for sainthood, I'd do it right now."

The woman with the white collar looked up at me with a hardness in her eyes I hadn't seen before. "I'm not a saint, Mister Knuckles," she said. "Right now, I don't know who or what I am."

At that moment, even my craving for gorgonzola couldn't mask the shame I felt. Being an aggressive private eye sometimes required you to do things that caused grief in good, innocent people, and sometimes, it changed them. I felt Reverend Amethyst would no longer be able to ignore the sins of her husband and his family. That'd be a big help for me in the long run, but I still felt bad.

Chapter Seventeen

I left Reverend Amethyst's office and its air of overwhelming sadness almost at a trot. Admittedly, a powerful hunger continued to hover over me since The Rev had no gorgonzola, but my guilt at busting the woman's illusions also lifted my feet. Maybe Lizabeth West could convince me I was only being a professional investigator, not an insensitive clod. Throwing in the existence of her impressive cheese collection and stopping at Lizabeth's cottage was the smartest thing I could do.

"I say, Nic, will you share some news or only eat my cheese?" Lizabeth asked after I'd crashed her cottage with an excited promise of a substantial advance in our case.

"Yes, yes, I'm sorry," I said. "I spent an hour with Reverend Amethyst, and I gotta tell you, that is one unhappy woman. It appears the heat Myles had for his wife was never as intense as what he carried for Gloria."

Lizabeth harrumphed. "Reverend Amethyst made her choice, so I don't feel sorry for her. Those religious types enjoy being helpless so they can nurture that pathetic dependence on a God."

"Yikes, Lizabeth, does the spirit of Bertrand Russell live in this house?"

"Never mind about that. Tell me what excited you, other than learning Amethyst Bethard is a doormat of a woman."

I swallowed my mouth full of cheesy proof that God existed and answered. "The Rev Amy agreed to try and help me get into The Rock. I am getting close to finally having that face-to-face with Myles. Who knows, it might even lead to meeting Rosemond."

Lizabeth snorted. "The wanna-be preacher only said she'd try and help you. Trust me, Nic; bloody Rosemond will put that church mouse in her place. Don't get your hopes up."

Wowzer, why such hostile feelings for The Rev, I wondered. Lizabeth had suggested going to the chapel for the Rev's service. She felt that might be a better way to get to Myles than banging my head against Melba's skull. Why all the hate for the Reverend now? I'd better change the subject. I'd already failed to read one woman's inner emotions this morning.

"There's one big gap in my knowledge that I need your help with, Lizabeth. In Gloria's last letter, postmarked the first of January, she talked about an upcoming New Year's Eve party hosted by the Bethards. She was super excited and planned to turn things around with Rosemond. Could you dig through Aunt Jane's documentation pile and see if you can find anything on that night?"

Lizabeth turned her contempt for Reverend Amethyst into anger toward me.

"Are you daft? What have I been doing since I last saw you?"

I absorbed Lizabeth's level-five stink eye, and she finally stood and left the room, returning a minute later with what looked like a faded party invitation. "I found the actual invitation to that New Year's Eve party, and fortunately, Aunt Jane wrote a lengthy summary of her experience on the back of it. But it was hell finding it. I should go on strike for better wages."

Having never dealt with an employee threatening a work action, I sat quietly and hoped her desire for collective bargaining would peter out. It did, and Lizabeth read Aunt Jane's notes from the back of the invitation.

"I arrived my customary five minutes prior to the official opening of the reception and planted myself on the most comfortable piece of furniture in the Great Hall, a peach-colored upholstered chair. The Colonel thrusted a cocktail into my hands, rudely saying, 'come on, old girl, loosen up.' I did not feel I needed to loosen up in any form or way. Nonetheless, I must admit, the cocktail was surprisingly tasty."

Lizabeth looked up. "Trust me, my aunt enjoyed a few cocktails in her life."

Nic Knuckles tried to avoid drinking any form of alcohol while working, although a beer or two was consumed when it was necessary to blend in with an unsavory crowd at a college sorority kegger. I think it was Gamma Ramma Mamma, or something like that. Some girl was pledging, and her parents hired me to investigate if it was a safe environment. I went undercover and survived to the last day of Rush Week before being found out.

Lizabeth brought me back to the present when she started reading again.

"Aunt Jane wrote that Gloria came over and sat with her, and they continued their conversation from the chance meeting in the village. Aunt Jane asked if Gloria felt more included in the family, and the girl demurred."

Lizabeth squinted and complained about faded ink. "Okay," she said, "then Gloria asked whether Aunt Jane had ever heard of Myles having an issue with his temper. Aunt Jane claimed to be only a passing acquaintance of the Bethard family, being invited to their New Year's Eve event and one social during the summer."

That comment brought me up straight. "Why would Rosemond and the Colonel include your Aunt Jane when she had no pedigree to speak of?"

"Oh, Aunt Jane had more than pedigree," Lizabeth answered. "She had information that Rosemond valued and the Colonel feared," Lizabeth grunted, apparently satisfied with her insight. "Aunt Jane wrote she prepared to leave the New Year's Eve party via cab at 9:30 PM, and Gloria stopped her on the way out. She said the American asked if she could have lunch before returning to the university."

Lizabeth raised her right hand and laughed. "Poor Gloria said she was desperate to get Aunt Jane's help understanding Rosemond. Oh boy, was that mission impossible?"

"Did they make a date?"

Lizabeth slowly rolled her head back and forth as she studied the note. "Other than asking Gloria to ring her later and schedule a meeting, that's all my aunt wrote."

I fell back into my chair and wiped my hands of gorgonzola crumbs. "I guess that has to be your next priority, Lizabeth. Find out if Gloria met Aunt Jane, and if so, did she offer a way to win Rosemond's favor or told Gloria to give it up?"

"Knowing Aunt Jane the way I do, I'm betting she suggested the girl catch the next plane back to America. We might be wasting time looking for more."

I didn't know if Lizabeth's opinion was just thoughts untethered to facts, or her interest in the case was wavering. With my mold-induced bronchial conditions, I couldn't take on digging through the remaining musty piles of Aunt Jane's notes.

"I tell you what, Lizabeth, I'll bump up your daily by five quid. Would that add to your motivation?"

"I won't say I'll enjoy looking in those chests," she said. "But I'm less disgruntled."

Chapter Eighteen

ram Edwards welcomed me downstairs the next day with her usual mix of local euphemisms baked into a Scottish burr. I mumbled good morning and took the cup of tea she handed me. I wasn't happy that my first instinct was to sip a hot cuppa in the morning. In England a week, and I'd already acquired another bad habit. My self-recrimination immediately ended when Gram said, "A wee lad came by this morning with a letter for you. He claimed it was from Rockingham Manor. Can you imagine a hand-carried message from someone livin' up among the high and mighty?"

I apologized to Gram for spitting my tea and snatched the letter from her hand. My name appeared in purple ink on the envelope in a woman's handwriting. I quickly opened it.

"Dear Mister Knuckles," the message began.

My practice was to keep any correspondence confidential, and I would not have usually read the Rockingham Manor letter aloud. However, Gram's look of anticipation was so strong that I was afraid she'd stuff me in a dryer if I didn't share the letter's contents.

"My husband, Myles Bethard, asked me to extend an invitation to meet with him today. Please arrive promptly at eleven this morning. Kind regards. Amethyst Bethard, Reverend."

"Well, blimey, me boarder has gotten himself invited up to the big house for a fix," Gram said as her eyes slowly examined me. You should let me help make your coat more presentable.

I did allow Gram to press my sports coat with a hot iron. It hadn't fully recovered after yesterday's soaking in the rain. Maintaining a noir look was more challenging than people thought. The fedora bent out of shape easily; the sports coat had to have enough inner pockets to carry a notebook and pencils, and the slacks had to match the coat in color, at a minimum. While Gram freshened my sports coat, I ate an excellent smokey cheese she provided.

"Bring me up to date on your investigation, Nic," the landlady said. "You haven't shared two pence worth, no chin-wagging or nothing, since you showed up at my door."

Gram didn't realize that loose lips, sunk ships, and snitches got stitches, and a talkative private eye was soon working parking lot security at a Taylor Swift performance. But the woman could help me if she knew what I was working against. I opened my notebook and shared the goals I needed to achieve with today's visit to The Rock.

"Number one," I said, "I have to get the dope on Myles and Gloria when they were the village's hottest romantic couple. Did Myles love Gloria as much as Gloria implied in her letters, or was the young woman fooling herself? Was there an actual engagement? Did Myles give Gloria the Swizlelback necklace as a sign of his intentions, or was it something Gloria wanted him to do?"

"Aye," Gram said. "Maybe the American lass convinced herself that a stuffy old Englishman had the hots for her. You know that happens a lot. And don't be surprised when you learn that there's not much jewelry left in their family vault, especially since the bloke struggles to keep the hearth heated. It's possible that the Swizlelback necklace was sold off long ago."

I took my pencil and jotted down Gram's comments. Nic Knuckles always looked for that local, low-level source that most people disregarded because they were minor characters used to add some color or toss out a red herring here and there. Gram was different. She offered some excellent insights, and maybe something she'd say would be an important puzzle piece.

"I also need to know what happened during that New Year's Eve party. Who did what to whom? Where was Myles while all of this was going on?"

Gram nodded her head as the iron hissed. "Aye, folks drinkin' to excess, and you never know how they'll behave. Me Jimmy would let his geggie run away with him until some bloke took offense. That was never good for Jimmy's fine face."

"I also hope to find out why Myles let his supposed love leave the country without a fight?"

Gram held my coat up so I could slip it on. "And take a gander while you're in there to see if the furnishings have gone shoddy. I'm thinking of expanding me business and offering upholstery cleaning. The old laundry just ain't cutting it, money-wise, you know what I mean?"

"Got it, Gram. I'll give the place a good look-see."

Two hours later, looking spiffy, I stood outside the main entrance of Rockingham Manor, my notebook and pencil in the side pocket of my neatly pressed sports jacket. I held Reverend Amethyst's invitation in my left hand, and my right hand was tightly wrapped around the heavy iron knocker. I was ready if that she-devil, Melba, the Housekeeper, tried to prevent me from meeting Mister Bethard.

A thunderous sound from the dropped knocker rattled the wooden front door. Seconds later, someone pulled it open, and I was looking into Melba's pasty face. Before I could flap Reverend Amethyst's invite in front of her eyes, she waved me in. "Mister Bethard awaits you in the parlor," she croaked. I followed Melba down a dark hallway where several suits of armor stood on exhibit. Oil portraits of what I assumed were Bethard family kin hung on the wall. I also realized The Rev had been right about the Manor being uncomfortable. I could almost taste the humidity and heat that had failed to escape the building during the night. We stopped at the entry to a small room, and I saw a man standing next to a dark fireplace.

"Hello, Mister Knuckles. Please come in and join me."

Myles Bethard was slender, with a small nose, pale green eyes, and heroically styled thinning hair. He gave off an odor of unwellness, like a teenage boy's dirty socks. To avoid catching anything contagious, I stretched my arm to its full length and shook his hand.

"Thank you for meeting with me, Sir Myles," I said.

A jagged smile revealed a set of grey teeth arranged in a way that reminded me of Stonehenge. "I have not been knighted, Mister Knuckles," Myles said, a soft chuckle slipping through those neolithic teeth. "I am just the humble master of Rockingham Manor, one of the most prestigious and honored country estates in the county of East Essex."

I knew Myles wasn't a knight, but I wanted to open with one of my most effective techniques: over-the-top flattery. I like my suspects to think they're more intelligent, better credentialed, more vital, less in debt, and prettier than Nic Knuckles. Once they fell into that trap, I could eventually play upon their overconfidence and trick them into revealing their secrets.

"Yes, sir, Rockingham Manor is an outstanding structure," I said. "But as you might know, I'm not here to study mid-19th-century English architecture. I'm working for a woman who fears her older sister, Gloria Butterfield, met her demise in your company on or about January 1, 1977."

"Oh, you Americans, always direct and to the point." Myles placed his open hands together and slowly clapped. "Bravo, sir, bravo."

Nic Knuckles appreciated the compliment, but the man's hands drew my attention. They were impressive—oversized and muscled for such a skinny guy.

"Please join me over here by the window," Myles said, "so we can enjoy the delightful country air while I try and quench the thirst of your curiosity."

I followed him over to some old-timey furniture that proved to be as uncomfortable as it looked. The purported country air wasn't delightful but smelled of distant agriculture, as best as I knew what farming smelled like. Myles sat across from my chair, offering me neither tea nor cheese.

"I suppose, as an investigator, you want me to share some insights into my early years," Myles said. "Isn't that how Sherlock Holmes proceeded? He was always looking and listening for that one clue that inevitably led to the damning revelation, wasn't he?"

"Yes, sir, all private investigators have sat at the feet of Sherlock to learn the fine art of sleuthing," I said as I pulled out my notebook and pencil and turned to an unmarked page, labeling it Myles Bethard. My first entry was short—*a know-it-all who didn't offer a snack.*

"Okay, Master Myles. Let it pop, and tell me all about Gloria and you."

Myles switched into storytelling mode, and I started recording his words. "I was the first child and only son of Colonel Jeremy and Rosemond Bethard. As a boy, I had enough cleverness to succeed in school, and that fact, combined with the family name, got me through university. When I celebrated my twenty-second birthday, I was a graduate student and teaching assistant at the local university in Brighton, not far from Village-In-Thistles."

"What was your major?" I asked. "What was your course of study? You know, the stuff you were interested in becoming an expert in?"

Myles tilted his head to the side. "My official field of study was economics, but most of my time was spent messing about with my chums."

"Did you do any sports?"

The man smiled. "While I was on the university rowing team for four years, my true sport was drinking too much and pursuing young maidens with the hope they'd surrender their chastity."

"Chasing chicks and drinking brewskis," I said. "You sounded like a typical American college guy."

"Yes, I probably was," Bethard said before lifting his suddenly damp gaze upward and sighing. "But then I met Gloria."

Holy Provolone, the man's eyes misted as he mentioned Gloria's name. Poor Rev Amy might be right. Even though it had been decades since he last saw her, Myles still had a soft spot in his heart for Miss Gloria Butterfield.

"It was July of 1976, and I saw this pretty young American undergraduate student at a pub, celebrating the two-hundredth anniversary of the colonies' humiliation of King George III. I introduced myself to Gloria Butterfield, who I learned was studying in England for the year. I was immediately drawn by her looks and her puckish sense of humor."

"How did she take to you?" I asked.

Once again, Myles's eyes flittered toward the ceiling as he searched his memory.

"It may not appear so now, Mister Knuckles, but I was quite the catch when I was younger. So, of course, Gloria was drawn to me. She seemed to have a romantic view of English gentlemen from large country estates. It's famously called the Mister Rochester syndrome."

I scribbled a note. *Take time to read Jane Eyre.*

"Gloria and I immediately connected, and I don't think there was a day after the meeting that we weren't together. It was intoxicating for both of us. We were like fire and oxygen, feeding and consuming each other. By November, I was convinced she was the one I wanted to share my life with."

Myles introduced Gloria to his family several weeks later, and the Colonel and Rosemond were congenial yet distant. Gloria assumed it was because they were typically reserved Brits, and Myles admitted he reinforced her thinking.

"I wanted to give my parents a chance to know Gloria and see what I saw in her."

"How'd Gloria and Cissy get along?" I asked.

"Cissy was a good sport, showed Gloria about the estate, and entertained her by sharing my most embarrassing exploits as a lad."

He admitted that his sister's kidding did not amuse him, but since Gloria found them funny, he ignored Cissy's behavior. "I'd do anything to make Gloria happy."

Everything he said so far confirmed what Gloria had written in her letters. She and Myles were hot and heavy from the start. Rosemond and the Colonel were cool toward her, and she and Cissy had gotten along.

"It sounded like the visit went better than you expected," I said.

Myles straightened his back, and his eyes iced over. "No, not really. It went as expected. It went *precisely* as I anticipated."

Myles explained that behind the scenes, the Colonel pulled his son aside and suggested he enjoy sowing his wild oats with this American, but not assume she was worthy of him. Rosemond added her acidic commentary, belittling Gloria's looks, mannerisms, and intelligence. Myles responded angrily, faulting his mother for snobbery and classism. Rosemond returned fire, accusing him of purposely working his way down the peerage ladder and hitting rock bottom with a foreigner with no worthy lineage.

"I was very despondent," Myles said. "I told Gloria that Rosemond expressed reservations about our relationship ever achieving success. I must say, Gloria's reaction was amazing. She thought that with some effort on her part, she could win over my mother. 'Surely, she wants her son to be happy,' she said."

Myles admitted that was the first time he experienced unconditional support from someone important to him. He and Gloria returned to the university more in love than ever, and their days settled into long walks in the woods and hot sex in the dormitory.

I looked up from writing to see Myles smiling as his mind floated among those happy, youthful memories. Gloria Butterfield was a hundred percent correct about the intensity of her relationship with Myles Bethard. Even after all those years, she still pulled the man's heartstrings. My feelings for Reverend Amethyst climbed a notch higher on the empathy scale. How could she compete with Myles' first and most genuine love?

Myles looked out the window, plucking his bottom lip. "A few weeks later, I took a call from my father. He'd received a back-channel message from one of his old chums at the university who reported on my academic performance."

Myles said his father raged over how his son's grades had cratered since meeting Gloria and issued a scathing lecture. Then, the older man completely shocked Myles, claiming the family estate had become a money trap because the farm was failing. The Colonel swore Rockingham Manor ran the risk of bankruptcy and would do so for the foreseeable future.

"You didn't suspect the Manor was in financial trouble?" I asked. "It was never discussed with you?"

"The Colonel might've lacked the talent to make Rockingham Manor a success, but he was a superb keeper of secrets." Myles snapped, spittle forming in the corner of his mouth. "That was when he told me I had an obligation to marry into a fortune, or the Bethards would lose everything created when my Great Gram Dame Swizlelback married Colonel Pepper Bethard and moved to the Rockingham Manor estate. I was devastated by having this obligation suddenly thrust upon me."

"I guess you were about to do some quick growing up."

Myles turned his watery gaze back at me. "Oh, bloody yes, and the pressure only increased thinking of how Gloria would react when I shared that conversation." Myles slowly shook his head. "I was utterly afraid my father's demands and my mother's opinions would drive her back to America."

"You got me hanging here, Myles. Is that why Gloria Butterfield so quickly and mysteriously left England?"

The man clasped those big, sinewy hands together and delivered. "Later that evening, Gloria talked about her excitement at entering the British High Society after we married. She was enamored with the idea of living at Rockingham Manor and eventually becoming mistress of the estate."

Myles paused to fill his lungs with air twice as if he were about to dunk himself underwater.

"I confessed that with the perilous financial condition of the Manor, the likelihood of her dream coming true was nil. I expected an emotional outburst, but I was absolutely flabbergasted at how she reacted." A soft smile nestled between his sunken cheeks. "Gloria was amazing. She claimed her family had successfully farmed for decades and felt that agriculture was in her blood. 'Together, my dearest, she said, we can turn the Rockingham farms into a source of steady revenue and keep the Manor in your hands.'"

"Wowzer, Gloria sounded like the type of can-do middle-American woman a weak-kneed fancy boy like you needed."

Myles vigorously nodded and said, "Gloria's optimism so took me; I proposed that we marry as soon as possible in the new year."

My hand started cramping as I furiously scribbled down what Myles said. Gloria accepted his proposal, and they decided to hold on to the news until December, when he and Gloria returned to Rockingham Manor for the university's holiday break.

"That must've made for a very merry Christmas," I said. "How'd the folks take the yuletide news?"

"Better than I expected," he said. "My father's stiff upper lip quivered, and my mother fainted, but otherwise, they managed the announcement quite well."

"How was Gloria feeling?"

Myles admitted the American woman was in a less celebratory mood.

"Mother's behavior deeply hurt my fiancée. I reminded Gloria of our plan to make Rockingham Manor a successful enterprise and challenged her to stay with the dream. Gloria gave me the most perfect answer. 'Yes, love, you are right. We'll never make it if I let your mother run over me.' After that night, I was more in love with Gloria than ever."

Myles Bethard had a radiant glow on his ragged face as he sat back in his chair. I tried to guess what was going on inside the man's head. Obvious to me, he was feeling some gooey sentiment. Maybe that night was one of the last times he stood up for what he wanted. Perhaps his memory of Gloria reminded him of a deep love he never duplicated. What if, instead, he was recalling a holiday buffet that included a spread of different cheeses? Whatever induced that combination of longing and joy on his face suddenly disappeared, taking with it, the man's vitality.

"You okay there, Myles?" I asked as his face lost its coloring, and he shrunk into himself.

"You're looking kind of sick."

"I...I utterly failed Gloria," he said, tears brimming his eyes. "The poor thing had no idea the hold mothers have on their sons."

I nodded as a hot bolt of emotion blew through my chest. "Like the piston-driven steel talons of an eight-hundred-pound hawk," I said. "Am I right?"

Myles nodded. He then drew a breath and continued his storytelling.

"It was the day before Christmas Eve," he said, "and I was busy with estate business and couldn't attend to Gloria. Cissy was off doing something, so Gloria had to fend for herself. She was anxious about being alone in the Manor with my parents, so I suggested she visit the village."

Myles added that was exactly what she did. Gloria went off alone and returned hours later, eager to share all her adventures in Village-In-Thistles. Myles was not happy with what he heard.

"Gloria found the shop operated by my step-sister, Pauline, and she introduced herself. She said Pauline was indifferent to the prospect of becoming sisters-in-law. That only made Gloria feel even more insecure about my family." Myles narrowed his eyes. "But what angered me was my love's interactions with Pauline's husband."

"We're talking about Bristol, right?"

Myles confirmed it was Bristol, a man he held in low opinion.

"Bristol would have to work too hard to be a successful scoundrel, so he settled on being average."

Myles continued complaining about Gloria's choice of new friends. "And if that weren't enough, later, she met an older woman who claimed to be dear friends with Mother. She offered to help Gloria understand my mother's thinking, which got Gloria quite excited."

"Let me guess," I said. "It was Aunt Jane."

Myles's lower lip rolled into a pout. "Yes, yes, it was. I warned Gloria that Aunt Jane was the village busybody. And while she and my mother did go far back in time, it wasn't because they were social equals. In my mind, the woman was a horrible peddler of gossip and half-truths."

I scribbled his comment in my notebook, wondering how much of Aunt Jane's gossip and half-truths had been about the Colonel.

"Gloria was cross with me," Myles said. "She said I'd sent her off to the village full of strangers, and when she socialized, I criticized her associations. She was absolutely right. I'd behave horribly, and in a desperate attempt to repair our relationship, I surprised her Christmas morning with a beautiful necklace that once belonged to my great-grandmother, Great Gram Dame Swizlelback."

Ah, the famous necklace of eternal love that the Reverend Amethyst had never seen, let alone worn around her throat.

"That's a pretty rich way to make amends," I said. "Did it do the job?"

Myles' narrow shoulders settled up around his skinny neck. "Gloria's mood was greatly improved, I guess you could say. But then Mother saw the necklace on her, fainted, and rolled under the holiday tree. Working together, Father, the Housekeeper, and I took twenty minutes to extract Mother. I think we lost half of the ornaments that Christmas morning."

Myles continued telling me about the Yuletide disaster. Gloria ran from the room in tears, and Myles eventually found her whimpering in the library. To soothe her hurt feelings, he promised to be at her side every moment of the week between Christmas and New Year's. And Myles was a man of his word, as the newly engaged couple spent those wintry days and nights attending luncheons and parties at various estates in the county.

"According to one of Gloria's letters sent home," I said, "she met a man during one of those shindigs who accused you of being a hot-tempered brute prone to violence."

The skin on Myles's face flushed, giving the man's mug some desperately needed coloring. After sputtering his first half dozen syllables, he regained control of his voice.

"It was complete rubbish," Myles added. "I told Gloria that man was a drunkard and had a long history of lying to besmirch the reputation of his betters. I did admit to a fight with a lad as a teenager, but it was your schoolyard fisticuffs, and my opponent's pride was far more bruised than his face."

"Did she believe you?"

Myles's big left hand pulled on his chin. "Yes, she laughed, saying she found it difficult to believe I'd ever do anything that might bruise my hands. Of course, that inference offended my male ego, but the discussion was over, so we went back to the party, which Gloria was delighted to do."

"How soon after was the New Year's Eve party your family was so famous for hosting?"

The smile on Myles' face slipped away, and he started to slink in his chair.

"Oh yes, I suppose we should discuss that horrible little affair," Myles said. "It was New Year's Eve, and I arrived at my parents' party with Gloria on my arm. We mingled comfortably with the other guests, and I remember Gloria being enamored with the Maple-Sriracha Devils on Horseback. She couldn't eat enough of them."

Nic Knuckles didn't enjoy hearing about hoity-toity social gatherings and their hoity-toity snacks. Not when your childhood New Year began begging on the frigid streets of New York City for money so you could buy some beef jerky for breakfast. I pushed the man to talk about Gloria confronting Rosemond.

"It was soon after we heard Big Ben chiming on the radio and life felt filled with joy and promise," he said. Then, the man's mouth drooped, and his eyes moistened. "That was probably my last happy memory of Gloria." His voice thickened with emotion, and he added, "Then, my poor lover made the mistake of approaching Mother."

Gloria Butterfield sought out Rosemond Bethard, seeking a reconciliation. Perhaps the young woman had consumed too much champagne, Myles speculated. Maybe it was a sincere motive that made her do it. Whatever her reason, it proved disastrous.

"My dear fiancée found Mother and proposed that they try to have a better relationship in the upcoming year. I was aghast, fearing what my mother would do. I watched from afar as Gloria spoke to Mother and then witnessed Mother unloading on Gloria. Gloria looked mortified and ran out of the room in tears."

Myles claimed he felt enraged and approached his mother, accusing her of being a wicked woman. He then went to find Gloria, who had left the house through the kitchen entrance. His concern about her safety was enormous because it was a frigid evening, so he rushed to find her.

"The moon was a waxing crescent, making seeing more than a meter before my face impossible. I found a torch and walked the perimeter of the manor house, looking for Gloria. After twenty minutes of frantically calling out, I found the poor dear, shivering and unable to raise her voice."

Myles told me they returned to the kitchen, where he insisted she drink hot tea. Once warmed, Gloria poured out her grief. She wasn't sure how she and Myles could live at Rockingham Manor when his father was distant, and his mother actively hated her. I stopped writing to look at the man because it sounded like Gloria's telling him to stand up and be brave was a make-or-break moment.

"She...she didn't appreciate what it meant to be the sole male heir responsible for Rockingham Manor," he said, his eyes tearing. "I couldn't ignore my birthright. I was groomed since childhood to eventually take control of Rockingham Manor."

"I imagine it was tough," I said, although I was only guessing. Even though I was technically the sole male heir to the Knuckles family fortune, my mother and three wretched sisters could take care of a fourth-floor walkup and didn't my help. We all preferred it that way.

"I felt trapped by her demand. Our argument grew heated, and I covered Gloria's mouth so as not to disturb the guests still celebrating in the ballroom."

Myles dropped his face into his hands, mumbling how Gloria pulled away and slapped him. He admitted he grabbed her by the wrists, but only to constrain her. They stopped tussling when they realized Melba was in the kitchen watching it all.

"I took Gloria by the arm and ushered her out of the kitchen and to her bedroom. We continued to argue, and she demanded I promise to leave England and live in America after we married. I was absolutely opposed to the idea. While I swore my love for her, I told Gloria she would have to adjust if she wanted a marriage."

"I'm guessing she didn't agree with you."

Myles shook his head. "She threw herself onto the bed, tears pouring from her eyes, screaming, 'leave me alone.'"

Usually, when Nic Knuckles issued an ultimatum to an angry woman, I flopped on the bed, crying my eyes out.

"I returned downstairs to the party and poured a stiff drink," Myles said.

The man stopped talking and sighed deeply as if about to give up the ghost. I worried that he'd lose steam and leave me hanging, but then Myles' chest rose as he filled his lungs, and he continued.

"I stayed up drinking until the last guest left, which meant I was thoroughly pissed by then. Somehow, I found my way to bed, fell asleep, and awoke sometime around noon. After cleaning up, I went to Gloria's bedroom, where I found a note addressed to me. She wrote that she could not spend another minute in the Manor and had Bristol take her to the university dormitory."

"How'd that make you feel?"

I didn't think Myles could shrink further into the chair without taking on the color of the upholstery, but he did.

"I have to admit a great sense of relief," he said so softly I had to lean forward to hear him. "I feared Gloria had gone to breakfast to show everyone she was no pushover, and there'd be a second go-around between Gloria and Mother."

A chuckle escaped from my mouth. "I understand, man. How many times could your mother roll on the floor before seriously hurting herself?"

"And yet, I felt devastated because I knew I'd never find another woman like Gloria."

Myles said he spent the rest of the day recovering from his previous night's excessive drinking, and it wasn't until two days later that he went to the university to find Gloria. He discovered Gloria had cleared out the dorm room. Soon, his father called to tell him that his university contact reported Miss Butterfield had withdrawn from school. He said a later inquiry confirmed that a one-way ticket was issued for a London to New York City flight to a young woman fitting Gloria's description by an agent of British Airways.

"And that, Mister Knuckles, is my story of youthful heartbreak."

Myles reached over to the side table and picked up a silver bell. He rang it three times, drowning out my question about why he had never followed up on Gloria's return to America. Melba materialized in the doorway before the last peal of the bell quieted. She had to be the fastest septuagenarian in England.

"Yes, sir."

Without looking up at me, Myles waved his right hand and said, "Please show Mister Knuckles the way out. I'm terribly fatigued."

I felt the woman's fingers grip my coat collar, and I was suddenly on my feet, my notebook and pencil pressed to my chest. "This way, Knuckles," she said.

"Can I come back tomorrow, Myles? I want to know why you never tried to contact Gloria."

Bethard didn't answer me. His big hands covered his face, and he sat shriveled in the chair.

Chapter Nineteen

I followed Melba as we walked from the room where Myles had done a data dump. Approaching the front door, she suddenly stopped and pointed toward the kitchen. "Go in there and sit," she said. "You ain't done yet, Knuckles."

What did she mean I wasn't done? Why was she steering me into her lair? With my loins girded, I entered the kitchen. The soot-covered yellow tile walls enclosed a four-burner stove, a large wood block table, and three stools situated around a circular table covered with oilcloth. The place looked like it hadn't seen an update since World War II. I wouldn't have been surprised if buried somewhere in the attic was an unexploded German V-2 rocket.

"So, this is where The Rock's culinary magic is performed," I said, sitting on a stool and pulling out my pencil and notebook. "I heard your cabbage stew was to die for."

The woman didn't respond, making herself busy with some kitchen stuff. Why had she planted me in her domain? Did she finally want to talk to me? Maybe this was the alpha break all investigators hoped for, the unexpected one that cleared an open path to the answers that solved your murder case. Yeah, Melba wanted to spill and only needed some encouragement.

"I'm guessing all the family secrets about Gloria Butterfield's disappearance are weighing heavily on you," I said. "I'll be happy to relieve you of your burden."

Melba grunted. "Not bloody likely."

Based on her previous hostility toward me, that comment had a microscopic improvement in tone. That's all an expert interrogator like Nic

Knuckles needed. After all, a termite needs just one nibble to start destroying a wooden house, and I was about to take my first bite out of Melba's stockade.

"What are your recollections of late 1976, when Gloria Butterfield was visiting Rockingham Manor as a guest of Myles Bethard?"

"I got nothin' to say," she said, dropping a chipped teacup before me. "Here's your bloody cuppa."

The tea Melba served me looked like it was the offspring of a thoroughly tapped-out teabag. I'd been in England for eight days now, and I'd stared into many a teacup, and this was the first time I could see the bottom. I also didn't feel the heat coming off it when I raised the cup to my mouth.

"Gosh, Melba," I said. "Could you trouble yourself and make me a hot-splosh, the cup that lifts and cheers, as Gram says?"

"Oh, sorry about that," she said, her upper lip curling to her nose. "I thought you Americans liked your tea ice cold."

I didn't need to check my notebook to know the source of that misinformation. Rufford mentioned Gloria liked her tea with ice and how his mother found that preference irritating. If Melba could remember a minor annoyance from decades ago, God only knew what else she had stored in her memory bank. Unfortunately, God wasn't working this case with me, so I had to use my skills and talents to pry answers from the woman.

"Speaking of tea," I said, "Your boss, Myles, told me about the New Year's Eve party where Gloria Butterfield was last seen. He claimed he brought the American in from the cold outdoors and served her hot tea to warm her up. Now I know you were working the kitchen that night and understanding how spoiled these Bethards are, I gotta believe you served that hot beverage. Am I right?"

Melba slipped a new cup of tea before me, the rising steam indicating that it was a drink worthy of an Englishman.

"That was a long time ago," she said. "But yeah, I recall that American woman in me kitchen she was, and barking mad."

"What do you mean?"

Melba's lips twisted. "Nothin', I met nothin'."

I didn't believe her. She wanted to talk about Gloria, and all I had to do was find a way to free her from her restraint. Maybe a little flattery would work. I sipped from my teacup and said, "Hmmmmm, Melba. This might be the best tea I've tasted since arriving in England. You truly are a gift to these Bethards."

The frown on the housekeeper's face lifted, and a tiny smile appeared. It might've been the first recognition of her talents she'd gotten in a long time.

"So, tell me what happened between Gloria and Myles that night after you served Gloria the hot tea?"

"Those two got into a right old argie-bargie, and that's all you bloody need to know."

The best offense is an even more aggressive offense, so I kept going at her. "What was Gloria and Myles fighting about?"

Melba seemed to have an extensive collection of interchangeable facial expressions because, with that question, she transformed from an irritated English country kitchen staff into a gargoyle right in front of me.

"Are you bloody daft, Knuckles? I ain't one to air the family's dirty linen in public, and I surely won't do it now to you, wanker."

Apparently, the positive benefits of complimenting Melba had a short shelf life. Now, I'd have to employ my most successful technique, the endless questioning. "Answer one question, and I'll leave you alone," I said. "Was there anyone else besides you, Myles, and Gloria in the kitchen when all this happened?"

Melba emitted her endearing rumble of discontent before delivering an answer. "No, no one else."

The housekeeper turned her back to me, her hands performing some mayhem on a slab of unknown animal protein.

"Did you notice if Gloria wore a coat or a man's jacket when Myles brought her in?"

"No, I don't think so. Okay, maybe she did have something over her shoulders. The bird was indecently dressed, as I recall. Now, sod off. I have to prepare a meal for the family."

"Okay, just one more question, and I'll be done with you," I said. "Was Myles still wearing his tuxedo jacket?"

Melba turned toward me, the skin on her face as red and sweaty as a day-old wiener rolling under a heating lamp at a Seven-Eleven. "Of course, Master Myles had his jacket on, you idiot. He's a gentleman, always was. Now stop with your pryin' into the family affairs."

It seemed Rufford's sighting of a man offering Gloria his coat that cold night, someone he thought wasn't Myles, had some truth. I wondered why that mysterious man didn't come into the kitchen with Myles and Gloria to retrieve his coat.

"I appreciate you keeping the family history confidential. There's a lot about my kin that is so secret that I can only recall it under deep hypnosis. Something about my Nana and razor blades creeps up from the depths of my memory. But we're not here to talk about the Knuckles family."

Melba's growling intensified. "I sure the bloody hell hope not. Now stop bothering me."

"Please answer just one more question about that night. Did Gloria threaten Myles that if he didn't leave Rockingham Manor and move to the States with her, she would never marry him?"

Melba's lips trembled, and her rotund frame shook. I held my breath. Would her long-held animosity toward the Butterfield woman override her loyalty to the Bethard family, or would she keep their secrets? It was my lucky day. Hate triumphed over virtue.

"That horrible girl was all tits and teeth, and when she demanded Master Myles give up his stewardship of the Manor, that was too much, even for that love sodden young lad."

Bingo, Myles's story was holding up, and Gloria had been capable of a good, old-fashioned shakedown.

"Myles must've felt cornered by Gloria's demand. I imagine the argument got heated."

"That bird was winding up, Master Myles, good n' proper. I'd never seen him so upset."

"Did either one of them lay a hand on the other?"

"I saw that girl slap Master Myles, and I was about to crack my iron pot over her head when he ordered me to leave the room."

"What happened next?"

"Nothin'. I went through the back stairs and to my quarters and saw nothing more."

"What did you hear?"

"Like I said, nothin', and I got nothin' more to say about that night. Stop flapping your lips and leave me alone."

"Just one more question, Melba. Did you see Gloria leave the Manor the next morning?"

I ducked as a soup ladle soared over my head. "No, I never saw that woman again. Now shut that beak up and let me do my work."

And that's what I did. I stopped talking, opened my notebook, and wrote these few lines. Gloria had demanded Myles leave Rockingham Manor, and their relationship showed signs of violence when she slapped him. Melba claimed she saw it, but no one else was in the kitchen to witness Gloria poppin' Myles across the face. Myles swore he and Gloria left the kitchen and went upstairs to Gloria's bedroom. If so, why'd Melba leave the kitchen after the initial altercation, especially with a big party still cranking in the ballroom?

I closed my notebook, but the questions kept coming. Was that fight and Gloria slapping Myles the critical event I'd been looking for? Was that the incident that clarified in Gloria's mind that Myles would never stand up to his parents and that she had no future with him? Was it enough to motivate her to pack her bag and depart Rockingham Manor? Or was the slap the beginning of an escalating cycle of violence that culminated in the murder of the American?

I looked up at Melba, chopping a big onion, and wondered how she'd react if I asked her if she happened to have any cheddar cheese handy. I was hungry and didn't want it to get out of control. Before I could form my words, the tingling of a tiny silver bell attached to the kitchen wall distracted me from my cravings.

Melba stopped her chopping and turned to me. "Okay, Knuckles, gather up your papers and come with me. They're ready for you."

"Who's ready for me?"

Melba didn't answer my question, but she did express her feelings. "Thank the Almighty I won't have to put up with all your bloody questions, you annoying pillock."

Chapter Twenty

Melba escorted me from the kitchen upstairs to a sitting room, where I saw a snowy-haired elderly woman who looked like an over-fried chicken wing. Next to her was a well-dressed woman who appeared to be in her sixties. She remained seated as she raised her hand for me to take, which suggested someone used to being pampered. The cluster of a half dozen big gold-plated bracelets covering her forearm suggested she loved costume jewelry. I hoped the two were who I thought they were.

"Hello, Mister Knuckles, I'm Cissy Bethard Dinwiddie," the younger of the women said, "and this is my mother, Miss Rosemond Bethard."

Slap my pet monkey and call the ASCPA; things were finally going my way. Nic Knuckles scored time with Myles Bethard in the morning, squeezed some good scoop out of Melba soon after, and now I had Momma Bear and the little sister all in one place. Either today was my lucky day, or something was up.

"Hello, ladies. I appreciate you giving me the time to chat. I'm the private eye investigating the disappearance of…"

"Gloria Butterfield," Rosemond said, finishing my sentence. The older woman grinned and extended her hand. "Welcome to Rockingham Manor, Mister Knuckles."

Any concern that Rosemond didn't have all her lights on in her attic was dispelled immediately.

"It's nice to finally meet you," I said as I gently grasped Rosemond's hand. Her skin was the color and consistency of tissue paper, but what held my attention was that, unlike her daughter, she was completely absent of jewelry. I didn't know women who quickly gave up their bangles regardless of age. As Gram had suggested, maybe her husband and then her son had sold it off.

"Could you give me your opinion of Gloria Butterfield?" I asked.

"Oh my, I haven't thought of that poor girl in decades. What a nuisance she made of herself those many years ago. I hope she found happiness with some dreary American man and lived happily among her equals."

"Sadly, Madame Mistress Missus Bethard, that is why I'm here. Gloria Butterfield never returned home."

Rosemond looked confused. Not knowing how to address the top lady of the Manor, I combined everything I knew about formal female greetings. Cissy came to my rescue. "I suggest you simply address her as Miss Rosemond."

"I'm sorry, Miss Rosemond. As you might suspect, I'm not from around here."

Rosemond looked at Cissy and snickered. "We couldn't have guessed, could we, dear?"

Cissy snorted and then invited me to sit with her on a red velvet sofa. I planted my tush but politely refused her offer of tea. "My hands will be busy with my notebook and trusty writing implement, recording your detailed and truthful answers."

Cissy pressed her lips together in one of those half smiles that the aloof among us love to use. She removed a teacup and saucer from a silver tray on an end table. She tilted a teapot's spout over the cup and asked, "Now, Mister Knuckles, how might my mother and I help you?"

I ignored Cissy and turned to Miss Rosemond. I thought Cissy could be afraid the elderly Rosemond might blurt out some uncomfortable truths, which I was all for. A good investigator often learns more by people putting their feet in their mouths than not. I leaned toward Rosemond, who was sitting in a chair across from me.

"Miss Rosemond, I understand you were upset when Myles brought Gloria to the Manor and announced his intention to marry her."

"Yes, the idea of Myles marrying the American aggrieved me greatly. He was young and silly and needed his parents to guide him through that awkward stage of life. That is what my husband and I did. We captained our son through dangerous romantic shoals and safely delivered him to sanity's shores."

I turned around to face Cissy. Her eyes were focused, and that same thin, disdainful smile was still riding on her lips. "According to your brother, Cissy, you and Gloria seemed to hit it off when she visited Rockingham Manor."

Cissy nodded and shared that she remembered Gloria as a nice girl, but provincially American. They enjoyed each other's company, but Cissy was concerned with Gloria's intense curiosity about the Bethard family status.

"It seemed to me that the girl was as interested in securing a possible hereditary title as anything my brother offered her, emotionally." Cissy softly chuckled. "Of course, my brother had no such title, and I think Myles played upon her naivete."

"I understand that Myles announced their engagement and gave her a big showy family heirloom. That sounds pretty serious to me. And based on Gloria's letters to her family, she felt the same way."

Cissy raised the teacup to her lips and cooed. "I doubt it was an official engagement, Mister Knuckles. More like an intention to ask her hand in marriage, perhaps. Do you recall that moment, mother?"

"Myles was such a silly romantic back then," Rosemond answered. "I knew his infatuation would pass, and we only needed to wait. That American could never wear something like the Swizlelback necklace. She was too common. Even her neck was common."

I made an entry in my notebook summarizing Rosemond's opinion. I was beyond the ability to distinguish a common neck from an uncommon one.

"If we could switch topics, Miss Rosemond, could you tell me about the party you hosted on New Year's Eve, 1976?"

The woman's eyes lit up. "Our holiday parties were highly sought-after invitations back then, Mister Knuckles. We served the best food and drink, and the entertainment was extraordinary. I miss those days. We always had such fun."

I let the older woman enjoy her happier memories for a few seconds before jumping into less pleasant things, like when she ripped poor Gloria a new one when the younger woman tried to build a civil relationship. "I understand Miss Butterfield approached you that evening, asking for the chance to prove she was worthy of your son's affection. And you rejected her like an eight-foot basketball player terrorizing a team of pee-wee hoopsters."

The joy on Rosemond's face vanished. "I must say, Mister Knuckles, you're being extremely unfair with that accusation. I was very polite, considering how the girl was an affront to my standards of decorum."

I turned to Cissy. "Do you recall witnessing any incident between Gloria and Miss Rosemond?"

Cissy resorted to the old foggy-memory excuse used by suspects for centuries.

"That was so long ago. There were so many men at that party, and it seemed they all were doing their best to seduce me. It was disturbing yet exciting, so if anything went on between Mother and that American, I most likely missed it."

"So, you telling me you have no memory of your mother behaving rudely to Miss Butterfield on New Year's Eve?"

Cissy lowered her teacup to the saucer before returning her gaze to me. "All I recall is that my brother was quite enamored with that Butterfield girl and may have spoken rather impetuously about her and his affections, but no one took him seriously." Cissy returned the teacup to her lips. "Least of all, my mother."

Rosemond agreed, the volume of her voice stretching her brittle vocal cords. "I can't be held accountable for the emotional instability of that girl. I'm sure she'd consumed an excess of alcohol by then." A dreamy look came over Rosemond, and she hummed. "Oh my, did we have the best wine and whiskey at our affairs? Nothing but top-shelf for our guests. You know, our parties were a much sought-after invitation."

I told the woman I was aware how grand her parties had once been and then asked, "Miss Rosemond, did you and your husband witness Gloria and Myles argue in the kitchen later that night?"

The right corner of Rosemond's mouth rose in a way that suggested she might be juggling how best to answer. "I didn't see anything, Mister Knuckles, but I heard plenty. I sent my husband to investigate and stop whatever rumpus was happening."

I fired off more questions, and Rosemond answered each with a clear voice and hearty conviction. Her husband reported that Myles and Gloria had left the kitchen when he entered and had taken their argument upstairs. No, he did not see anyone slapping another. And she swore she never saw Gloria again.

"I never rose before ten on most mornings back then," she said. "I indeed slept very late, considering our last guests probably didn't depart until three in the morning. I couldn't retire as long as guests were in the house, could I?"

I turned my attention to Cissy and that damnable grin.

"After my conversation with Myles this morning," I said, unable to mask the irritation in my voice, "it was clear that your brother still has fond memories of his love affair with Gloria Butterfield. Perhaps you and your mother are hiding something about the man's relationship with the young American that you don't want me to know."

Cissy was no slouch at banging heads and came back strong. "We're hiding nothing, Mister Knuckles, don't be ridiculous. My brother suffers from what polite people call emotional issues. I'm sure he holds deeply felt sentiments for the American woman, but he was a very immature young man. We all know those early romances are driven by animal desires rather than true love built up over decades."

I didn't understand how a woman called the Yellow Widow by the locals could talk about decades-old relationships when hers never reached the ten-year mark. But then, I never had a girlfriend, let alone a wife, who kept up the hugs and kisses for longer than two years. Was I no better? I decided to switch gears and verify what I'd learned about Cissy's brother's personality.

"This emotional issue you mentioned, would that explain your brother's reputed hot temper as a young man?"

Cissy laughed. "Oh my no. Myles always ate his anger like a silkworm chewing tea leaves. I'd never seen my brother; how do you say it, mother, go off his trolley."

Rosemond emitted a squeaky giggle. "Oh my, Myles slept with a night light on until he left for university. He was a gentle boy."

She rose from her chair, stepped to a table, and pushed a small black button. "I must get back to my life, Mister Knuckles. Is there anything else?"

I also stood, not wanting to give her a head start if she tried to scamper away. "How did you convince your close friend, Aunt Jane, to squash any investigation of Miss Butterfield's disappearance? I understand that woman had a powerful thirst for transparency regarding matters in and about Village-In-Thistles."

I wasn't sure if that thin black line over Rosemond's left eye was an eyebrow or something inked on, but it climbed halfway to her hairline. "First of all, Mister Knuckles, Aunt Jane was neither a dear friend nor the paragon of honesty you're implying. If she was snooping in our family affairs, I was unaware of it."

Cissy nodded, and that infuriating smug smile returned to her face. "As you can tell, Mister Knuckles, your investigation isn't as dramatic as you might hope, regardless of what you're learning from the American girl's love letters. And, as far as anything the locals might say, remember that people love to gossip, especially about their betters."

I slowly closed my notebook and pocketed it in my sports coat. "You're a very observant woman, Miss Bethard Dinwiddie," I said. "What do you think happened to Gloria Butterfield?"

Cissy stood and looked me in the eye. "I believe the American realized she had no future with Myles and simply took her leave."

"You saying she just packed up and scooted out of the country without anyone seeing her go?"

Cissy gave me her slick smile again and slowly nodded. Rosemond filled the silence with her opinion. "'I agree with my daughter," Rosemond said. "The young woman finally realized she would never be accepted."

I have a mother who does not have one but three daughters. And these women have never agreed on anything other than I was a waste of a good ovum.

"I appreciate your comments, Miss Rosemond and Miss Cissy, but I still have too many questions to give up my investigation."

Both women clasped their hands, their Bethard smirks gone from their faces. "You're wasting your time, Mister Knuckles," Rosemond said. She looked at the figure that had suddenly appeared in the doorway. "Melba, please show Mister Knuckles to the door."

I felt Melba's grip on my arm, and she pulled me out of the room. "Off you go, wanker."

Chapter Twenty-One

Melba clucked with short bursts of glee as she nearly lifted me off my feet and guided me down the hallway.

"I couldn't help but notice that the sofas in the parlor look pretty sad," I said. "Gram Edwards is offering an upholstery cleaning service that you might be interested in."

The woman was not curious about Gram's new service, even when I offered her a twenty percent discount on the first cleaning.

"Good day, you piece of rubbish," the housekeeper said as she pushed me through the doorway and onto the gravel drive. "Go stick that bloody nose up someone else's arsehole."

"Ah, come on, Melba. You and I could get along if you just gave me a chance."

"Not a chance," she said, shutting the wooden door with a decisive-sounding thud.

Dang, I sure wished Melba wasn't so opposed to us developing a friendship. I imagine she'd seen and heard a few things while employed at the Manor for all those years. How could I charm my way back into that kitchen and Melba's memory? I didn't think gifting her a day at the spa would work. She didn't seem like the kind of woman who liked being touched.

"Roll me into a ball and spit me out of a straw," I said. "Nic Knuckles knows another way to tap that old gal's memory."

I jogged from the big house to the dilapidated outbuildings that sheltered the farm equipment. Being from New York City, I didn't know what they were for, but it looked like they hadn't been used in years. Over in the corner was something else that appeared not to have been working in a long time.

"Hey, Rufford, you got a minute?"

"Hey, back at you, Mister Knuckles," he quietly said, his index finger rising to his lips. "But I can't talk because I don't want the chickens to know I'm around."

"Which of those darn chickens are questioning your intentions now?" I asked. "The Sussex or the Dorkings?"

Rufford sighed. "They joined forces, those damn hens, and wanted to know what I'm doing with their eggs. They don't believe I'm enrolling them in a finishing school. I fear what they might do to me if they knew better."

"I understand your concern. I once investigated a children's zoo on Staten Island and was attacked by a turkey. Did you know those things can chase down a screaming man?"

Rufford smiled, seemingly happy to have someone near him who appreciated the evil intent of animals. Now that I had his attention, I pulled him in. "How about we escape down to the Pissin' Pint and compare notes on our issues with fowl?"

"That'd be wicked fun, Mister Knuckles."

Rufford and I slipped away from the Manor without the chickens noticing, greatly reducing Rufford's anxiety. We arrived at my favorite pub as the lunch crowd was thinning out. A table in the corner was available, and within minutes, he and I had our pints in hand and an order for a load of fish and chips delivered to the kitchen. My notebook and pencil lay on the table, ready if Rufford said anything remotely worthwhile.

"I visited Myles Bethard just this morning," I said. "He shared very fond memories of Gloria Butterfield."

Rufford took a hearty swallow of his ale and said, "Aye, Miss Gloria was special; she was."

"I feel your mother was less impressed with Gloria. Am I wrong there, Rufford?"

"Aye, me mum didn't fancy Miss Gloria."

My questioning of Rufford stopped when the fish and chips arrived. After a generous sprinkling of salt and vinegar on the cod, I switched my mouth from yakking to eating. Rufford must not have been hungry because he kept talking.

"Miss Gloria sometimes acted all posh. She'd complain about things she missed from America, like decent heating and bigger loos and air conditioning. Once, Miss Gloria set Mum's hair on fire, asking her to make ice cubes for her tea. Can you believe that? Putting ice cubes in your tea?"

I mumbled a half-hearted answer. "Yeah, yeah, that's outrageous, a national insult." I then got to the important stuff. "Can you recall anything about the week Gloria last visited Rockingham Manor? It was around New Year's Day."

Although Rufford was only a youngster when Gloria visited, I knew he could be a valuable source of information. In one of her letters home, Gloria mentioned the young son of the woman who managed the house and referred to him as a cheeky little fellow who knew a surprising amount about the Bethard family.

"Blimey mate, do I remember that week?" Rufford said. "Me mum was barking mad, what with all that was going on. Miss Gloria and Mister Myles in the Manor, making demands, Miss Rosemond hosting her big party, and the Colonel cussin' and ramblin' about how much wonga was being spent. I remember because my mum would as soon clip me around the ear as to look at me, so I stayed out of the way."

Rufford continued downloading his memory, telling me he kept a low profile but was still too curious not to listen and look at who was doing what. "I know Miss Pauline's husband was up making deliveries all week, although she never came around."

"I understand that the Bethards kept the What Not in operation, which Pauline felt was charity. Was that the only reason Pauline refused to visit her father or half-siblings? Or was it because Rosemond didn't want her up there?"

"Oh no. Miss Rosemond was decent toward Miss Pauline. You know, Miss Rosemond hired Miss Jane to locate the girl after hearing her mum died. Or, that's what me mum once told me."

I paused my scribbling. Lizabeth West told me Rosemond tasked her aunt to find Pauline, as well. It was always good to have a second confirmation.

"How'd Rosemond treat you as a kid?"

Rufford looked down at his fish and chips and shrugged. "She didn't like me much. As a lad, she called me a sneaky bugger, so I stayed out of her way. I don't see her much anymore, not since she took up living in her bedroom."

"I'm guessing she's quite elderly; what near ninety years old?"

"Easily."

"How's her health?"

"I don't know for sure." Rufford swallowed the last of his pint and looked up at me. "But I hear things, you know."

Rufford might have once suffered a blow to his brain, but he still had enough of his synapses working to wiggle another free pint from me. I waved at the waitress, who quickly delivered another foamy-topped glass to our table.

"Now, Doctor Johnson comes to the big house about once a week to check on everybody because something is always going on with somebody."

"Do you mean he visits Rosemond once a week?"

"Miss Rosemond, Mister Myles, and probably Miss Cissy, or at least her husband. You know, Mum never knows how long before Miss Cissy's husbands get sick."

"I know you have socialized health care here in Kingdom of the United, but having a private physician on call must cost the Bethards some coin."

Rufford, his mouth stuffed with chips, mumbled a reply. "You bet it costs them. I heard a rumor that Mister Myles is in the market to sell the ol' Bentley; things are so tight up there at the Manor."

At the rate I was feeding and hydrating Rufford, money was getting tight here in Knucklesland.

"Going back to that last week of the year 1976. Did your mother mention Myles and Gloria announcing their intentions to marry?"

"Oh, bloody hell! Do I remember? Miss Rosemond lost the plot over it. Me mum had to make her a special tea with a pour of whiskey to calm the woman's nerves."

More verification that Rosemond found Myles and Gloria's matrimonial plans most unwelcome, and she wasn't as nonplussed as she told me.

"Did your mother ever talk about the New Year's Eve party hosted by the Bethards?"

Rufford stuffed some crispy fish into his mouth and talked as he chewed. "She worked her fingers to nubs, she did, just gettin' everything together."

I wasn't interested in Melba's many kitchen chores that evening. I wanted to know if she saw Gloria and who the young woman interacted with at the event. Rufford finally washed down the last chew with a swallow of beer.

"Now, Mum was in the kitchen supervising the cookin', but I was catchin' the goings-ons from the upstairs banister."

"What did you see?"

"People talkin' and drinkin' and showin' off."

"Geez Louise, Rufford, stop playing me. What about Gloria? Did you see her or not?"

The man's lips pressed together tightly enough to disappear in his face. Was he trying to get me to buy him another pint? How many more could he drink before whatever he told me was nothing more than a drunk's blathering nonsense?

"I saw her talkin' with Miss Jane and some fancy folks I didn't know, and she and Mister Myles would say stuff."

"Were the exchanges between Myles and Gloria edgy, friendly, loving?"

"S'not like they were snoggin' each other. At least not when I was awake."

"You're saying you fell asleep?"

Rufford slid his shoulders to one side. "I was ten years old and knackered long before midnight, so I didn't see nothin' all the time."

I sat back in the chair and closed my notebook. If the fish and chips hadn't been so tasty, I'd have wasted an hour with Rufford trying to understand what happened at The Rock on New Year's Eve, 1976. I was done with buying food and drink for the man. I stood up and grumbled. "If you ever recall anything from that night that might be useful, let me know, okay?"

Rufford seemed surprised. "Hey mate, I said I didn't see nothin' going on in the ballroom, but that doesn't mean I didn't see nothing."

As I've often said, Nic Knuckles was a proud Bernie Madoff High School graduate, finishing in the upper third of my graduating class. While I didn't earn awards for my mastery of the English language, I knew Rufford was guilty of high crimes against our shared mother tongue. "I don't care if you saw something or nothing. Just tell me what you remember."

Rufford said he was awakened by the horn blowing and cheers from the partygoers as the clock struck midnight. He watched for a while before climbing the stairs to the staff quarters, where he and his mother lived. Even though the two rooms were on the building's third floor, an auditory oddity of the structure amplified any sound coming from the back garden.

"I swore I heard Miss Gloria's voice. So, I opened the window and looked out. That's when I saw Miss Gloria, and she was cryin'."

It was just past midnight, and Rumford was a good twenty-five feet up and swore he saw the woman crying. That testimony could be picked apart like a vulture plucking the flesh off of an Oklahoma roadkill.

"Wasn't it pretty dark?" I asked. "I doubt they had street lights illuminating the neighborhood."

"It was a full moon."

"You sure it was the Butterfield woman? I know many females who start crying when they've had too much to drink."

"She had an American accent, and I know me mum complained that only one guest had to have ice cubes with their cocktail, so I'm pretty sure Miss Gloria was the only Yank in attendance."

"You were pretty far up from the action, and maybe you didn't hear what you thought you heard."

Rufford snorted. "Me ears were twenty-twenty back then. I knew it was Miss Gloria, and she wasn't sloshed. The bird was gutted, mate, gutted."

I sat back down in my chair and opened my notebook. Such clarity for Rufford had been rare until then, and I wanted to get it all written down. If what he said was true, I'd have Gloria still alive as 1977 rolled in.

"Did you see anyone come out and talk to Gloria?"

"I did. A man, but he whispered like he didn't want to make a ruckus, and I couldn't tell you who he was."

"Could it have been Myles?"

"I don't know. He seemed bigger than Mister Myles, and he never snogged her, you know, like he was tryin' to make her feel better. He hung back in the shadows like he didn't want to be seen."

Rufford told me that Gloria and the man turned toward the house.

"Miss Gloria started movin' to go back, and as she got close to the bloke, he put a coat over her shoulders. Then I couldn't see or hear them."

"Was that the last time you ever saw Gloria?"

"Yeah, pretty much."

I finished filling the page with Rufford's recollections.

"You have anything else to add?" I asked.

Rufford shook his head. "Sorry, that's all I got for you."

I wondered aloud if a fresh pint of Bass Ale would encourage his memory. He surprised me when he again shook his head. "I need a clear mind, mate," he said. "Those bloody chickens are throwin' their trick questions at me right now, and I gotta think carefully."

Rufford excused himself and left the pub. I paid off the tab and walked out, feeling the lunch with Rufford had quickly gone from a waste of time to a good investment. I had an eyewitness confirmation that Gloria attended the Bethard New Year's Eve party, and something happened that got her so angry that she left the manor and stood outside in the cold darkness. And if it wasn't Myles who retrieved Gloria from the cold night, who was this mystery man?

Hopefully, my partner and highly paid archivist, Lizabeth West, had found something in Aunt Jane's dusty collection of notes that might answer those questions. Otherwise, my investigation rested on the word of a man who was bullied by chickens.

Chapter Twenty-Two

I left the Pissin' Pints anxious to find out if Lizabeth had located any more of Aunt Jane's recorded observations of Gloria Butterfield's time at Rockingham Manor. I had zero doubt that Gloria attended the Bethard party on New Year's Eve, and hoped Aunt Jane had written the skinny on what happened to the American at the party.

As I approached the gate to West's property, I saw that big, fancy automobile I'd seen several days ago on the street in front of Doc Johnson's place. Behind the steering wheel was Roland, the chauffeur. Why in the world was he parked outside Lizabeth's place? I heard two women's voices coming from the side of the cottage, where a small patio was situated between the house and a stone fence.

"Hello there," I called out, not wanting to startle them. "You got Nic Knuckles approaching."

"Hello, Nic," Lizabeth said, "come back here, please. I want you to meet someone."

I came around the corner and ran face-first into this greeting. "Hello again, Mister Knuckles."

Holy Provolone, it was Cissy Bethard Dinwiddie.

"Boy, Miss Cissy, you don't let the grass grow under your feet, do you?" I said, pointing to a stool near the small wrought iron table where she sat. "May I join you?"

Lizabeth moved a potted plant from the stool, swept it clear of leaves and dirt, and slid it toward me. "Mrs. Bethard Dinwiddie was in the village and stopped by to renew acquaintances," Lizabeth said, her cheeks pinking up.

"Wasn't that lovely of her?"

Bethard Dinwiddie waved her hand in protest. "Oh, please call me Cissy. It was a long-overdue visit to my friend, Lizabeth West. I'm embarrassed to say I can't recall the last time we had tea."

Lizabeth gently patted the woman on the knee. "Now, Cissy, life gets busy for all of us, whether up there at the Manor with your daughter and husband or in Village-In-Thistles with our dreary lives."

Something was going on between the two women, and Lizabeth's kowtowing to Cissy confused me. Then it was Lizabeth's turn to be confused. "I appreciated you coming to the Manor this morning," Cissy said, "and giving mother and I the opportunity to answer your questions."

Lizabeth did the old fashion double take. "What?"

"I had what I call the Bethardpalozza this morning, Liz," I said. "I interviewed Myles, Cissy, and the indomitable Miss Rosemond."

That thin, phony smile that Cissy employed so frequently back at the Manor made an appearance. "And I believe we set Mister Knuckles on the correct path to the truth, that nothing malevolent happened to that American girl."

"You and Miss Rosemond were helpful, but I was rushed out before asking about your father, the Colonel."

"What did you wish to know?"

"Other than the Big Papa thinking Gloria was unworthy of your brother, and he drove the estate into the ground, I haven't heard much about how he reacted to the prospects of Gloria becoming his daughter-in-law."

"While Father was not pleased, I never saw or heard him speak harshly to Myles. And I'm sure he treated that American woman respectfully, as he was a gentleman from the old school."

Okay, she was dishing no dirt on the Daddy Bethard. Not that I'd eliminate him as having nothing to do with Gloria's disappearance. Nic Knuckles knew from sorry experience that those tightly packed individuals were even more deadly than the crazed maniacal killers. His name was Prince Washami, and he ran an ashram called the Temple of Perpendicular Delights. Prince Washami was trying to maintain a continuous state of meditative bliss when a student asked him for the meaning of life. Washami had been asked that question a million times over four reincarnations, and that day, he just blew. Saying heads rolled would be an understatement.

"You told me you thought Gloria Butterfield realized she had no future with Myles and simply took her leave. How did she get from the Manor to wherever she departed Great Britain?"

"My half-sister's husband, Bristol, might have had a hand in the woman leaving the country. I'd take a good, long look at him. He seemed attracted to the American, or that was my observation."

I recorded Cissy's opinion and then asked a question that might crack the woman's frosty demeanor. "I understand that Bristol was very handy at addressing sticky family situations. Hasn't he been your go-to guy when your husbands mysteriously died?"

Cissy was surprisingly not offended by my directness. Lizabeth West, however, angrily grumbled, "I must say, Nic, that is a most insensitive question."

"No, no, my dear," Cissy said. "I am comfortable discussing what seems to be the curse of Rockingham Manor. And yes, Mister Knuckles, Bristol was once there to assist the family in our hour of need."

"Hours of need," I said. "Didn't at least three hubbies leave The Rock with their toes up?"

Cissy straightened her spine and, through thinned lips, answered, "Yes, three of my beloved husbands have passed before their time. But I carry on as each of my deceased husbands would've wanted."

Cissy's words hung briefly in the air before she stood and announced her departure. Lizabeth mumbled her disappointment while eye-rolling me with a master look of irritation. The two women walked to the front gate, and I closed my notebook, satisfied that it had been a productive day. Nonetheless, I was at that stage in an investigation when getting answers only produced more questions. People had different recollections about the past, and determining which ones had the most validity was challenging. The air suddenly felt electrified, and I looked up to see Lizabeth. Boy, her face was red.

"Why did you bring up Cissy's husbands and their premature deaths? That was tacky, and you embarrassed me."

I waved my pencil at her. "Listen up, Lizabeth. Nic Knuckles is a professional sleuth who incorporates proven private investigative techniques. That aggressive move was what I call the old Fancy Pants Jujitsu. Cissy was trying to control the conversation with her cultured persona, which added weight to her suggestion that there was nothing to Myles and Gloria's romance. You know how the Brits get away with things because you sound smarter than Americans, so we think you are. I was throwing her off her game by exposing her dirty laundry."

"That is not how we do it here, Nic. We make the culprit reveal themselves through impeccable data collection and cunning analysis."

I felt my nose crunch up like when I learned the ingredients for making black pudding.

"And that's why you never caught Jack the Ripper," I said. "Too much polite yakking' and not enough unequivocal whacking'."

Our squabbling continued for another minute before Lizabeth gave up, and her native instincts took over. She offered me a cup of tea, which I gladly accepted. "Why did Cissy come all the way into the village to visit you?" I asked. "I didn't know you were tight with the Bethards."

"I'm not," Lizabeth said. "We met many years ago when Aunt Jane took me to Rockingham Manor, and while she and Rosemond socialized, Cissy entertained me. She was only three years older, so we did pretty well. Honestly, I've only sat and talked with her a half dozen times in all my life."

"Sounds like my visit to Rockingham Manor triggered a need for Cissy to reacquaint herself with her dear friend, Lizabeth West. What'd you two talk about?"

"Mostly, we shared memories of Aunt Jane and Rosemond and their unusual relationship. Two women, one older who survived on her wits, and the younger on her beauty and social standing."

"Did you share how you thought Aunt Jane had the upper hand with Rosemond since she knew the Colonel's secrets?"

"No, that would've been impolite." Lizabeth stood and topped off my teacup. "But Cissy mentioned several times how Rosemond treasured my aunt's discretion."

"There you go, girl. That's the purpose of Cissy's little unexpected pop-in. She's expecting the same from you."

"Oh, yes. Cissy was as clear as the crystal chandelier that hangs in the grand ballroom of Rockingham Manor. But what does she think I know?"

I sipped my tea, and for a brief moment of bliss, the appeal of an afternoon cuppa made so much sense.

"I don't know what Cissy is thinking, but when she tried implicating Bristol in Gloria's disappearance, I knew she and the family must be worried," I said. "That's why I wanted to throw her off her game. Now she knows that Nic Knuckles is no one to trifle with."

Lizabeth slowly dipped her head. "I see. A strange approach, nonetheless."

"Now, let me unload all the scoop I learned earlier today."

I read from my notes and told Lizabeth about my meeting with Myles and Cissy and Miss Rosemond. I added the key points I secured from Melba, and additional information from Rufford. Lizabeth said nothing more insightful as I read than, "That's curious" or "That's interesting."

I closed my notebook. "That's all I have, my friend. What do you think?"

Lizabeth's head bobbed up and down, and she whispered. "Very good, Nic."

"That's all you gotta say?"

"Yes, I guess your competence stunned me into wordlessness."

Lizabeth West better get used to being knocked senseless by my skills. Hopefully, her work ethic would knock me off my feet as well.

"Did you find anything else in Aunt Jane's old doodling that shines light on what happened to Gloria?"

A toothy grin filled the lower half of Lizabeth's face. "Yes, Nic, I might have found something rather noteworthy," she said. Lizabeth stood and left me, returning a few minutes later and handed me a single sheet of paper filled with a woman's handwriting. "I found this piece stuck between the pages of a playbill. I think it's hugely significant."

"Boy, I like the words, hugely significant, Liz. Let's see what you got for me."

The date at the top of the page read, January 27th, Thursday, 1977.

I'm sad to write that my investigation of the American woman has reached a conclusion. At my own expense, I took the train to London and arrived at the office of British Airways by late morning. I met a lovely young man named Hebert, who, I'm embarrassed to write, I victimized with a clever ruse. I told him my niece, Miss Gloria Butterfield, had purchased a one-way ticket to New York City on January 1st and asked that I compensate her for the cost, as promised. "I intend to keep my word, Hebert," I said, "but I fear my niece might try and nick her dear aunt with a significant overcharge."

My trickery worked, and Hebert confirmed that Gloria Butterfield had purchased a one-way ticket to America on January 1. He also verified that she'd boarded the flight by calling in a favor from a friend inside the record-keeping department. Hebert was such a marvelous young man, and I felt ashamed having to lie to him.

I shall not share my discovery that Butterfield had departed England with Rosemond Bethard. I refuse to give that woman the satisfaction of being correct. She'd told me to stay out of her son's business when I approached her weeks ago about Miss Butterfield's sudden departure. Her rudeness only spurned me on, I must say.

While my tendency to find a crime in every human action has served me well, I might have been wrong about Miss Butterfield meeting an unnatural end, or at least here in Village-In-Thistles.

Not to worry, however, as a cold corpse was reported found sitting at Catherine Steeplebrook's dining room table yesterday morning. I intend to visit poor Catherine as soon as I finish my tea.

I rocked back and forth on my stool, trying to get comfortable. My undershorts suddenly felt too snug, and my socks too loose. Lizabeth had hit the nail on the head. This was a huge development. Aunt Jane dug deeper into Gloria's disappearance than anyone knew and found evidence that the American had left England.

"Wowzer, Lizabeth, this might not tell me where Gloria was after January first of 1977, but it sure seems to say she wasn't here in England."

"I'm sorry, Nic. I guess you'll have to take your search back to the States."

I lifted the document in the air, allowing the midafternoon sunlight to bounce its illumination off it. "This doesn't look like it's an original, Lizabeth. Is this a photocopy?"

Lizabeth eagerly nodded. "Yes, it is. I thought you'd want a photocopy to take back and share with your client. It might come in handy to prove you gave her case a bloody good try."

I appreciated Lizabeth's forethought and sensitivity, but I still struggled to accept that there might not be a crime to solve.

"I must admit my interviews with the Bethard clan have been enlightening," I said. "I was beginning to see they had good reason to dislike Gloria and want to see her leave the country. Families go to great lengths sometimes to protect each other. However, that doesn't always include murder."

Lizabeth chuckled and patted my hand like I was a five-year-old who'd correctly spelled the word, obviously.

"I know a private investigator hates to think they've wasted their time searching for a crime when one didn't exist," Lizabeth said, "but finding the truth is why you're getting paid, not to have a story you can later serialize on a podcast."

"I can't argue with you, Lizabeth. You've given me something to think about."

"Now, you can return to America instead of being trapped here. Trust me, Nic. The quaintness of Village-In-Thistles grows stale after about two weeks. You should consider yourself lucky."

I should've pointed out to my crime-fighting partner, Lizabeth West, that she was wrong. Nic Knuckles and Lady Luck had been estranged since I was born. My mother gave birth to me while lying under a ladder as a herd of black cats crawled over her. The midwife, Stretch McAuliffe, dropped a mirror, breaking it into thirteen pieces. Sure, she used one of the shards to cut my umbilical cord, but only because she couldn't see her razor because a dark moon was rising. Bottom line, Nic Knuckles was seldom a fortunate son.

"I'll go back to my room and ponder the situation. I don't want to be rash, but right now, I don't have much of a reason to hang around."

"I know, Nic, but reread Aunt Jane's record of events, and you'll realize Gloria left England. You'll find the evidence irrefutable."

I shook my head. "Yeah, Liz, I might be out of refutes."

Lizabeth stood and began clearing the table, her signal that she wanted me on my way. Only later, when I was back in my room, would I create a new page in my notebook, titled Coincidences. I added names and places, and facts and guesses and clues of all color, and value. I then organized and ordered and correlated it all. When I was done, I still had too many coincidences, and my friend Lizzy was associated with too many of them. I'd better keep an eye on her, I decided.

Chapter Twenty-Three

I left Lizabeth's place with a bad case of acid reflux from my earlier lunch with Rufford. The idea that my investigation had come to an end, and one I hadn't anticipated, also contributed to the war zone in my digestive tract.

Lizabeth seemed pretty certain that Aunt Jane's last attempt to find Gloria proved the American had departed England, and there was no crime. Maybe assuming that everyone *could be* innocent was a new British thing. It's possible that after a century and a half of detective stories always having an unexplained death being a murder, the automatic assumption of a killing had run its course. Maybe Lizabeth was at the forefront of a new movement in murder investigation where, after 80,000 words worth of digging, there wasn't a crime but an accident or an unlucky coincidence.

A twist in my intestine convinced me I needed some primary medical intervention. Warford's What Nots was up ahead, and I assumed they'd have a tummy medicine for sale. I soon stood face-to-face with the Pauline Warford.

"Hello, Paulie," I said. "You're looking lovely."

Actually, Nic Knuckles wasn't being sarcastic. Pauline looked like she had slept well, and a half-smile gave her appearance a lovely-looking vibe. Her tone of voice was another matter.

"First of all, only me husband calls me Paulie, so it's either Pauline or Mrs. Warford to you. And, secondly, are you here to buy something, or waffle about and waste my time with your silly questions?"

"I'm desperate for calcium carbonate to settle an upset stomach."

Pauline pointed to the back wall. "You'll find some Rennies on the lower shelf. That'll ease your indigestion."

I pulled the product off the shelf, paid for it, and popped a few tablets in my mouth. My curiosity rose to the surface as my indigestion eased, and I went after the only human in the room, Pauline. "I spent some time at The Rock talking with your step-family today. Could you tell me what makes those folks tick?"

"Buyin' a box of stomach medicine doesn't earn you my free time," Pauline answered. "I have better things to do than blather on about those three."

"I'd gladly be doing a little shopping, Pauline, and the more questions you answered, the more time I'd spend buying whatnots sold in Warford's What Nots."

The woman seemed to appreciate my quid pro quo offer because she handed me a basket. "Here," she said. "We can chat while you make your purchases."

I juggled my notebook and pencil while my left arm slipped through the basket handle. Walking around the shop was awkward, but Pauline kept her word and answered questions as the basket slowly filled with stuff I didn't need, like a pair of hot pads and a box of soap chips.

"Why the animosity toward Rosemond? Did she not find you after your mother's death and take you in?"

My question caused the woman to start chewing her bottom lip. "Yes, Rosemond did push the Colonel to find me," she answered softly. "That was a kindness, I suppose."

Whatever Pauline recalled from that time seemed to have a calming hold on her. At least for a few seconds, and then, whoosh, she went up in flames. "I was surviving alone and didn't need bloody saving by her or the Colonel. And living with them was no holiday for me. I didn't like how my father, Myles, or that shrew Cissy treated me. They were horrible, acting like I was ruining their happy little family."

Pauline's face further darkened. "They still feel that way, claiming what little money the Manor earns is sucked away, supporting me and Bristol and our store. But let me tell you, my husband earns every quid we clear."

I could relate to Pauline's feelings. My mother often complained about how my childhood bedwetting had prevented her from pursuing a career as an astrophysicist. Later in my life, I learned how much education you had to get to be one of those scientists, so I came to think Mom met her not becoming an astrologist. That reduced my guilt somewhat, although I often feel like a lousy son when standing at a urinal.

"Moving on to your step-brother, it's my observation that Myles is an unhealthy critter, prone to fainting and falling. Was he like that when you lived with him?"

Pauline grimaced. "There was always something wrong with the bloke, for sure."

I took a jar of olives from the shelf and dropped it in my basket. "Was there a medical condition or some psychosocial diagnosis that might help me understand how and why he behaves the way he does?"

"Not that I ever heard," Pauline said. "When I first arrived at Rockingham Manor, I was warned not to irritate him, or he'd go all mental on you."

My left arm was growing numb from the weight of the shopping basket, so I laid it on the counter. Hopefully, Pauline would keep talking even if I wasn't pulling stuff from the shelves.

"I saw him getting wound up a few times," she said, "but either someone from the family or that witch housekeeper would shuffle me away before he blew. I never saw how bad he got."

"That old witch of a housekeeper you mentioned. Was that Melba, or was another sorceress working there before her?"

Pauline narrowed her eyes. "Oh no, it was Melba. She was very protective of Myles. They all were, and they still are. I could never understand why they did it."

I scribbled her words in my notebook while Pauline ran up my purchases. Maybe everyone living in Rockingham Manor was covering for Myles, but Pauline wasn't. Did something happen between Myles and poor Pauline that made her so angry? Might it have some connection to Gloria Butterfield's disappearance? Hopefully, I'd be able to decipher my scrawl when I later returned to my room.

"Do you remember a young scamp named Rufford?" I asked. "He'd been about six or seven years old when you lived there."

"Oh, do you mean the bastard child of Melba and the driver, Roland?"

Holy Provolone, we have scandalous behavior among the working class.

"I didn't know who Rufford's daddy was," I said, "but I'm sure we're referring to the same boy."

Pauline showed me a receipt for forty-four pounds and sixteen pence. "Didn't he grow up to be a half-wit living in the barn or something?" she asked.

I felt offended when Pauline slandered my primary source and rose to his defense. "I believe he once suffered a farm accident that made him peculiar, but he's a productive member of the Manor staff. Although he does love the sauce a bit too much to be totally trustworthy, he does have a decent memory."

Maybe my defense of Rufford didn't rise that high, but it was elevated nonetheless.

"Yes, I remember him. Always getting into things, he was. I believed his mum, Melba, used him to spy on the house."

I handed Pauline a pound sterling with the numeral fifty and some Englishman's face printed on it. It was enough to cover my bill because she handed back some coins.

"I heard the New Year's Eve shindig was a much sought-after invitation. Were you ever tempted to show up for free food and drink? From what I heard about the spread the Bethards put out for folks, I would have been tempted."

I was surprised by Pauline's heated response. "I never sought an invitation, not in this life or the next. We'd never attend such an event. We hated that bloody place and the tossers living there."

"Sorry to argue with you, but I understand Bristol attended that New Year's Eve party back when Gloria did. Was that not true?"

The woman shook her head and hissed. "No, no, no, Bristol wouldn't attend as a guest. With even my tainted pedigree, Rosemond would've never allowed him into one of her parties. But I'm sure he was there making a late delivery. The fool would do anything to keep in Rosemond's good graces."

"Did Bristol say anything about the New Year's Eve party?" I asked. "Anything at all about an incident between Myles and Gloria?"

I'd again triggered another bad memory because Pauline vigorously shook her head and spat out an answer. "Good Lord, no, we didn't discuss what he'd done. I was not in a talkin' mood back then, as I recall. The wanker didn't show up until late the next day, claiming he'd drank too much to drive home safely. It was a bloody miserable way to start the new year."

If I had the time, I'd match Pauline's terrible New Year's Day story with a dozen of mine, but she had more to say.

"I don't know what happened up at the Manor, but whatever it was, it changed my husband from an easygoing bloke, where not much bothered him, to a man who couldn't get through the night without wakin' me up with his nightmares."

Put the brakes on my rapid eye movement, sister. Did she say nightmares?

"Sounds like something horrible happened to him," I said.

Pauline drilled me with a cold stare. "Bloody hell, yes somethin' happened."

"Does he still suffer from the nightmares?"

Pauline shook her head as she stuffed my purchase into small plastic bags. "He woke me less and less that first year, and then they became rare. That is, until last week when he started having them again, and I swear, it's almost every night."

Chapter Twenty–Four

Gram Edwards and I caught up the following day over a hefty cup of Earl Grey and a platter of almond biscuits. I'd yet to tell her I'd soon be checking out, only because yesterday's conversation with Pauline had enough stuff that failed to make sense. Did Myles have a hair-trigger temper or not? Why'd happy-go-lucky Bristol suddenly lose his spirit and start having nightmares? And coincidences be damned, why did his nightmares return after I arrived in the village and started asking questions?

Maybe I was grasping for straws, but I was not ready to close the book on the Gloria Butterfield investigation. Nic Knuckles never quits when there are still straws to grasp.

And if I did want to tell Gram I'd soon be checking out, I couldn't because her mouth was running on about her new upholstery cleaning endeavor. My ears perked up when she mentioned that Doctor Johnson had requested her services.

"With all the pandemic bugs evolvin' and spreadin' willy-nilly, old Johnson wanted to be sure his waitin' room chairs weren't the source of any new plague." Gram shared the doctor's concern that, with an aged population making up much of his clientele, he couldn't afford to lose anyone. At least not until the bloke retired.

"Let me know when you're going over to clean Doc Johnson's waiting room," I said. "I'd like to tag along."

Gram grunted. "Tag along nothin'," she said. 'You'll be lending me a hand, you will."

It's not that Nic Knuckles was above doing manual labor, but my client back in America paid me to find out what happened to her long-lost big sister, not to steam-clean upholstery. I said nothing to reinforce Gram's expectations of me getting my hands dirty, and when she paused to refill her morning drink, I wished her a good day and left.

A competent private eye had to be suspicious when things were too easy, so anxiety yanked my lower sphincter when a small delivery van pulled in front of me as soon as I stepped from the launderette. Bristol Warford hung out the open driver's side window, smiling.

"Cheers, Knuckles. Paulie told me you stopped by the shop yesterday."

"Cheers back at you, Bristol. Yes, and I had a delightful shopping experience. Your wife is quite the salesperson."

"You gotta minute, mate?" Warford pushed open the passenger-side door of the van and invited me to ride to the train depot to pick up fresh stock for his shelves. "We can catch up."

I happily hopped in, and before he released the clutch, my notebook and pencil materialized in my hand.

"What's with Pauline and her seemingly outsized animosity toward Rosemond?" I asked. "Her eyeballs almost popped out of her head as she talked about her."

"My wife is a proud woman who never forgave the old Colonel for deserting her and her mum. On top of that wound, she's angry at herself for accepting Rosemond's invitation to live with them, although me Paulie was in desperate straits at the time."

"Why do you think Rosemond took the girl in? From what your wife told me, no one in the family liked the idea."

Bristol slipped through the only stop sign in the village, taking us outside the boundaries of Village-In-Thistles. Warm air carrying the musty smell of agriculture blew through the open vehicle windows, flapping my notebook pages.

"Rosemond is a complicated bird. Some might say she took in Pauline to show off her kind heart, while others might think she did it to remind the Colonel of his weak character. Rosemond could've used me Paulie to control Myles and Cissy, threatening to give her a share of their inheritance."

I felt a cold shudder climb up my spine and take my second vertebra hostage. Stories about manipulative mothers always pushed me back into the dark memories of my own. There was a time when Mom ran a traveling farm rodeo that showed up at county fairs on Long Island. She'd strip me to my underwear, grease me up with petroleum jelly, and have the rubes try and catch me as I raced around an enclosure of barbed wire. Mom told me it was the only way I'd have friends.

Bristol's baritone brought me back to the moment. "Me Paulie was pretty lonely living there at the Manor. Cissy ignored her, and Myles was at Uni, so he was indifferent, although he felt she cost part of the monthly stipend the Colonel sent him. Pauline stayed at the Manor not more than a year before we found each other, but she was unhappy the whole damn time."

The van jumped hard as the cobblestone gave way to a rutted country road. We were now driving through the countryside with the stone fences and yellowing pastures clotted with sheep.

"You know, Bristol, you told me about how you, a farm boy without prospects, got hooked up with a girl living at Rockingham Manor. You said you owed the Colonel and Rosemond for providing you a wife, a shop with a comfortable home above it, and a steady livelihood. It sounded like the Colonel and Rosemond did you a huge favor."

"Innit true?" Bristol said. "I'd do anything to show my gratitude for the Bethards giving me a better life than my mum or pop could've."

"Did you have an opportunity to show your appreciation to the Colonel and Rosemond on New Year's Eve when Gloria Butterfield was a guest at the Manor?"

Bristol Warford suddenly stopped the van and stared at me with the same cold eyes he had shown me days ago at the end of Reverend Amethyst's Sunday service. "Listen, mate, whatever I did that night, I did because I felt sorry for Gloria. As I told you before, I thought Gloria was a sweetheart, but her relationship with Myles was doomed."

"Oh, I believe you, my friend. I'm sure you had Gloria's best interests at heart. Tell me, did you intercept Gloria out in the cold after she and

Rosemond fought?"

Warford didn't answer, looking into the side mirror as he accelerated the van and got us back on the road.

"You gave her your jacket to wear, am I right?"

"What if I did? Myles wasn't going to come out and do the right thing. She was freezing."

"Did you bring her back into the kitchen, or did Myles finally retrieve her?"

"Yeah, it was me. I brought her back in and had Melba make her some hot tea. And then Myles came in and told me to leave, so I did."

"You didn't see or hear anything that indicated Gloria and Myles fought?"

"I didn't see anything but heard them screaming at each other. They both sounded pretty gutted."

"Was that the last you saw of her until the next morning?"

Bristol didn't answer.

"Come on, man. What happened between you getting booted from the kitchen and Gloria sneaking off The Rock the next morning? Fill in the gap so I don't have to go back and interrogate Pauline, who has a very unhappy memory of that New Year's Day."

The man slowed the van and pulled off to the side of the road. He shut off the engine and turned to me. "Okay, mate, here's what happened. I was celebrating the new year like everyone else at the Manor. Rosemond and the Colonel's boozy party was the dog's bollocks! It was easy to get pissed, and I did; I was shredded."

"You were in the ballroom, boozing, and dancin', with everyone else, huh?"

Bristol laughed. "No, I wasn't in the party. I got shit-faced in the pantry drinkin' the whiskey Melba kept aside for her and Roland and any other staff still awake. I made me a little bed among the bags of potatoes, and woke late in the morning, and that's when Gloria asked me to take her to the dorm in Brighton. She said something about her and Myles fightin', and she wanted to stay in the dorm."

Sometimes, a suspect stumbled over what they said previously, and Bristol was practically falling to the ground.

"When we first talked at the shop, you told me Gloria wanted to know if a bus was available back to London on New Year's Day. You said nothing about her wanting to stay at the university."

The eyebrows on Bristol Warford's forehead jumped with that comment.

"I said that? You sure?"

I nodded, authoritatively waving my notebook. "Yes, you did."

A slow rumble of a laugh rose from Bristol's chest. "Blimey, mate, you got me."

You're dang right, I gotcha mate; I wanted to shout. Who did he think he was dealing with, a man living in a dark cave without decent internet access? Of course, I knew his latest story didn't agree with his first one.

I opened my notebook to a fresh page, determined to record Bristol's confession.

"No more games, Warford. How'd Gloria Butterfield get from The Rock to London that morning?"

Bristol drew in a raspy breath and told me Gloria woke him up from his drunken stupor early in the morning of January 1. He couldn't be sure of the time, but the sun was coming up, so it must've been about seven. She begged him to drive her to the dorm in Brighton, which he agreed to do.

"Wasn't anyone else up at the time?"

"No, everyone was nursing their hangover."

Bristol claimed he pulled himself together and drove Gloria to Brighton, where she entered her dorm and threw together her belongings. He helped her move her luggage to his van, and they left Brighton for London.

"Did she say what she intended to do?" I asked.

"She hoped to be able to find a seat on the first flight back to the US."

"What time did you drop her off at the airport?"

Bristol sucked his teeth and answered. "Oh, I dunno. We left the dormitory in Brighton about ten, and the traffic on the A23 wouldn't been heavy on a holiday, so yeah, add another hour and a half, so around noon."

"Did she say much?"

"She wasn't in a mood to talk, but I tried to make her feel better. I said she was lucky to get away 'cause sharing a life with the Bethards would've been hell for her."

"Do you feel that way? Has living a life beholden to the Bethards been hellish for you?"

Bristol stared ahead for a few seconds before answering. For once, I felt he wasn't trying to fool me.

"When a man knowingly makes a deal with the devil, he's a pillock for complaining about it. How else could I marry a fine woman like Paulie and own a lovely shop with a comfortable flat above it? I have no regrets, mate, no regrets at all."

Bristol and I arrived at the train station, and I helped him load boxes of whatnots sent from factories producing whatnots for human consumption. As the sweat darkened my shirt, Bristol filled the air with minutiae about operating his store, living in Village-In-Thistles, and some gossip about its inhabitants.

"You know I wasn't the only villager making a fair share of me living income from Rosemond, don't you?"

"I heard Aunt Jane did pretty well, keeping track of the Colonel and his indiscretions," I said.

Bristol laughed. "True, mate, and when that old gossip passed on, the Colonel and Rosemond celebrated. He no longer had to worry about being hunted like a fox, and Rosemond saved herself a pretty penny, not paying Aunt Jane to keep her mouth shut."

"It sounded like everyone was using each other back then."

"Innit, true?" Bristol mumbled. "Ain't that much different now, mate."

As we approached the village, I turned to Bristol and asked, "Why didn't you come clean the first time I asked you about Gloria? Why all the effort to mislead and confuse me?"

The man didn't take his eyes off the road as the vehicle vibrated from the tires on cobblestone. "I dunno. Maybe because whenever you get your answers or whatever you're looking for, you'll be gone, never to be seen again. Me? I'll still be livin' here trying to keep my business goin', keepin' Paulie happy, growin' old, and gettin' buried in the old village graveyard."

I didn't say anything. Everyone in living the Village-In-Thistles probably felt the same way. I probably shouldn't expect anyone to be completely truthful, what with the risks of losing income, or community standing.

Chapter Twenty–Five

I was exhausted when Bristol dropped me off in front of the launderette after we'd completed his run to the train depot for his new inventory of whatnots. I hadn't done that much lifting and hauling since I climbed to the top of the Empire State Building while fulfilling my Nana's personal Make-A-Wish. She wanted to experience completing all 1,860 steps from the street to the observation platform before she passed. Her feet started hurting her on the fifteenth floor, and she demanded I carry her to the top. "Make my damn wish come true, or I'll put a deathbed curse on you, boy," she screamed. The woman made wishes every month for years before croaking, and the tears I shed at her burial were ones of relief.

As Nic Knuckles was prone to do after a rigorous physical workout, I returned to my room for a short nap that stretched until midafternoon when Gram Edwards tapped on the door and woke me up.

"You've got a visitor, Nic. Looks like you've done something again to get the attention of those folks up at the Manor."

I wiped the fuzz from my eyeballs and trundled down the stairs to the entryway. Gram had it right. Standing in front of me was another resident of The Rock.

"Hello, Turquoise," I said, "What's up, girl?"

Turquoise Blix-Vixen's lips went crooked on her face, seemingly surprised at my informal greeting. I couldn't blame her. She didn't know that Nic Knuckles needed time after waking up before his brain fully engaged. That's why I had better success solving late-night crimes than those committed before noon.

"Uh, good afternoon, Mister Knuckles. My Grandmama asked me to hand-deliver this letter to you."

I took the small envelope from the woman's hand.

"Do you normally serve as Grannie Rosemond's errand girl?" I asked as I eyeballed the unaddressed envelope.

"Oh, we all run errands for Rosemond Bethard."

I slipped her delivery into my back pocket and suggested she join me for a stroll around the village. "The fresh air will clear my head, and maybe you can answer some questions that bother me."

"I'll tell Roland to park the Bentley, Mister Knuckles. I'll save Uncle Myles fifty quid by not having Roland run the engine while we chat."

"I bet that Bentley doesn't get more than ten miles a gallon, does it?"

"Our gasoline is sold by the liter," Turquoise said. "And, yes, the Bentley is very costly to operate. Hopefully Uncle Myles can find a buyer and unload that behemoth."

"I imagine a collector would pay a pretty penny for such a fine car."

Turquoise nodded. "You'd be surprised what people would pay for a Bentley T-Series."

I wasn't interested in old cars. I wanted to talk about an old gal living at Rockingham Manor, instead, "I spent some time with your grandmother," I said. "She's pretty sharp for her age."

"Yes, she's probably the quickest mind in the family. Always was, I believe."

"How do you get along with her?"

The woman loudly sighed. "We get along as long as I do what she wishes."

"Was that always true?"

Turquoise brushed the hair off her forehead. "I have very fond memories of Rosemond as a child. She was attentive and fun, but it changed when I was seven and Poppa died. She shuttled me away to her cousin in London for six months so my mother could mourn without the burden of caring for me. It was rather traumatic."

The woman easily gave up her memories of growing up at Rockingham Manor, suffering through the deaths of her father and then stepfather, and the frequent absence of her mother as Cissy pursued possible mates. "I was raised by my Grandmama, you might say, but it didn't eliminate my fear of abandonment."

"Does that explain why such a bright woman like you hasn't left The Rock for a more adventuresome life?"

She stopped walking and looked me in the face. "That's not the reason. The tantalizing taste of Melba's cabbage soup has kept me there."

Turquoise's laughter echoed against the buildings and up the street. "Oh, Mister Knuckles, if you could have seen the expression on your face," she said, "it was hysterical."

"Oh, I'm glad I could make you laugh," I said, the words dry in my mouth. I wasn't happy with her pulling my leg like that. Not that Nic Knuckles didn't enjoy jokes and humor. I was a regular at the best comedy clubs in New York City and saw some lesser-known acts perform. There was the guy who read obituaries while standing knee-deep in a tub of lime Jell-O. He bombed, but watching two bouncers trying to get him off the stage was hilarious.

"I'm sorry, Mister Knuckles," Turquoise said, dabbing a tear from the eye, "but my family is so void of mirth that my sardonic sense of humor comes out among strangers."

"Yeah, your family isn't exactly the fun bunch. I know because I spent several hours with your Uncle Myles,"

"Ah, yes, my uncle is an odd man, isn't he?"

"Did you get along with him while growing up?"

The laugh lines activated by Turquoise's cabbage soup joke quickly faded, and her gaze turned downward. "I didn't interact with him much," she said. "I'd see him only on Sunday nights when we joined the Colonel, Rosemond, Myles, and his wife for dinner."

"What were those meals like?"

"They were horrible."

I stopped, and my notebook and pencil appeared with a sleight-of-hand worthy of any magician.

"It seemed every conversation would turn to money. The Colonel would whine about expenses, and then Uncle Myles would take issue with my father's contribution to the Manor's operation. Too many times, Poppa would storm off. I hated those dinners."

Turquoise wrapped her arms around herself. "That's probably why I have eating issues."

Nic Knuckles was known throughout the civilized world as a hard-boiled private investigator, yet Turquoise's story put a lump in my throat. I couldn't imagine having my relationship with cheese ruined by bad memories.

"There was one particularly nasty argument between Poppa and Uncle Myles that I can't forget because it was the night that Poppa died."

Her remarks were quickly transcribed into my notebook. I asked whether she ever forgave Uncle Myles for provoking her father that night. The woman stopped walking, her eyes scanning the space in front of her. "Forgiveness isn't something the Bethards do very well, Mister Knuckles."

Turquoise turned hard on her feet and started back toward the launderette. I jumped in behind her.

"Give me a proper answer, Turquoise," I said. "With your smarts, looks, and connections, you could be doing something exciting, like running a small press putting out cozy mysteries and an occasional humor book."

Turquoise laughed. "Yes, I'd rather fancy a life like that, but if you don't cultivate your dreams, they're easily stolen by time."

I continued peppering the woman with questions, and she responded with vague, uninformative answers. I felt I was dealing with someone who'd spent her life dodging difficult queries with clever responses. As we reached the Bentley, I popped one that she happily provided details.

"You referred to Myles's spouse as his wife but never Amy, Aunt Amy, or the Reverend. I'm guessing you don't like the woman."

Roland opened the door of the Bentley, and Turquoise slid onto the leather back seat.

"Everyone living at Rockingham Manor carries an aura of banality, and we're comfortable with that. Myles's wife is the opposite, with her earnest spirituality and quest for earthly accountability. It's all rather tiresome being around her, even if it's only once a week."

Before I could ask a follow-up question, Roland shut the car door. Now, most private eyes would shrug, go to their favorite dive, and muse over what they'd heard while sipping whiskey. But not Nic Knuckles. If a warm body with an operating mouth was nearby, potentially valuable information could be gathered. I called out, "Roland, my friend, surely, you drove Myles Bethard and Gloria Butterfield around the countryside in 1976. What can you tell me about those two love birds?"

Maybe the man had a hearing problem? Perhaps American English was unfamiliar to his ear. Whatever it was, the man stepped into the driver's side of the Bentley, closed the door, and fired up the engine without answering my question. 'We'll catch up later, Roland," I shouted. "Don't feel bad about your job getting in the way."

After the Bentley cleared the corner and was out of sight, I wanted to read the letter Turquoise had hand-delivered. I took the necessary number of steps to get to the Pissin' Pints, shouting at the barmaid as I entered. "Cheers, lass. A glass of your best ale, love."

Yeah, I spent almost ten days in Merry Old England, and it didn't bother me that I was sounding like a local. As I waited for the pub staffer to bring me my drink, I quickly jotted my thoughts about Turquoise Blix-Vixen into my notebook. The woman seemed to have deep-seated issues with her family and confused feelings toward Rosemond and Cissy. Although unstated, my super sensitive hearing picked up that she might hold Myles responsible for her beloved father's premature death.

A small voice in my head spoke up. It asked why I was spending my energy trying to learn more about the Bethards. Hadn't Aunt Jane's investigation notes confirmed that Gloria left England? Cutting through Bristol's hocus pocus revealed he drove Gloria to the airport on New Year's Day. Lizabeth thought the American had gone home; even Gram felt it was highly likely. Why was I still working on the case?

That little voice is what I call Homesick Nic. He wants Nathan Hot Dogs and Coney Island in the summer, not tea and sausages. The baseball playoff races were heating up, and not being in the city to witness the collapse of the Mets or the Yankees was excruciating. Homesick Nic wanted accents he grew up hearing, not nonsensical colloquialisms spoken in a clipped manner.

"Thanks, love," I said as the waitress placed my beer on the table. A quick sip of alcohol seemed to mollify Homesick Nic enough to allow me to tear open the letter from Rosemond. The message was written in surprisingly strong strokes, reinforcing my thinking that behind Rosemond's frail exterior was a battle-hardened older woman.

Dear Mister Knuckles, I understand that my son-in-law, Bristol, spent a delightful morning with you as he secured new inventory for his fine shop. He reported that you had multiple curiosities that he did his best to satisfy.

Bristol answered your questions honestly and sincerely; however, the man's recollection was incomplete. This was not because he was disingenuous. Sir, Bristol is as transparent as the Swarovski champagne flutes we used to toast the new year. Nonetheless, the man does not know everything that occurred during the early hours of 1977.

"Well, ain't this something?" I muttered before drawing a hard swallow from my glass. I continued reading.

Soon after midnight, the American woman, Miss Butterfield, approached my husband, the Colonel. She asked him for assistance in returning to America. Not surprisingly, this assistance included money to purchase airfare from London to New York. I believe in your business, Mister Knuckles; it's called a shakedown. It is a very sordid behavior, regardless of what you name it.

My husband requested Bristol's help in assisting Miss Butterfield, which he did. However, my son-in-law is easily confused, especially after drinking excessively, which he'd had done that evening.

While your efforts to reconstruct the past undoubtedly have painted an unfair picture of my husband and me in dealing with our son's romantic misadventure, I wish to emphasize that we provided the American girl the means to leave Rockingham Manor and England with her head high.

Sincerely, Rosemond Bethard

I stared at the letter as my mind raced. Why didn't Rosemond provide those details when I spoke to her back at The Rock? Why was she bad-mouthing Bristol? Did she intend to make the man's faulty memory a blanket excuse for explaining away anything he's told me that was inconvenient?

With my brain working hard, I knew my stomach would soon demand attention. I lifted my hand and caught the barmaid's eye. "Hey, love, can I get some chippers?"

"Chippy, that's chippy, you scrote!"

"Yeah, sure, whatever," I said. I didn't know what it was with waitresses and barmaids, but whether in New York City, small-town Indiana, or Village-In-Thistles, the restaurant help staff hated Nic Knuckles. I knew a secret network of waitresses tracking bad tippers existed, but I didn't think it had an international branch. Geez, a man leaves a 5% tip once, and forever, he's branded a chiseler.

I pocketed Rosemond's letter and sipped my beer. My mind was like the Long Island Expressway on a rainy Friday night. My thoughts were bumper-to-bumper, each driven by an irritated neuron. A lot of effort went into writing that message, and to have her granddaughter deliver it to me was clever. Rosemond knew I'd flood Turquoise with questions, allowing her to spin the family story favorably. More importantly, the woman might learn where my investigation was headed. But why go to all that trouble if there was no mystery to cover up?

Poor Homesick Nic couldn't argue with my thinking. He realized everything appeared too orchestrated for me to close the Gloria Butterfield case. Homesick Nic faded as I waited for my order of fish and chips. Private Eye Nic took his place and joined me in plotting my next move, finding that weak spot in the Bethard family defense.

Chapter Twenty-Six

After another satisfying meal of fish and chips at the Pissin' Pints, I headed out to visit Lizabeth West. I wanted to see if she found anything in Aunt Jane's third chest that might help my cause. I'd maneuvered about fifty feet of that ankle-busting Village-in-Thistle's cobblestone when I saw Gram Edwards coming up the street carrying a vacuum cleaner on her back. Her arms were stretched long by a big bucket full of gear and a gallon container of some cleaning chemicals.

"What the heck you doing, Gram?" I asked, unable to hide the concern in my voice. Her usually pale Caledonian complexion was aflame with exertion. I was afraid she'd drop at my feet right then and there.

"Blimey, Nic, the Lord blessed me by sending you my way," she said, the words riding puffs of breath. "I could use those manly American hands right now, dearie."

I grabbed the bucket and the plastic container with the skull and cross-bones on the label. "Are you headed to clean Doctor Johnson's place?" I asked.

Gram nodded at a red door ahead of us. "Yes, lad, he wants me to purify his waiting room. I sure could use some help."

"Of course, Gram, anything for you."

In America, Gloria Butterfield's little sister would not be happy knowing I was using her paid time to help kill germs in a medical office. I'd explain to her that it wasn't any old office. Nope, Doctor Watson Johnson was the attending physician for Myles and Rosemond Bethard. If I could get into his building and maybe have a chance to snoop around, I might learn about

Myles' mysterious ailment.

"Oh dearie, you helpin' me would be much appreciated," Gram said. She unlocked the door to Johnson's office, and we stepped inside, where it was dark and quiet. "The place is closed for a few hours while we do our work, but we can't dilly, lad."

"What do you need me to do?"

"I don't want you poisoning yourself applyin' the chemicals, so if you'd vacuum the surfaces of the waiting room, that'd be a bloody big help."

I swung the mobile vacuum on my back, found the starter button, and swiped the surfaces of the waiting room chairs, carpets, and drapes. Gram busied herself, putting on a mask, a pair of goggles, rubber gloves, and plastic booties. I finished vacuuming and turned to find Gram bent over a bucket, carefully pouring yellow-colored liquids. That was the break I needed.

"I'll get to work here in Doc Johnson's office," I said. "And I'll close the door so I don't get overcome by those toxic fumes." Gram waved her hand in approval and continued mixing her concoction of virus and bacteria-destroying solvents. I closed the door behind me and turned on the light switch. Johnson's office was typical, with a desk, chair, and framed diplomas hanging on the wall. I immediately got to work.

I propped the vacuum against the door, its motor roaring to cover my misbehavior. Along the back wall of Johnson's office was an old wooden four-drawer file cabinet, and its lock feebly resisted my pick. Like any good private eye, Nic Knuckles had weak principles regarding other people's privacy. I believe that if you don't want a dick digging through your life, don't do stuff that a dick might need to know to solve his case.

My fingertips scurried across the tops of the folders, and one labeled with Bethard, M. was quickly removed. Sitting at the desk, I pulled out my notebook and pencil and prepared to read and write down anything that might explain Myles' multiple medical conditions.

Folks untrained in medicine would be challenged to understand the terms presented in Johnson's reports, and discerning which ones were important would intimidate most investigators. Knowing you only had minutes before Gram Edwards checked in, the average private eye would be overwhelmed.

But not Nic Knuckles. I knew more about medical conditions than half the staff at Sloan Kettering Hospital.

I credit my mother for my encyclopedia-like knowledge of health issues. The woman spent her life violating every sensible rule ensuring good health and, consequently, developed conditions and diseases rarely seen outside the most isolated jungles. To address her illnesses, Mom read every mailer pitching unproven cures, as long as they cost less than ten bucks. She also was a big fan of nightly TV pitches by medical quacks. I inadvertently mastered a massive vocabulary of medical conditions. That knowledge allowed me to quickly read Myles Bethard's file and note only conditions that might be relevant.

Myles's file was lengthy, and his ailments were numerous and common to a man of his age. But one condition caught my eye because I'd never heard of it. When the man was a teenager, he was diagnosed with something called misophonia. I pulled out my notebook and transcribed the details of the doctor's summary of the condition.

The astute reader might wonder why Nic Knuckles wasn't using his cellphone to snap photos. Wouldn't that allow him to quickly record the necessary images for later study? Or was Nic a technological neanderthal and didn't possess such a device?

I live in New York City, where even the subway rats have a low-cost data plan. Of course, I used a cellphone. The truth was I forgot to pack the phone charger. Because I bought the device from a Senegalese guy selling them off a blanket on Queens Boulevard, it was impossible to purchase a replacement charger here in England—even Warford's What Nots couldn't help me.

Nonetheless, Nic Knuckles made the best of violating Myles Bethard's privacy, and I'd finished recording any interesting tidbits when suddenly the vacuum toppled to the floor. Gram Edwards pushed open the door and poked in her goggled face, asking, "Are you done in here, dearie?"

I jumped from the chair and stood between my landlady and the open file folder on the desk. "Almost done," I said. "Step outside so I can vacuum the carpeting behind the door." Gram complied, and thirty seconds later, the carpet had been swept, and the Bethard folder was stuffed back in the file drawer.

"I'm done with you," Gram said. "You can go about your way." She pointed at the vacuum cleaner and said, "Could you kindly carry my kit back to the launderette? That'd be a bloody kindness."

"Of course, Gram. Anything to ease your earthly burden." I hoisted the device on my back and exited the room. I kept walking even when Gram shouted at me. "And I'll lock that cabinet, so no one wonders what you were doin' in here."

Chapter Twenty-Seven

I delayed returning to the launderette because I wanted to visit Lizabeth West and complain and whine. Hopefully, she'd spot anything in what I had to say to point me in a more fruitful direction. I found her at her cottage, kneeling while doing something horticultural. She didn't seem too happy to see me.

"What is it now, Nic?" she asked as she pointed to the cleaning equipment on my back. "Are you selling vacuum cleaners?"

"I'm doing my landlady a favor, and I hoped you could do one for me."

The woman loudly sighed and waved me onto the property. "Come on in. Can I fix you a cuppa?"

Lizabeth and I entered her cottage, and I sat in what had become my usual spot in her living room. She returned with two steaming cups of tea.

"You look perplexed, Nic; what is it now?"

"I gotta tell you, Lizabeth. For days, I couldn't get past the Rockingham Manor front door, and in the last forty-eight hours, Bethard family and friends have been falling out of the sky, wanting to talk to me."

Lizabeth sat across from me, gardening pads still on her knees and an impatient expression on her face. "I understand why the family is so helpful," she said. "Surely, they wish to be done with the new rumors your investigation has created. They haven't had to address in decades the whispers that that American girl met an unnatural end."

"I can understand that, but I got concerned when Rosemond used her granddaughter to go to great lengths to correct Bristol's testimony. I sense I'm being closely monitored here in the village."

Lizabeth didn't think the Bethard family's behavior was suspicious, considering neither Myles nor Bristol was known for their memories. "Brits like to keep things tidy," she said. "I can see why Rosemond sent you a written clarification. And, if it saves you time and effort, is that so bad?"

I sipped my tea and mumbled a response. "Crime isn't tidy, Lizabeth, not in America or the land of the Beatles. I think I'm being played."

The woman sucked in a breath but said nothing.

"I know something happened to Gloria right after midnight on New Year's Day. The crime was most likely committed in the kitchen, maybe the garden, but not too far from the Manor. My number one suspect is Myles. I've gotten different opinions on whether he had a temper. Those who claim he doesn't are family members. Everyone like Gloria, Pauline, and The Rev were warned to stay clear of him if he was triggered. So, I gotta ask, what gives?"

"I hear you, Nic, but did any of those women ever see Myles get physical?"

I shook my head. "No, but with the size of that man's mitts, he should be considered dangerous if used in a way they weren't designed for."

Lizabeth sipped from her cup. "All speculation, Nic, please."

"Myles also suffers from a psychological condition that makes him unpredictable. I've heard that from his wife, sister, and niece."

"Unless you define the supposed affliction, you have nothing."

"I think it might be something called misophonia," I said. "You ever hear of it?"

"It's a nerve disorder, I believe, but nothing serious, as far as I know."

"Okay, then, there are the different stories about what happened in the kitchen after Rosemond snubbed Gloria. Myles had one story, Melba pitched a slightly different version, and Bristol told me another, more revealing one."

Lizabeth waved me off. "People never remember things exactly the same way, Nic, especially after so many years. You have to excuse the slight variations in their stories."

I didn't argue with Lizabeth because her point made sense. I wasn't done pitching reasons why I couldn't give up, however.

"Okay, here's something else. Myles told me that he and Gloria had a big argument in the kitchen, and Gloria slapped him. Melba also pretty much substantiated the story. I can't shake the feeling that the assault went further than a slap."

Lizabeth brushed the mud from her knee pad and leaned closer. "Maybe, but more likely that was when Gloria finally realized she had no future with Myles. A woman can only fool herself so long."

I knew from experience that women's affection have limits, because most of my girlfriends quickly dumped me after a few dates. One of them excused herself soon after we sat down for our first movie date, snuck out of the theatre, rented a Quiki-Haul truck, drove to her apartment, loaded her belongings, and left town. I wasn't that upset. The movie was pretty good, plus I got to eat her bucket of popcorn.

"And there's Rosemond," I said, jumping to my feet. "She told me what she wanted me to hear and expertly stiff-armed any further questions. That woman is a champion manipulator and liar."

"Yes, she is a prevaricator of the first order, no doubt, but you have to prove she's lying, not just complain because you're being bested."

I dropped back into my chair, feeling like I had the wind knocked out of me. Holy Provolone, I *was* being bested, wasn't I? The Bethard clan came at me with a unified front, and Nic Knuckles was rolled like an Easter egg on the White House lawn.

"We can't forget that they had the greatest motivation to take out Gloria Butterfield, am I right?"

Lizabeth tilted her head to the side as her look of exasperation reappeared. "True, Nic, but that doesn't mean they murdered the young woman."

"I doubt Rosemond has lost her manipulative touch with age," I said. "I'm convinced she's the mastermind behind this cover-up."

I heard Lizabeth taking in a deep draw of air through her nostrils before blowing it out of her mouth. She didn't say anything.

I sat further back in my chair, my hand rubbing my forehead. "I'm stuck, Lizabeth. What am I missing? Where is that loose thread, that weak link, the deuce of hearts that brings the house of cards tumbling down?"

Lizabeth swallowed the rest of her tea and gently touched a napkin against her lips. "Perhaps it is time you admit that any reasonable person would say the only crime committed at Rockingham Manor was petty classism."

I bit my bottom lip while my mind tried to come up with something to refute Lizabeth's argument. Nic Knuckles didn't believe in unsolvable cases. They could be cracked if you worked harder and longer. But what if I'd so convinced myself that I end up ruining an innocent person's reputation or life?

"Maybe it's time I make Homesick Nic happy and go back to New York City," I said.

Lizabeth cocked her head as if she was trying to make sense of my comment. She didn't seek clarification and signaled it was time for me to go by standing. "Before you leave, Nic, I have something important for you."

I felt my heart jump. Had Lizabeth discovered a critical piece of information in Aunt Jane's third trunk of notes that would keep the investigation alive? My palms grew slippery as I waited for Lizabeth to return. Within a minute, she handed me a single piece of paper.

"Here you go, Mister Knuckles."

My eyes quickly scanned the document. I slumped and crushed the paper in my hand.

"Good Lord, Lizabeth, you don't need to submit an invoice. Just tell me what I owe you, and I'll pay."

"Okay, I think two thousand should cover it."

I almost fell out of my chair. I wanted to challenge the number of hours she charged me, but was too embarrassed to uncrumple the invoice and argue. The woman asked to be paid in cash, which emptied my wallet and money belt. Lizabeth thanked me for the experience and wished me safe travels. All in all, I left Lizabeth West's cottage feeling depressed and defeated.

Homesick Nic was cheering, however.

Chapter Twenty-Eight

I left Lizabeth West's cottage with Gram's vacuum on my back, Lizabeth's invoice stuffed in my pocket, and a boatload of disappointment. I returned to the launderette and poured myself a lovely cuppa from Gram's continuously brewing kettle, riding on one of her dryers. I entered my room, a cup of tea in one hand and a plate of cheddar cheese scrounged from Gram's lauder in the other. I sat at the tiny window-side table, and after a nibble and a sip, I mused.

Sometimes, I preferred musing instead of thinking, hoping to add a certain panache to the Nic Knuckles brand. I also promised to look up the word panache to ensure it wasn't French for silly poodle.

I figured I could probably be home in two days, sweating like ten million other New Yorkers in the late summer heat and humidity. By comparison, the last nine days spent in southeast England were comfortable. The food wasn't bad, and the evolution of my affection for tea was complete. It had been a good travel experience, and I should've brought a camera and taken photos I'd never look at. Nonetheless, my mind drifted from planning my return to New York City to the disappearance of Gloria Butterfield.

Why couldn't I let go of this investigation? I guessed, based on her letters, that Gloria Butterfield would never give up. She didn't sound like she'd be easily deterred once she'd set a goal.

Was there anything I might have missed in any of Gloria's letters home? Maybe she expressed doubts in her later correspondence, but I didn't catch them. I went over to my bed and pulled from underneath the mattress the Gloria Butterfield collection of letters. I read them more carefully than my previous readings to ensure I didn't miss anything. Several themes appeared throughout the whole bunch. Gloria was determined from that first kiss that she'd be Mrs. Myles Bethard and live in a big mansion. She frequently whined about Rosemond, the Colonel's indifference, and how Cissy was mischievous with her affection, but she was convinced she could win them over.

Her last letter, dated December 31st, 1976, wished her American family a prosperous new year before diving into Gloria's plans for the evening.

I am getting ready for the New Year's ball hosted by my boyfriend's, or should I say, my fiancée's parents. It should be a fabulous kickin' good time and much different than lighting fireworks and drinking PBR like we did. Huh, Mom?

I might have to pound down a couple of highballs before midnight because I intend to have a come-to-Jesus meeting with Myle's mother. I've bent over backward being nice to her and her husband, Sir Stick-Up-the-Butt Bethard, and they still treat me like dirt. Myles has made promises I intend to make him keep if his mother doesn't treat me better. I know he loves me, but he can be wobbly under pressure, so I intend to help him stand tall.

But what the hey, I'm not letting that thought ruin my good time tonight. I met this old lady in the village a few weeks ago, and when I told her I was engaged to Myles, she got all buggy-eyed. She also said the Bethard New Year's Eve party was legendary for great food, fancy people, and plenty of booze. She said she'd be there as well. It was her favorite social event because she could stay up late and watch the fancy people getting drunk and misbehaving. What a hoot!

The letter ended with complaints about the unheated bedroom and lukewarm bath water in the mornings. Gloria admitted struggling with university classes but thought she'd avoid academic probation. She ended the letter by adding a row of Xs and Os and signing her name.

I sat back and sighed. The young American woman was headstrong and determined, but could she go ten rounds with Rosemond Bethard? Did she stay on after she and Myles fought, or did she give up and leave for London and the airport the next morning, as everyone seemed to believe?

After all my digging, Nic Knuckles had not punched enough holes into the story coming down from Rockingham Manor to sink it. As Lizabeth said, any reasonable person would conclude Gloria left England in 1977 with a broken heart but still standing on two feet.

However, Nic Knuckles wasn't always reasonable. I couldn't answer why the woman never contacted her family if she came home. Gloria was too close to her parents to slink away because of a humiliating end to a romance. I guessed something could've happened to Gloria once she landed in New York City. If anyone knew the criminal capabilities of thugs and lowlifes of the Big Apple, it was Nic Knuckles. I'd looked into too many bad things happening to young women around train stations and airports over the years not to wonder if Gloria could've been a victim of home-grown criminality.

Speaking of criminality, the amount Lizabeth charged me for her assistance sure seemed excessive. Why'd I so easily accept her charges? I pulled the crumpled invoice from my pocket and smoothed it on the table. My so-called partner listed the dates and the hours spent doing research. She averaged six hours a day over a week, and billed me a consultation fee whenever I stopped by and chatted. Well, bounce me between two paddles and call me pickleball. The woman even made me pay for the tea and refreshments I consumed at her cottage.

Holy Provolone! Could that be? Was that possible?

I bolted from my chair and pulled my sports jacket from the hanger. I snatched the Rosemond letter from the inside pocket and read. A quarter of a page in, I mumbled. "Holy hot Provolone, can that be?"

My heart pounded blood to my brain so loudly I was afraid Gram might hear it from across the street at Doc Johnson's office. I spun around and pulled my luggage from beneath the bed. Inside were some of the whatnots I was compelled to buy while questioning Pauline. What I was looking for was the photocopy of Aunt Jane's reported visit to the British Airways office at Heathrow Airport in late January 1977.

Holy mother of Provolone, I couldn't believe what I was looking at. Lizabeth West lied, and worst of all, I paid her nearly two thousand pounds to make a fool of me. Maybe she and the Rockingham Manor folks could pull one over on Nic Knuckles every day for a week, but sooner rather than later, I'd see through it. And, what I just seen through made me angry, and then hungry, and then hangry. So, I went down to Gram's kitchen and snatched any remaining cheese from her fridge, slapped a couple of slices of bread around it, and ate.

Once my brain realized I was no longer starving, it shifted gears and started ruminating and plotting and planning. Nic Knuckles, America's premier private investigator, wasn't going to let a handful of deceitful Brits get away with murder. We showed the English in 1776 and again in 1812 that America would stand up to the Redcoats and secure justice. All I needed was an hour of thinking on a full stomach, and I had the plan.

Chapter Twenty-Nine

Early the next morning, I sat in a chair in a small anteroom just off the chapel on the grounds of Rockingham Manor. Across from me was Reverend Amethyst, her hands pressed as if in prayer, and although she'd evoked the name of the Lord, it wasn't in a religious sort of way. It was more in a dockworker's kind of way.

"That is so disturbing," she said, "although I must say, not surprising."

I'd just shared with her how I'd been a victim of a conspiracy to prevent me from proving that Gloria Butterfield never left The Rock in 1977. The Rev admitted there had always been some unspoken guilt and shame hanging over Rockingham Manor and that she'd given up trying to penetrate the family's secrets to understand it.

"I always assumed the source of this malaise was from the other side of the Manor, where Cissy's husbands mysteriously died. I believed Myles' despondency came from a different source."

For years, Reverend Amethyst assumed Myles's embarrassment at failing at everything he pursued in life discouraged him. She never suspected it had anything to do with Gloria Butterfield's disappearance.

"I know something horrible happened to that young woman decades ago," I said. "But I'm facing a tightly orchestrated resistance to finding all my answers, and I need your help."

Reverend Amethyst nodded. "Oh, I understand the difficulty breaking through the Bethard family shield all too well, but I'm willing to help you if I can."

I felt the weight of desperation lift from my shoulders, replaced by one of hopeful high anxiety. My plan was still a long shot, but I'd secured the critical component – a pulpit-pounding preacher.

"I believe at least three guilt-ridden people want to gain absolution but are afraid to go against Rosemond. Using your preaching skills, Rev, if you can get one or more of them to confess, I think…I hope, it opens a floodgate of admitted culpability, and we'll secure justice for Gloria Butterfield."

A frown appeared on the Reverend's face. "My mission has always been to save souls," she said, "not imprison them."

Yikes, a hint of doubt. "A body or two might spend time in the slammer," I said, "but their conscience would be liberated, and their soul would soar with the angels."

Reverend Amethyst gave me a weak smile. "You'd do well on the pulpit, Mister Knuckles." She drew a deep sigh and said, "What do you need me to do?"

The plan I proposed was simple. I would promote next Sunday's service as the grand reveal. After nearly fifty years, the question of what happened to a young American woman visiting Rockingham Manor would be answered.

"You'll have a full chapel by Sunday, I promise," I said. "I mean the in-laws, staff, and villagers, not just the Bethard family principals. All you need to do is craft a sermon that shakes loose at least one repentance-seeking soul, and I'll take it from there."

The Rev was all in and suggested the sermon title she'd post outside the chapel for all to read. I loved the directness of it. Those little white letters would be pressed into the black slots of the board to read: Sunday We Bring Gloria Home.

Reverend Amethyst excused herself, explaining that preaching was like running. You had to stretch before you gave that full-throated sermon, or you risked pulling a muscle. She'd pray long and hard for divine inspiration to help her craft her message, then draw from her bag of sermonizing tricks to ensure she captured and maintained the audience's attention. "I'm going to isolate myself to prepare my absolute best sermon," she said.

Nic Knuckles, however, didn't need to stretch any muscles to do my task. In the short time I'd been in Village-In-Thistles, I'd become familiar with how quickly word could spread. I left the chapel and strolled the village, and chatted with Gram, Rufford, Bristol, and anyone who'd listen at the Pissin' Pints. "Did you hear," I'd whisper, "This Sunday morning, Reverend Amy and I will together solve the long-ago mystery of Gloria Butterfield's disappearance."

As rumors about Sunday's sermon picked up strength like a hurricane over warm seas, people's tempers seemed to flare easily. The waitress at the Pissin' Pints grew even nastier after I refused to hint at what would happen at Sunday's service. Gram plied me with cheese and warm biscuits, which shook my resolve to its core, but I held firm. "You'll have to attend services, Gram," I said. "I truly don't know what will happen."

"Why should your landlady wait like any chapel punter to hear the news," she said, pulling the last biscuit from the plate before I could take it. "Bloody disgraceful, Nic, bloody disgraceful."

Bristol Warford ignored my warm greeting when I gave him a shout-out as I passed his store. The ultimate snub came last evening when Rufford refused to let me buy him a pint. It felt like my first day in the village when every citizen gave me a long, judgmental look as they silently walked by me. I checked bus, train, and airplane schedules, figuring I might have to quickly escape Village-In-Thistles if I came up empty-handed on Sunday.

I learned I wasn't the only one under pressure. Reverend Amy reported that Myles was beside himself with curiosity, and Rosemond's frosty disdain toward her had grown colder. Cissy and her offspring were friendlier than usual until they realized The Rev had nothing in the gossip bank; they could withdraw. Even normally standoffish Melba made a play, over-salting the Reverend's porridge when the Rev failed to provide the housekeeper with answers.

"I don't know what Mister Knuckles is going to reveal," she'd reply to the questioners, "I'm only there to offer the opportunity for immediate confession and absolution."

By the time I crawled into bed Saturday night, the village's rising excitement and fearfulness were at a feverish pitch. The buzz of speculative conversation overflowed from the pubs and filled the street until midnight.

The noise didn't matter because Nic Knuckles couldn't sleep anyway. Even thinking about eating a decent pastrami sandwich once I got back to New York City couldn't keep my mind off tomorrow. I felt confident that The Rev would deliver. Whether any of the guilt-stricken folks would come clean was the unknown. Maybe it would be Bristol, who now struggled with old nightmares, or Rufford, who saw and heard more than I suspect he'd already shared. Turquoise had the most ethical fiber of any of the Bethard clan, and she might talk. I might be stunned, and Roland or Doc Johnson or even Gram Edwards could be a surprise witness. You never knew what might be the big surprise in a story like this.

It was my usual anxiety dream that startled me awake at five the next morning. Not only was I standing in the front of my old seventh-grade class in my underwear, as I tried to explain why I didn't do my book report, my front teeth fell out.

Chapter Thirty

S unday morning's sky was cloudless, and the air was warm and humid, making my job harder. Since I typically drew clues from how much a person sweat, if they were already perspiring because it was eighty-five degrees and humid, I'd lose the advantage. How could I tell if a flushed face was from guilt or the heat? It was one more challenge for Nic Knuckles.

The chapel was packed with people when I slipped in from the back. Sitting in the first row was Myles, dressed in a beige colored suit that matched his complexion. His mother, the indomitable Rosemond, sat beside him, an angry aura simmering around her snowy head of hair. Cissy and Turquoise filled out the pew. The wrist of the older woman jangled with big bracelets, while the younger woman was dressed more appropriately for an afternoon at a bowling alley.

In the second row was Gram, a skeptical expression on her face, Melba, outfitted as shabbily as humanly possible, Lizabeth West, looking out-of-place not wearing gardening overalls, and Dr. Watson Johnson in a coat and tie. A man sat directly behind Cissy, and judging how they continuously whispered to each other, I figured it was Wilton Dinwiddie, Cissy's current husband. He looked healthy, so I guessed his finances were equally robust. The angry barmaid from the Pissin' Pints made a late entry and claimed the last space in that pew. She walked by and hissed at me. "You better not botch it up, mate."

The third set of pews contained the Warfords, Bristol and Pauline, Rufford, Roland in his chauffeur uniform, and two field hands and their wives. I sat in the last row, sharing space with a half dozen regulars from the Pissin' Pints.

One said he was running a pub pool on who'd be exposed as a criminal and was here to hear it firsthand. I laughed when he asked if I wanted to place a quid or two. Did that guy think he'd gain a betting edge by tricking Nic Knuckles into revealing his bias? Honestly, I wasn't sure who ended the life of Gloria Butterfield, although I had narrowed it down to three possibilities: the Colonel, Myles, or Bristol.

A rustle at the front of the chapel silenced the chatter. Reverend Amy charged through the chapel's side door, looking as determined and focused as a hungry shark in a bathtub full of ducklings. She jumped to the front of the altar and greeted us in a strong, warm voice. "Blessed be God, the Father, Son, and Holy Spirit. And blessed be his kingdom, now and forever. Amen."

The rest of us mumbled a collective ah-men, and Reverend Amethyst sang a hymn in her sweet melodic tone. She instructed everyone to open a copy of The Book of Common Prayer and the room filled with murmured voices. I held my book open, but my eyes scanned the folks before me, looking for clues to how people might be feeling.

A perspiration stain forming on the back of Myles' dress jacket was a good indicator that someone either over-dressed or knew his day of reckoning had arrived.

Bristol stood motionless, Pauline's left hand with a tight grip on his elbow. Did that suggest someone's spouse might soon be going off to prison, and she was clutching him close one last time? Could it mean Pauline was holding back a man filled with guilt who might sprint to the front of the chapel and disrupt everyone's life?

Cissy's voice rose above the rest as she sang the hymns with gusto, and her daughter shrunk in embarrassment with each refrain. Was the Yellow Widow immune to feeling any remorse after successfully snuffing three husbands, and feared nothing from today's revelations?

"Greetings to all who come to taste the succulent peace that our God willingly grants us," Reverend Amethyst said. "All the Lord asks is that we humble ourselves and atone for our sins."

The Reverend continued, announcing that we could gain the Lord's grace, if we knelt down and atoned for our indiscretions. She raised her voice, and her words bounced off the chapel's unadorned stone walls. "Atonement has no best-used date like an egg. Whether our sin was committed last year or fifty years ago, confession still frees the heart of its burdens and guarantees us eternal salvation."

The Reverend glowered and stepped closer to the edge of the altar. "Who among us this morning will take the first step to help this community send Gloria Butterfield home to her long-suffering family?"

First, Cissy's head turned side to side, then Turquoise looked over her shoulder at Bristol. Everyone in the first row twisted around and stared at the folks behind them. Rufford mumbled, "not me, mate," and nudged Pauline, who pushed him back. The third and fourth rows of attendees nodded toward the folks in the first and second rows. When Reverend Amy growled, everyone's attention returned to her.

"In the winter of 1976, a young woman arrived to our fine village and eventually fell in love with my future husband, Myles Bethard. I never met this woman named Gloria Butterfield, but many of you did. For the short time she lived among you, she cast a spell of intrigue over this community that has lasted decades. Today, we must look deep into ourselves and bring peace to Gloria Butterfield, Village-In-Thistles, and Rockingham Manor."

The air in the chapel suddenly shifted, and my eyes were drawn to the figure of Lizabeth West rising to her feet. "Enough of this rubbish," she shouted. "We have nothing to confess because the only crime was a brash American woman thinking she could get what she wanted by throwing a tantrum."

Reverend Amethyst looked stunned as a wave of congregational murmuring swept over her. West must've sensed the same confusion as she increased her aggression. "I became acquainted with Mister Knuckles soon after his arrival as he approached me to assist in his efforts. His stated objective was to determine the truth about Gloria Butterfield's last days in England. I soon realized, instead of searching for truth, he intended to slander the good names of our citizens by digging up ancient rumors and bawdy speculations. I listened carefully to his arguments, reviewed the letters Butterfield penned, and found nothing to convince me there was anything worth pursuing."

Someone muttered. "He's a bloody wanker then." Several voices grumbled in agreement.

"Mister Knuckles, an admitted mercenary hired by scurrilous Americans, was not deterred by this lack of credible evidence. So, I went the extra kilometer and provided him with the notes from my beloved Aunt Jane, an extraordinary sleuthing talent who herself had investigated the whereabouts of Gloria Butterfield. Aunt Jane proved the woman had returned to America, yet Knuckles refused to accept what one of Britain's greatest detectives had determined fifty years ago."

The chapel exploded with angry words. "Them Americans think they're so smart, they do." "Did those Yanks ever thank us for John, Paul, George, and Ringo? I think not!" "The bastard showed up, with his perfectly straight teeth, accusing our betters of murder."

By now, the blood had drained not just from Reverend Amy's face, but every other one of her organs as well. She reached for the pulpit to keep from falling. It was time for Nic Knuckles to stop this chaos and reveal to the unruly crowd of villagers and elites that Nic Knuckles was the premier investigator working in Village-In-Thistles, not Lizabeth West.

"Ladies and gentlemen, please cool your jets and listen up, for I will reveal the fraudster who lives among you."

And that's what I did. The letter delivered by Turquoise from her grandmother, Rosemond Bethard, appeared in my right hand. I read the contents of the letter to an attentive audience and offered a summary.

"As you heard, Rosemond's letter did clarify the storyline that Gloria had decided to depart Rockingham Manor after realizing Myles would never give up his position to marry her and live in America."

Then, whipping my left hand like a magician about to materialize a dove out of thin air, I pulled another document from my inside coat pocket.

"This page," I said, "Is a photocopy of Aunt Jane's investigation written almost a month after Gloria's disappearance. Aunt Jane made contact with British airline personnel, who had evidence that a young woman left on a flight to the United States on the first day of January, 1977. Aunt Jane concluded that Miss Butterfield departed the Manor, traveled to London, and eventually Heathrow Airport, in reasonably good health."

I stepped from the pew and slowly meandered toward the front of the chapel. Outwardly calm looking, inside my chest, my heart was pounding. Nothing was more exciting and gratifying for a private eye than the grand reveal, and my time in the limelight was now.

"Why was Nic Knuckles not persuaded by this evidence?" I asked. "Let us look carefully at the letter written by Rosemond Bethard." I handed the paper to Dr. Watson Johnson. "Please note the fine penmanship, Doctor, and how those words were laid down by a firm stroke of the old quill."

Johnson nodded. "Yes, I see that," he said.

I turned toward the front row. "Miss Rosemond, please raise your right hand for me."

"I have to do nothing you ask, you shameless cad," the woman said, her words clipped tight by her anger. "Leave me and my family alone."

Fortunately for me, Rosemond was so irritated by my request, she raised her right hand in a clenched fist. Her hand shook like a seismometer during the 1905 San Francisco earthquake.

"As you can see, ladies and gentlemen, Rosemond Bethard, as most anyone her age, has a significant hand tremor. That begs the question, how could she compose her letter with such perfect penmanship when she was afflicted with the shakes?"

"Maybe Rosemond dictated it to Cissy," Lizabeth called out. "Or, it could've been the granddaughter who wrote it."

"Those are two possibilities, Miss West," I said. "I propose a third one."

Handing Dr. Johnson the photocopy of Aunt Jane's diary, I asked him. "Would you kindly look at the handwriting of Aunt Jane's investigative notes supposedly from 1977?"

The man's eye shifted back and forth between the two documents.

"What do you see there, kind doctor?"

Johnson harrumphed like a backfiring motorbike. "Why, the handwriting is the same."

The rumble of discomforted villagers swept through the chapel.

"Aunt Jane of Village-In-Thistles was indeed an outstanding solver of criminal mysteries," I said. "Sadly, her skills did not transfer over to her niece."

I reached into my coat pocket and removed a wrinkled piece of paper. "This my gossipy friends, is a handwritten invoice given to me by Lizabeth West for services rendered."

"I hope she over-charged the pillock," a man from the Pissin' Pints shouted.

"She did, my friend, but now it's my turn to collect."

I asked Doctor Johnson to carefully examine the handwriting of the invoice.

"Oh my, the handwriting is identical to the other two documents."

I slashed the air with my right index finger. "You were sloppy, Lizzy," I said. "It was you who wrote Rosemond's dictation in a letter, and it was you who created that fraudulent Aunt Jane notes to mislead me. But Nic Knuckles has the eye of a New York City pigeon pecking at bagel crumbs scattered after a Sunday brunch at Izzy's Deli; and when I saw the distinct handwriting of your invoice, I realized you'd been working for the Bethards from the start."

Red-faced and quivering, Lizabeth pushed her way from the pew and left the chapel through the back door. Rosemond pulled a shawl tighter around her shoulders and stared at her shoes. The rest of the attendees sat quietly, perhaps embarrassed at how easily they'd turned into a howling mob.

Reverend Amethyst looked to have regained her composure and softly called for a public act of contrition. The only sound to be heard was squeaking pews as people shifted their weight. Then, a sob slowly rose from the front row and ascended to the ceiling and shook the rafters. All eyes turned to the bent figure in a beige jacket spotted with sweat.

"I can't take it anymore," Myles cried, "I must make testimony."

Chapter Thirty-One

Myles stood and turned to face the congregation. If he tumbled forward in a faint, I'd not be surprised, but the set of his jaw suggested he was determined to beat back any anxiety attacks. His voice was surprisingly firm.

"Let me offer this preamble before I testify," he said. "I dearly loved Gloria Butterfield, but I was only twenty-two then. What did I know about life and love?"

Rosemond mumbled. "Amen, brother."

"I thought she was the one I wanted to spend my life with, but I soon learned she wanted something I couldn't give her: my destiny."

Covering her face with her hands failed to mute Turquoise Blix-Vixen's snickering, but her mother's elbow in her ribs did. Myles continued his speech, rubbing his big, sinewy hands as he spoke.

"On the last night of 1976, Gloria planned to tell my parents we intended to marry, regardless of whether we got their blessing or not. My mother and father, however, thought I was too young, and in retrospect, they were right about my immaturity."

The people in the chapel leaned forward as Myles went on with his story. "Immediately after the start of the New Year, Gloria approached my mother with a peace offering and the hope she'd accept her as part of the family. If she didn't embrace Gloria living in Rockingham Manor as their daughter-in-law, Gloria threatened to live in America after we married."

"Blimey, just like Harry and Meghan," the Pissin' Pints barmaid shouted. "Those bloody Americans just can't leave well enough alone, can they?"

Myles ignored the unsolicited social commentary and continued.

"That night, I watched as Gloria spoke to my mother from afar. I couldn't hear the conversation, but I knew what was said from the flushed expression on Gloria's face and the sneer on my mother's lips."

Myles shared how Gloria ran out of the Manor in tears, exiting through the kitchen and into the garden on a bitterly cold night. He claimed he chased after Gloria and eventually found her deep in the garden, shivering and crying.

"Your mother told me she'd do everything possible to prevent us from marrying," Gloria cried to me. "Will you stand up to her and your father?"

Myles suggested that Gloria go back inside with him to have a civil conversation. He covered her bare shoulders with his jacket, escorted her to the kitchen, and instructed Melba to prepare Gloria some hot tea to warm her. Myles talked about how his and Gloria's discussion grew more animated, with Miss Butterfield pushing him to leave England for a new life in America. He told her he could not, that he would not, give up his inheritance to live in some small town in Indiana.

"That was when Gloria lost her temper and slapped me across the face."

The old wooden pews stopped squeaking as people sat motionless, waiting for Myles's next revelation.

"Her violence took me aback," he said. "I told her I could never marry if she'd resort to pugilisms every time we disagreed."

Myles dropped his head, and a shiver crossed his bony shoulders.

"What happened next?" Reverend Amethyst asked. "How did you react?"

In a voice now lower in volume and less assured in tone, Myles admitted to grabbing Gloria's upper arms and shaking her, which caused her to slip from the stool and fall to the floor.

"As she tumbled down, her head cracked against the corner of the stone table top. It was horrible watching her on the floor, unconscious and bleeding. I didn't know what to do. I was in a state of panic."

Myles said he then realized two people stood in the kitchen entry. His alarm was considerably lessened when he saw it was Rosemond and the Colonel. They'd witnessed the exchange between Myles and Gloria, from the harsh words to the physical altercations.

"My parents examined Gloria and announced that she was still breathing. Grateful the young woman was still alive, they expressed concern about what brain damage she might've suffered from the fall."

Reverend Amethyst appeared stunned and feebly asked her husband, "What did you do, Myles? Surely, you went to Gloria's aid."

Myles looked up at his wife and cried. "I did, love. I wanted to get Gloria to the hospital, and I begged my parents to call for medical assistance."

The Rev's eyes said what her mouth couldn't. What happened next, you dithering fool?

"My mother refused to call for a medical service, saying something like, 'What will our guests think seeing a supine young woman being carried from our kitchen? There'll be questions and rumors. There must be another way.'"

Myles admitted to being distraught at his mother's insensitivity. "I screamed, but I love her and can't continue without her. We have to do something."

Rosemond's expression remained unmoved, hearing her son's recollection. Her eyes were half closed, her nose pointed upward, her thin lips tightly clasped shut.

Myles, on the other hand, grew more emotional. Tears filled his eyes, and he wiped his hand under his nose. "My father told me to leave the kitchen and that he and mother would get Gloria the necessary attention. That's what I did. I returned to the festivities, retreated to a corner with a bottle of whiskey, and proceeded to get properly pissed."

The next day, after Myles slept off an epic bender, the Colonel, Rosemond, and Cissy told him that his father and Bristol took Gloria to the village doctor, who found she was only concussed, not brain-damaged. Gloria regained consciousness and complained of a mild headache, which the doctor addressed with aspirin.

"I was elated after hearing their news," Myles said. "I demanded I be taken into the village to see Gloria. But my parents warned me that the doctor was disturbed by the bruises on Gloria's upper arms and would have to report it to the police."

Myles' head dipped hard, and he muttered into his chest. "Gloria had asked the doctor not to go to the authorities. She was done with me and wanted to get as far from Rockingham Manor as possible. The doctor agreed because he didn't want to destroy my reputation, especially if Gloria was leaving the country."

Myles claimed to have been deeply hurt by Gloria's rejection but, fearful of reputational damage, never pursued the American woman. The doctor eventually retired and moved to the Lake District, and Rosemond and the Colonel never brought up the incident.

"I never forgot what I'd done," he said. "I still regret hurting Gloria, both physically and emotionally. Nonetheless, I believe she did depart England, and Mister Knuckles' inquiry is without warrant."

Myles had already seeded his telling of what happened with enough lies that I had no choice but to challenge him.

"That was a very interesting version of the events, Mister Bethard," I said, forcing Myles to turn toward me and make eye contact. "Did Melba, your dedicated housekeeper and cook, witness you shaking Gloria and causing her to fall?"

Myles's eyes flitted over to where Melba sat, desperate for a reaction from the woman. He got nothing. "I don't recall, but she most likely left the kitchen. Melba has always been a loyal member of the Manor staff, known for her discretion."

"Was there anyone else in addition to your parents?"

Myles shook his head. "No."

"How about Cissy?"

"No, again."

"Is it possible Bristol Warford was there after making a late delivery run? Perhaps toasting the new year with the staff?"

I didn't like how the color slipped from Myles's cheeks. I hoped he wouldn't faint, fall to the floor, and roll out of the chapel.

"Maybe, he was there," Myles said, "but I'm sure he didn't see anything."

I looked at Bristol. The man's face revealed no emotion.

"So, Mister Bethard, you're claiming the only people who saw Gloria strike you and then fall after you shook her were your parents, am I correct?"

"Yes, that is correct."

"Well, sir, another witness was there the night that Gloria and you had your little dust-up."

I stepped to the front of the assembled villagers; my fingers tightly intertwined to keep me from pointing an accusatory digit at the smarmy faces of the Bethard clan in the front row. "Back in 1976, a precocious young lad was known for his observational skills and brilliant timing, being in the right places at the wrong times. As an adult with an astonishing memory, he has been a reliable source for my investigation. I believe he will offer greater insight into what happened to Gloria Butterfield during the earliest hour of 1977."

I pointed at the man sitting in the third row, the person who'd I placed all my chips on. "Please stand, Rufford, and testify."

Chapter Thirty-Two

I hadn't seen that many gaping mouths since my last visit to Fulton's Fish Market. The village had written off old Rufford as an intellectually impaired man just because he heard the complaints of pigs and chickens about humans' treatment of them. They didn't realize he wasn't always that way, and his memory was phenomenal. They were about to learn how amazing his recollection of New Year's Day, 1977, was.

Rufford stood, his eyes wide and focused on me. Usually, when I saw that expression, a pint I'd just bought rested in front of him. I bet the man wished we were sitting at the Pissin' Pints right now, instead of in front of the local community.

"Please share with us, Rufford, what you saw happen at Rockingham Manor on and about New Year's 1977."

"I was up late on New Year's Eve night because me mum was so busy getting things done for the party. First, I watched from the upstairs hallway and saw everybody comin' in, and they were all fancied up."

"Did you see Gloria Butterfield?" I asked.

Rufford nodded his head. "I sure did see Miss Gloria. She was dressed nice."

"While watching the party, did you happen to see Gloria Butterfield approach Rosemond Bethard soon after midnight?"

"No, me mum caught me peekin' and jerked me by my ear and sent me upstairs to our little quarters."

Rosemond Bethard loudly whispered. "That was brilliant." Cissy chuckled.

"Did you see anything else between midnight and one in the morning?" I asked.

The earnest expression on Rufford's face made me smile. "Oh yes, sir," he said. "Just about ten minutes after I heard all the posh folks downstairs yelling about the new year, I heard a commotion outside me window. I saw Miss Gloria. She sounded upset, you know, crying and cussin'."

"Was she alone?"

"At first, she was alone, but then I saw a man come out and talk to her."

"Did you recognize the man?"

"No, it was too dark, but I knew it wasn't Mister Myles because this man was bigger by a lot. You know, muscles as you see on a plow horse and taller than Mister Myles."

I asked Rufford to continue with his recollection. He said the man removed his coat and put it around Gloria, and they talked some more. Then they left the garden, and Rufford no longer saw them.

It was time for Nic Knuckles to roll the dice, to trust his gut, to throw caution to the wind. I always felt Rufford knew more, and now I was about to find out if he would share it with the world.

"Was it Bristol Warford," I asked, "who retrieved Miss Butterfield from the cold night, not Myles?"

Rufford nodded. "I saw Mister Bristol bring in Miss Gloria into the kitchen. She was wearing his coat, and seein' it made me giggle because it was so big on her. I heard Mister Bristol tell me mum to make Miss Gloria some tea."

I asked Rufford how he witnessed this interaction if his mother had confined him to their small apartment upstairs.

"I left me bedroom when I saw Miss Gloria and the man leave the garden. I went to me hidey-hole where I could see through the old duct that looked down into the kitchen. It was me secret way to know if me mum was done workin'. I also heard Mum and Roland talk about stuff like the Colonel shaggin' the Duchess of Butterburrs, you know, stuff like that."

"Ya better shut that mouth, you flippin' idiot before I remove your teeth from that addled skull of yours."

Everyone in the chapel jumped when Melba loudly delivered that message to her son—everyone but Nic Knuckles. My mother used to wake me up on school mornings using a similar tone before throwing a bucket of cold water on my head. Although I still wake from sleep if I hear a faucet running, loud noises don't startle me.

Reverend Amethyst stepped to the altar's edge. "Please understand that my chapel is a refuge for everyone, and they're safe from persecution and harm. Go on, Rufford, tell us what you saw."

"I seen Mister Myles come in soon after, and he shouted at Miss Gloria about fightin' with his mum. Miss Gloria yelled back at him."

"Did Bristol and your mother witness this argument?"

"Well, Mister Bristol, he left, but me mum stayed. No bloke, even the Colonel, kicks Mum out of her kitchen."

"What happened next?" I asked.

"Lots of hot words and Mister Myles sayin' he won't ever leave Rockingham Manor, and Miss Gloria got all red-faced and slapped him across the mouth. Then Mister Myles grabbed Miss Gloria and used some swear words."

"Did you see her fall after he shook her?"

"No, she didn't fall."

The gasps in the chapel rolled back and forth like water in a carried bucket, and my stomach was just as unsettled.

I stepped closer to Rufford. "You did not see Miss Gloria fall after Myles shook her?"

"She didn't fall from Mister Myles shakin' her. She fell when he choked her."

The chapel exploded in a wild mix of cussing, complaining, yelling, and grumbling. Reverend Amethyst needed five minutes to regain control of her sanctuary. Once the crowd quieted, I approached Rufford, my nerves taunt like a guitar string on an old Gibson. "What do you mean, Myles choked Gloria after she slapped him?"

"No, mate. Mister Myles didn't choke her after she slapped him; he shook her after she slapped him."

Rosemond's frail little body let loose with a chapel-shaking laugh. "Ha, he's mental. What a waste of my time, this is."

I worked hard at swallowing a big ball of anxiety that suddenly filled my throat. "Rufford, did Myles shake or choke Gloria Butterfield?"

"Mister Myles shook Miss Gloria, and then he choked her."

The chapel loudly rumbled as if a motorcycle gang was cruising down the aisle. Everyone appeared confused by Rufford's response, but not Nic Knuckles. I realized the man was truthful, but I wasn't asking the questions in the proper sequence. Hearing talking farm animals wasn't Rufford's only cognitive issue.

"Rufford, let's start from when Bristol brought Gloria into the kitchen. What happened?"

"Me mum poured her a cuppa and Miss Gloria askin' me mum for some ice cubes to put in her tea."

The air in the chapel filled with a collective gasp. "Ice in your tea, had she lost the bloody plot?" someone said. Rosemond turned to the people behind her. "See, that was what we had to put up with from that horrible woman."

Reverend Amethyst hushed Rosemond and nodded at Rufford. "Continue, please."

"Then Mister Myles came in and Mister Myles and Miss Gloria started goin' at each other, you know, about leavin' the Manor."

"And is that when Gloria slapped Myles?"

"Yes, she did."

"And is that when he shook her?"

Rufford nodded.

"Is that when she fell?"

Rufford shook his head. "Nope. Mister Myles stopped shakin' Miss Gloria but she was still sittin' on her bun."

I drew a breath and squeezed my hands, a dribble of perspiration snaking down my back.

"What happened next, Rufford?"

"Well, when Miss Gloria crunched that ice cube, Mister Myles got all purple in the face and asked her to stop. But she didn't. She crunched down on that ice over and over again."

Rufford lowered his head and his voice. "Mister Myles screamed for her to stop, but she crunched on that ice, and that was when he grabbed her by the throat."

Rufford told how Gloria's eyeballs were popping from their sockets, and the veins in her face were bulging. "I was terrified," Rufford said. "I was so happy seein' the Colonel come runnin' in, and he pealed Mister Myles's hands off of Miss Gloria's throat. That was when she fell."

"Did she hit her head on the table as she dropped to the floor?" I asked.

Rufford shook his head. "No, Miss Gloria never hit her skull on nothin', but she was out cold when she landed."

My gabby witness rattled on about how Rosemond entered and was very upset with what she saw. He said Myles was crying, the Colonel was swearing, and Rosemond was shouting for someone to do something.

"The Colonel told Mister Myles to leave and that he and Miss Rosemond would care for Miss Gloria. The Colonel checked Miss Gloria and said she was still alive, but he worried she might've lost her brain because Mister Myles had been choking her air off for so long."

Rufford claimed Rosemond didn't want to take Gloria to a doctor because the bruise marks on her neck would raise suspicion and a possible police investigation. The Colonel supposedly worried the American or her family would sue them into the poor house once she recovered.

"The Colonel went to the back door and shouted for Mister Bristol to come into the kitchen," Rufford said. "He told Miss Rosemond that he and Mister Bristol would fix Miss Gloria and that Miss Rosemond should go back to the party so nobody would think something bad was going on."

"What happened after Bristol returned to the kitchen?" I asked.

Rufford's shoulders climbed higher. "I don't know. I felt like a laser beam was burnin' me skin when I realized me mum was looking right at me, her eyes all blazin' like she would reach into that vent and choke the life outta me like Mister Myles had done to Miss Gloria. I fell back on me arse and scooted into me room."

Melba's voice was unmistakable. "Bloody lyin' wanker. You'll get yours tonight, boy."

Rufford sat in the pew, his chin bent deep into his chest.

"Thank you for speaking up," I said to him. "I admire your courage, but I have to ask. Why didn't you tell anyone about Gloria getting choked into unconsciousness? You always talked about how kind she was to you."

"I dunno. I was a lad of about ten and me mum depended on the Colonel and Rosemond for our livelihood, you know."

Rufford bowed his face and loudly sniffled. "I always hoped she got well enough. You know, like me after I got hoofed in the old noggin' and turned out all right, you know what I'm sayin'? "

"I know what you mean, Rufford."

The man looked at me with tears bubbling in his eyes. "Once I got used to the pigs and chickens makin' me feel bad about what we do to em, it ain't a terrible way to live."

Rufford sat down, his face buried in his left shoulder. It seemed he'd unloaded a lifetime of regret for not speaking up with these statements. It was only fair, and he owed it to Gloria Butterfield, and considering all the pints I'd bought him, me as well.

I turned to the assembled gathering, planning on asking Bristol Warford to testify about what he saw and did on that fateful night many years ago. My momentum was stopped before it started when Rosemond stood and took control of the room.

Chapter Thirty-Three

Rosemond stood, like a stork slowly rising up on one bony leg, although she balanced on two stems, so maybe that's a poor metaphor. Anyway, she had everyone's attention, including mine. "I am outraged that this spectacle has been allowed in a supposed house of worship," she said, sending Reverend Amethyst a Class A stink eye. "I must ask you to consider the obvious facts, not fairytales told by a half-wit whom a British-hating American coached into making slanderous remarks."

The woman demanded that her son, Myles, stand. He did, of course. She then asked, "Look at this man. How ridiculous it is to think that he would've attacked the American woman just because she crunched ice cubes?"

Rosemond had a point. Myles's pale face hung from a head that appeared too large for his scrawny neck to hold up. His skeletal shoulders poked through the sweat-stained suit jacket, and he was bent at the middle of his back.

"My son is eighteen years younger than me," Rosemond said, "yet I could pin him to the mat two out of three times."

An undercurrent of giggling rippled through the attendees. I had to admit Rosemond was a master at winning over the audience with her sly, biting humor. Nic Knuckles knew, however, that facts, not jokes, won the day, so I'd let her finish her comedy bit, before exposing her as a liar.

"Seriously, good people of Village-In-Thistles," Rosemond said. "Can you see this man losing control and choking someone just because they crushed ice between their molars? You'd have to be bereft of common sense to consider such a claim."

"And we all know old Rufford ain't got no sense," the Pissin' Pint's barmaid called out, "common or otherwise."

Rufford sank deeper in his seat, not willing to risk any more ridicule by defending what he claimed he saw.

"Thank you, dear, for stating the obvious," Rosemond said. "I'm relieved I don't have to bring in one of Rockingham Manor's prized Berkshire sows to explain to Rufford how mistaken he was about what he claimed to have seen."

Laughter ripped through the chapel. Inside Nic Knuckles' mind, however, I was thanking Rosemond for the opening.

"Maybe I can help you with your dilemma, Madam Bethard," I said. "Why don't you stick your tushie back onto that pew, and I'll explain to everyone how Myles was more than capable of attacking his beloved."

I walked up to Myles and gently lifted his arms in the air. "Fine folks of Village-In-Thistles, please remember that the decrepit specimen you see before us was not always so feeble. In 1976, young master Bethard was a strapping young man, a big man on campus, and an accomplished athlete. Look at these mitts on him," I said as I lifted Myles's hands high. "When Miss Butterfield disappeared, Myles Bethard had been a university rower, a vigorous and powerful man. Even today, he has the hands of a longshoreman."

I looked at Rosemond. "Maybe you could wrestle your son to the floor today, but in 1976, Myles would have snapped you like a strand of uncooked spaghetti."

I released my grip on Myles' wrists, and they dropped like they were weighted, seemingly pulling him down onto his seat. I looked at the people in the second row and asked, "Would Doctor Watson Johnson kindly rise and answer my questions?"

Johnson appeared surprised I was dragging him into this discussion. He stood with his lips tightly pulled behind a well-trimmed goatee. "How may I be of service?"

"You can be of service by kindly explaining a condition known as misophonia."

Johnson's eyelids flickered in apparent astonishment. He must wonder how anyone would know to ask such a question, especially when it's so relevant. Nothing tickled a private investigator's sphincter more than seeing discomfort in a person's eyes during an interview.

"Well, it is a sensitivity to certain sounds, such as chewing, slurping, and snoring," Johnson said. "People suffering from misophonia might respond in various ways to these noises, including being irritable or even angry."

"How rare is this condition?"

"I saw a recent study that estimated nearly twenty percent of the population here in the UK suffer some form of misophonia. But you need to understand that this condition is more than just being annoyed by certain sounds. Some people suffer emotionally and physically."

"I find the noise of someone popping bubble wrap irritating," I said. "I also get the heebie jeebies when I hear a watermelon being cut open. And don't get me started on how I react when people use the word 'irregardless.'" A shudder skipped up my spine and raised the hair on my arms.

"Many of us indeed react to certain sounds," Johnson said. "But there are key differences between those with misophonia and the general population. For example, you may dislike hearing the slicing of a melon, but those who suffer from misophonia might react with panic because they feel trapped and unable to escape the noise."

"Might a sensitive person in such a situation explode in anger?" I asked. "Maybe even physically try and stop the source of the sound?"

Johnson nodded. "Yes, sometimes, those who suffer severe misophonia, if they're feeling helpless, might get physical, I suppose."

I placed my hands behind my back and slowly strolled around to the side of the pews so I was standing next to Doctor Johnson. "Doc," I said, "does Myles Bethard suffer from misophonia?"

Johnson shook his head. "Mister Bethard's medical history is confidential information I can't share without his permission."

From the front row, Myles Bethard's voice caught everyone's attention. "Yes," he said. "I've suffered from that dreadful condition all my life."

Rosemond reached over and pulled on the sleeve of Myles's coat jacket.

CHAPTER THIRTY-THREE

"Stop talking, you fool," she said through clenched teeth. "Shut your mouth."

Myles ignored his mother, a behavior Nic Knuckles greatly admired, knowing firsthand the difficulty of extracting a mother's talons from your soul.

"I hate the sound of a bird's singing, or the clatter of silverware," Myles said. "When I hear those sounds, the only way I can stop from exploding is to internalize my panic until my brain shuts down and I pass out."

"Blimey, mate," a man's voice from the back row exclaimed. "I must suffer misophonia from drinking ale, because after a dozen pints, I pass out."

The pub locals roared and slapped the man's back. "Good one, Chalkie."

Myles ignored the man's observation and continued sharing. "My misophonia has only grown worse since my youth. Back then, only a handful of things would set it off."

"And was someone crunching ice cubes a trigger?" I asked.

"Since Gloria was the only person I'd ever met who chewed ice cubes, I wasn't aware it would set me off until we met. It annoyed me initially, but the irritation became more powerful as time passed."

Rosemond swiped her open hand at Myles. "Keep quiet, you bloody dolt." The man scooted further to his left, far enough to escape his mother's pummeling.

"I was so angry at Gloria," Myles said. "She was acting unreasonable that evening, and then she slapped me, which was humiliating. But I loved her, so I held my temper in check. I was able to do that until she started with the ice. She knew it triggered me, but she wouldn't stop."

I moved closer to Myles, lowering my voice in a warm tone that had once talked a beautiful woman from Staten Island out of betting a fortune on the NY Jets.

"I can understand how trapped you must've felt," I said. "Did you do more than grab Gloria by the arms and shake her?"

Myles shivered.

"Did you grab her around the neck like Rufford claimed? Perhaps squeezing her so tightly she no longer chewed that ice?"

Myles's eyes filled with tears.

"Did you keep choking her," I asked, "until she passed out?"

A fat teardrop fell from the man's eye and splattered on the stone floor of the chapel.

"Did you choke her until she was no longer alive?"

Myles gathered enough outrage to shout, "No, no, she was alive. Even Rufford said she was still alive. I didn't kill Gloria."

"Who did, Myles? Who killed your beloved Gloria Butterfield?"

"My family told me that Gloria left for London early that morning. Father said he helped her buy a ticket to fly home. That is all I know." Myles wiped his coat sleeve across his nose. "I loved Gloria. I'll always love her."

I looked at Reverend Amethyst, and my heart lost a beat. The poor woman appeared so brittle that the slightest breeze might knock her over.

"You know, Myles, my shaky, inconsiderate friend, I believe that you did not kill Gloria Butterfield."

Myles dropped his face into his hands and sobbed. "Thank god."

"However, I do believe that someone did kill her, and the killer is sitting in this chapel."

"Blimey, mate," the Pissin' Pints barmaid screamed. "Get on with it. My shift starts in thirty minutes."

Chapter Thirty-Four

After assuring the ever more restless audience that I did intend to soon reveal who killed Gloria Butterfield, I called on Bristol Warford. I had questions to ask the man; the more important concern was whether my luck would hold, and Bristol, like Rufford, would speak truthfully and completely. Hopefully, the urge to shed decades-old guilt was contagious here in Reverend Amethyst's chapel.

"Good morning, Bristol. Thank you for attending today's services."

The man stood, his right hand hanging by his side, gripped by Pauline. His facial expression lacked its usual jocular merchant vibe.

"Please tell us what you witnessed over the twenty-four hours when Gloria Butterfield was harmed."

Bristol spoke in a firm voice, first sharing his memory of the woman, Gloria Butterfield.

"From the first day she arrived at Rockingham Manor, one of my jobs was to watch over her."

Bristol told how Rosemond and the Colonel added the task to his regular duties, as they worried Myles was in over his head with the American. Bristol made his introduction soon after and found the young woman to be seriously naïve about Myles and his family.

"Gloria was determined to make a bloody go of it. Tradition and class differences be dammed," he said.

Bristol admitted he found Gloria attractive and charming, and he once confessed that he was worried for her. "I told her it wasn't easy being an outsider married to an insider and dealing with the residents of Rockingham

Manor."

On the evening of New Year's Eve, 1976, Bristol had arrived at the Manor about eleven o'clock. Melba had earlier called him in a panic. They were running short on food, and she asked him to make a run and bring more ingredients for Toad in the Hole. Once he arrived, he decided to stick around. "I knew Paulie would never accept an invitation to party at the Manor, so I was curious to see what went on."

A smile danced on his lips. "And Melba had kept a nice whiskey aside for the staff to drink."

A minute or two after midnight, Bristol was still sitting in the kitchen finishing his traditional glass of whiskey when Gloria swept through the space in tears. She looked at him and mumbled. "You were so right," and ran out the back door and into the garden.

"She was wearing a flimsy gown, and it was a brass monkey of a night, so I followed her."

Bristol found Gloria in a highly emotional state. She was frustrated with Rosemond and worried that Myles would not support a plan to move to the United States. He covered her bare arms with his coat and convinced her to return to the kitchen. Once inside, they were intercepted by Myles, who chastised Bristol for acting overly familiar by giving his fiancée his jacket.

"He didn't offer his coat to her," Bristol said. "He was happy to let her keep wearing mine. I told Melba to give the woman some hot tea. Myles was too caught up yipping at Gloria to comfort the poor girl."

Bristol reported that Myles and Gloria started arguing. He said it was embarrassing to watch, and he took his coat from Gloria and left the kitchen.

"I must admit I was angry with the way Myles was slaggin' me and Gloria, so I sat in my motor waiting for it to warm up and for me to cool down."

"How long were you sitting in your van?" I asked.

Bristol suggested it might've been fifteen minutes, but no more.

"That's when the Colonel rapped his knuckles on the glass and asked me to come into the kitchen."

"How'd the Colonel look at the time?"

Bristol slowly rolled his head from side to side. "Oh, the Colonel was doing his nut. I'd never seen him that way before."

"What did you see when you returned to the kitchen?"

"I saw Gloria unconscious on the floor. I couldn't tell if she was breathing, so I asked the Colonel if he wanted me to take her into the village and find the doctor. He told me it was too late."

The chapel crowd had sat quietly as Warford spoke, but his last comment stirred their emotions. "Bloody hell, what did he mean by that?" someone asked. Others murmured similar questions. Once they settled, I asked Bristol, "Did the Colonel say why he thought it was unnecessary to get Miss Butterfield medical attention?"

Warford's eyes shifted from me to the back of Rosemond Bethard's head. I could see her face, and her eyes had gone dead. I suspected Bristol and Rosemond's decades-old understanding was about to take a hit.

"The Colonel said that he'd seen victims of asphyxia during the war and that they'd never recover. He felt Gloria was too far gone, and she'd be a blathering human vegetable if she received help."

Myles Bethard jumped to his feet, screaming. "You're a filthy liar. I'd choked her for a few seconds, that's all. Father swore she regained consciousness and decided to leave England. Mother and Cissy observed her standing and talking. I did not kill her. No one killed her."

Reverend Amethyst asked her husband to sit down. He held his hands out to her as if inviting her to come hold him up. She shook her head, and he heaved a sigh and dropped to his seat. The Reverend nodded at Bristol, and the man continued talking.

"I didn't know for sure what asphyxia meant," Bristol said, "but I felt pretty sure Myles had something to do with it. He did have a reputation for going all mental over nothing."

"If the Colonel didn't want you to take Miss Butterfield to a medical facility, what did he ask you to do?"

Warford stood motionless, drawing in ever-deepening breaths. Pauline whispered something I couldn't hear, but her words were enough to push her husband forward.

"The Colonel offered me an opportunity of a lifetime, as he called it. He said if I disposed of Gloria, he and Rosemond would ensure me and Paulie would always have a roof over our heads and enough business to keep our store operating."

"What did he mean by 'disposing'?"

"I think he wanted me to finish her off. You know…" Bristol placed one clenched fist atop the other and twisted violently, "finish her off for good."

Rosemond may have been pushing ninety, but the way she rocketed from her seat convinced me she'd live another fifty years. "How dare you besmirch my husband's reputation?" she screamed. "The man is not here to defend himself against your horrible accusation. How dare you!"

Pauline jumped to her feet and pointed her right index finger at Rosemond. "He dares to tell the truth because he's tired of carrying your bloody secrets around. We have had enough of being used and manipulated by you and Myles and Cissy."

Rosemond sputtered. "Oh, sod off, Pauline, why don't you?"

Bristol squeezed his wife's hand, and it seemed to calm her, and I continued with my questioning. "Mister Warford, you have admitted on multiple occasions that you and Pauline would've never survived all these years without Rosemond's business. Are you telling us that you killed Gloria Butterfield in exchange for your livelihood?"

Bristol shook his head and admitted he knew he'd risked his position with the Colonel and Rosemond by turning down the offer, so he suggested an alternative. "I told him I'd do anything to help them out of their mess, but it would have to be something that wouldn't get me a date with the hangman."

The Colonel agreed to Bristol's conditions and had him collect Gloria's belongings from the guest room, drive to the dorm, break into her room, and pack the rest before noon.

"Later that morning, Roland arrived with Cissy," Bristol said, "and she placed a fudged withdrawal letter on the desk in the dormitory room."

Cissy instructed Bristol to take Gloria's clothes, books, and toiletries and dispose of them.

"That's when I showed Cissy the letter I'd found in the guest room where Gloria stayed at the Manor. It was addressed to her mum and dad in

America."

"I assume that's Gloria's last letter home," I said. "How did it ever get mailed?"

"Cissy took the letter and said she'd handle it. But I felt horrible knowing her folks might never get that last letter, so I pushed Cissy to let me mail it."

I looked at Cissy, who was busy picking at the polish on her fingernails.

"Cissy thought about it for a minute and then promised to add the necessary overseas postage once she got to London. She liked the idea of having a London post office stamp marking. She thought it'd prove that Gloria was at Heathrow on January first."

"Poppycock," Cissy said, not bothering to look up from her hands. "The man is daft, he is. I did no such thing."

Bristol wrapped up his testimony, claiming seeing Gloria unconscious on the kitchen floor was the last time he ever saw her. The Colonel and Rosemond never brought up the topic, and for more than forty-five years, they ensured him and Pauline their business. He kept his actions to himself, and although he suffered nightmares, the disturbing dreams stopped after a year.

"I made a deal with the devil, so I don't expect much mercy," Bristol said. "But what I've said is the truth."

Chapter Thirty-Five

Bristol Warford dropped onto the pew, and Pauline slipped her arm around his neck and hugged him. The man's eyes and mouth pulled downward in relief, as if he'd thrown off a huge burden. Other than the Bethards, I thought everyone in the chapel would agree he had. Next up was a nut that'd be much harder to crack than Bristol or Rufford, since he'd never once shared a civil word with me.

"I wish to have Roland the Chauffeur testify before the assembled multitude," I said. Usually, Nic Knuckles would never use words like assembled multitude. Saying something like that in my native Borough of Queens would've earned me a fat lip for acting all educated. But since I was operating in the motherland of the English language, I thought I should be more adventuresome, so I scoured my Thesaurus last night and upgraded my vocabulary.

Roland was all decked out in his uniform, with its twin column of silver buttons running down the front. He stood with his little cap in his hands, his eyes blank circles of grey, and his lips thin strips of determination. I'm sure everyone thought old Nic Knuckles would fail to extract valuable details from this man. Roland had lived a long life of discretion, and some obnoxious Yank wasn't going to get him to spill secrets.

Rosemond, however, wasn't taking any chances. She turned to Roland, who stood behind her, sweetly smiled, and said, "Ah, our long-time chauffeur and loyal friend of the Bethard family. It's been a while since we've had the pleasure of your company."

Roland flinched. "I drove you and Mister Myles to the chapel, madam."

"Nonetheless, as my husband always said, 'Roland is a man of steadfast honor.'"

"Thank you, madam."

No one ever called Nic Knuckles a man of steadfast honor. I was known more for being a steadfast splinter in the soft tissue of the criminally inclined. Once I dug into a case, there was no way I could be plucked out until I brought truth, justice, and a dang good solution to the mystery. The people of Village-In-Thistles were about to find out how easily Nic Knuckles could get someone to talk.

"How long have you been driving for the Bethard family?"

"A very long time."

"Driving a beast like that Bentley T-series must be a pleasure," I said.

Roland nodded and left it at that.

"I'm from New York City, and my transportation is usually the M Train out of the Woodhaven station. That can be a crowded ride, you know what I mean, my friend?"

"Not really, since I've never ridden on a train."

"That subway train seat is a tight space. I guess you have a lot of legroom in that Bentley, don't you?"

"It's adequate."

"And I bet that car is as quiet as Westminster Abbey at two in the morning."

"I wouldn't know, since I've never been in Westminster Abbey at two in the morning."

Roland seemed unimpressed with my questions about the Bentley's fine qualities. That was okay. I wanted him to be relaxed when I whizzed my hardball question high and inside.

"Have you ever driven a Kia Picanto?"

The man's face locked up briefly, which told me he realized where I was going with my inquiry. Instead of his previous clipped, clearly enunciated responses, he answered my question with a muffled no.

"I understand the Kia Picanto is a fun, jaunty little vehicle," I said, "designed for the common man who wishes to commute unnoticed across the city. Are you a man who likes to drive unnoticed among the sheep of the English countryside?"

Roland's Adam's Apple gave him away. It rose up and down in his throat like a maniac's yo-yo. I had to believe he was swallowing his panic, trying to maintain his dismissive English chauffeur demeanor. However, it wasn't going to survive my probing.

"I imagine you won't be having much fun driving the Bethard family in a small car, will you?"

Roland's bottom lip disappeared, and his eyelids dropped like a widow's window shade at bedtime.

"You've spent much of your life babying that Bentley, haven't you. Lovingly maintaining the plush interior and polishing the deep blue exterior to a shine. I imagine your life would feel empty if Myles sold it off."

Roland looked away from me, so I stepped closer and whispered. "Why isn't Myles calling me a liar, Roland? If he has no plan to sell the Bentley, why doesn't he say so?"

Roland's bottom lip rejoined the upper, but not as a stiff slash of rectitude. Nope. His lips were now a wiggling, twisting set of muscles anxious to say something.

"What do you wish to know?" he asked.

A vacuum was briefly created when everyone in the chapel simultaneously sucked in their breath. They were shocked that a man of supposedly steadfast honor would cave so easily. The people didn't know what Roland and I knew, however. His beloved Bentley T Series was probably going on the auction block soon, because Myles could no longer afford the insurance, taxes, and upkeep.

Nic Knuckles understood that for working people like Roland, who'd labored for years to gain a position that elevated their status from their humble beginnings, certain things were very important. Roland's uniform and cap made him look dignified when he drove the Bentley. Chauffeuring Rosemond or Cissy in a small car, popular with the working class of Great Britain, would make him and his uniform appear ridiculous. Once Myles Bethard considered selling off the Bentley, the rumor eventually arrived in Roland's ear. It didn't matter who said it, or whether it was valid, Roland now understood the source of his self-esteem, driving a big beautiful automobile, was probably going to disappear.

Whether Myles intended to actually buy a Kia Picanto as the family's ride was just a guess. But it worked. The nut cracked.

"Tell us how you spent your time on New Year's Day of 1977."

Roland was uncomfortable talking, and to his credit, he didn't waste time jibber-jabbering about unimportant facts from that day. He admitted he drove Cissy to Brighton and the university later that morning. "I assumed Bristol was in there," he said, "as I recognized his delivery van parked outside the dorm entrance."

Roland admitted he could not be sure of what Cissy had planned to do once she was inside the dormitory, but he had suspicions.

"As I came around the Bentley to open her door, I saw Miss Cissy pull a plain white envelope from her handbag. She seemed determined to obscure my vision so as to keep me from seeing what she was carrying, but her wrist was so heavy with the multiple bracelets that she struggled to keep it out of sight."

"Is it possible she had the fraudulent letter announcing Gloria's withdrawal from the university?"

"I suppose."

"Speculation," a man yelled. "I am Alexander Wilton Dinwiddie the fourth, and I object to this man's accusation against my wife. He should've kept his eyes forward, not peeping at what his superior was doing."

Reverend Amethyst quickly responded. "This isn't a court of law, Mister Dinwiddie," she said, snapping off each word. "It's a group confession in my chapel, so I'll allow the comment to stand."

Dinwiddie quickly dropped back onto the pew, humiliated by the Reverend's aggressive response. It looked like the woman was funneling her marital hurt into anger and would run a tighter service going forward. She seemed as determined as me to get answers once and for all about what happened to Gloria Butterfield.

"Continue, Roland," Reverend Amethyst said, with an emphatic nod of her head. "We're anxious to hear your declaration of fact."

Roland twisted his cap as he continued talking. "It was maybe twenty minutes before Miss Cissy returned. I opened the car door as I always did, and she slipped in."

"Did she have anything in her hands?" I asked.

Roland leaned forward, which caused everyone to do the same. "Yes, she was carrying an envelope."

Dinwiddie snorted and said, "Obviously, Cissy hadn't delivered some false missive, as you've claimed. The man is a shameless liar."

Before Reverend Amethyst could admonish Cissy's husband, Roland growled and added, "It was a different piece, sir," he said. "It was a lightweight envelope specifically designed for overseas posting. Plus, a handwritten address was on the front, unlike the envelope she carried into the dormitory."

A triumphant buzz sizzled among the lower-class attendees at seeing one of their own score a goal against their haughty superior.

"After leaving the dormitory, I drove Miss Cissy to London, where we wasted a half hour trying to locate a postal office, but they were closed for the holiday. Fortunately, we found a bodega in an immigrant neighborhood that happened to sell overseas postage. Miss Cissy was quite relieved. I, on the other hand, was cheesed off by it all. I was wasting one of my few holidays driving Cissy Bethard around England."

Rosemond loudly whispered something to Myles about Roland being impertinent, by referring to her daughter as Cissy Bethard, not Mrs. Bethard-Dinwiddie. "Do we really need to keep a chauffeur?" Rosemond asked. "Couldn't Turquoise drive us?"

I feared that after hearing the top lady of Rockingham Manor threatening to dismiss him, Roland would go silent. I decided to help him stay the course using a proven investigator's technique: the bald-faced lie. "Don't let Rosemond's threats stop you from sharing your memory of that day," I said. "I have an old friend at Buckingham Palace who told me those Royals hate walking and won't go anywhere unless they're driven. I'll be delighted to put a good word in for you."

Roland smiled, which must have felt strange for his face. My suggested alternative to working for the Bethard family seemingly had the desired impact because the man plowed ahead.

"I drove to Heathrow Airport and let Miss Cissy out at the departure entrance," he said. "I could see through the glass doors her approaching the British Airways counter. She was there for approximately fifteen minutes, and when she turned, I saw her stuff something into her handbag."

"Perhaps it was a one-way ticket to New York City," I said. "Maybe it was for a flight leaving later that day?"

I got the expected response from Cissy. "That's ridiculous," she yelled, her metal bracelets clacking against each other as she raised her arms in protest. "I did no such thing."

I turned to my audience. "Cissy was about the same age as Gloria back then," I said. "Anyone who might've investigated Gloria's disappearance would've learned that, yes, a young woman in her early twenties had purchased a ticket."

I explained how buying an airplane ticket in 1977 required very little identification, if any. Cissy's purchase was an expensive way of creating false evidence that Gloria Butterfield had been in London and at Heathrow Airport late on the first day of January.

The skepticism on most faces in the chapel suddenly lifted. Bristol and Pauline, the barmaid, and the Pissin' Pints punters, and Rufford and Melba, Gram Edwards, and Doc Johnson, all realized that Nic Knuckles knew what he was doing.

Cissy did as well. "I demand to be heard," she said, her words rattling the chapel's stained-glass windows. "I had nothing to do with Butterfield's disappearance. Roland is behaving vindictively because my brother is selling the Bentley. How do you think I feel about stuffing myself into a tiny back seat like the meat in a steak and kidney pie?"

The mention of food caused my mind to skip from what was happening before me to what wasn't happening in my stomach. I told myself I'd buy a steak and kidney pie as my reward if I maintained my focus and completed today's inquiry. That seemed to help.

"Cissy," I said. "I understand your grief at having to give up the comfort of the Bentley. Once again, it seems, you are being asked to make the sacrifices for the family because Myles can't make a go at running Rockingham Manor."

The woman's head jolted higher on her neck, and a deeper natural blush appeared under her artificial application of color. My comment had struck the nerve I was aiming for. Nic Knuckles knew what living with incompetent and selfish siblings was like. My three sisters behaved like mad warthogs at a church yard sale, and, like Cissy, I was always expected to clean up their messes.

"You must wonder when it became your job to keep the Bethard family afloat," I said. "I suspect it began when your father told you to go to Gloria's dorm room, drop off a falsified letter of withdrawal from the university, and then purchase a one-way airplane ticket to New York."

"Well, I couldn't refuse my father," she said, sputtering her words.

I agreed with her that, at her age, it would have been difficult not to help the family.

"Sadly, for you, it was only the beginning of you covering up for your pathetic older brother."

A broken heart overrides the most vigorous measures of a person's self-control, and Cissy's face gave way to long-buried anger. Her eyes watered, and her chin trembled, but she said nothing. I went in with a second wave of brutal observations.

"It fell upon you to marry for money because, at first, your father, and then your brother, could not keep the Manor afloat without your spouse's money."

Cissy sniffed, and her bracelets clanged together as she wiped her nose with a tissue.

"You never married for love, did you, Cissy? The Colonel and then Myles insisted you marry the man with the deepest pockets, the greatest assets, the dodgiest of health."

Cissy answered in a voice thick with snot, "Yes."

"Well, that's a crock of shit," Alexander Wilton Dinwiddie mumbled.

I offered Cissy a reprieve from my inquisition if she admitted she'd been an accomplice in Gloria's disappearance. The woman lowered her head and agreed that everything Roland had said was true.

"Thank you, Miss Bethard-Dinwiddie, for coming clean."

"I always suspected something terrible had happened to the American woman, but I never wanted to know." Cissy sighed and dropped onto the pew, her bracelets clattering loudly when she landed.

"Now that we've established that Gloria Butterfield never left England," I said, "we must now determine if she was murdered, who did it, and what became of the poor woman's body." I rubbed my palms together and took several steps toward the one person I was sure had the answers.

"Rosemond, my frail but feisty adversary, are you willing to join your daughter and speak the truth?"

The chapel excitedly buzzed as Rosemond slowly stood, her joints popping like an uncoordinated twenty-gun salute. She gingerly shuffled around to face the attendees.

"It seems like discretion and loyalty are out of fashion this morning," she said. "I guess I'm no longer bound by them either, so I must say my piece."

Chapter Thirty-Six

Rosemond got straight to the point.

"It was neither Myles nor Bristol who applied the coup de grace to the American," she said. "It was my husband, Jeremy Bethard, also known as The Colonel."

Chop me into dog food and feed me to the old Queen's favorite corgi. Was Miss Rosemond dropping her defense of her husband so quickly? Had the mystery been solved with this admission? Of course, I thought, how convenient that the Colonel had been dead for over a decade. You can't prosecute dusty bones in a coffin.

"Very interesting," I said. "Would you be willing to tell your story, or do I have to get all aggressive with you before you cough up the facts?"

Rosemond steadied herself by holding onto Cissy's shoulder. "The Colonel and I were attending to our guests that New Year's when we couldn't help but hear a commotion from the kitchen. I immediately knew it was that American woman because she had just confronted me minutes prior and was hostile and rude. After putting her in her place, she stormed from the ballroom like a petulant child."

Rosemond shared how she and the Colonel entered the kitchen and saw Myles choking Gloria.

"My husband quickly pulled Myles off that woman," Rosemond said. "She collapsed and fell to the floor, unconscious. Myles was quite upset with what had transpired and wanted to call for medical assistance. He was all a flutter, and I feared he'd soon pass out, leaving us with two unconscious people in the kitchen. So, I insisted he return to the ballroom revelry and take a stiff drink to steady himself."

Myles took his mother's instructions to heart, she said, confirming his story that he got blackout drunk and didn't make an appearance until mid-afternoon the next day.

"What happened after Myles left the kitchen?"

"My husband and I discussed the woman's condition."

"What did you suggest be done?" I asked.

Rosemond's loose neck skin flapped as she emphatically shook her head. "Oh, I made no suggestions. My husband was a gentleman and insisted I leave the kitchen. He assured me he'd handle the situation and that I should return to the party and continue as the most accommodating hostess."

"When you left the kitchen, Miss Butterfield was still alive, correct?"

"Yes, that is accurate."

"When did you learn that she died?"

"It was surely after our last guests left. I somehow recall that Sir Eddie and his wife Pots were the ones who called the night. It must've been two in the morning."

"Who told you Miss Butterfield had died?"

"My husband. He said the woman was beyond help, and that her dying was fortunate and now she'd not burden her parents by arriving home in a vegetative state."

"Or not being a legal liability to you and the Colonel," I added.

Rosemond shrugged.

"Is that the total of your involvement in Gloria's death?" I asked.

"I did write the withdrawal letter as my husband requested, but that was the only contribution I made to the removal of that American from the Manor."

"You didn't ask your husband how Gloria died or how he intended to address Miss Butterfield's corpse?"

"I had no curiosity about such ghastly details," Rosemond said. "And I doubt the Colonel offered Bristol a free ride through life to kill the woman. Seriously, I ask you, why commit to such an expense when he could easily do it himself?"

Rosemond claimed she went to bed after writing the letter and didn't see anyone until later, when she came to the dining room for brunch. "As I recall, only my husband and I were at the table. It was rather quiet that morning."

I reminded Rosemond why her children weren't eating with her. "We know Myles was nursing his alcohol-induced hangover and guilt for choking out his supposed fiancée. And, Cissy was off chewing up Roland's holiday and buying an airplane ticket that would never be used."

"Yes, I suppose you're correct, Mister Knuckles."

"In that time alone, just you and your husband, did either of you express remorse?"

Rosemond closed her eyes and answered. "No, we had more pressing concerns, like whether our son would recover enough from this drama to return to university?"

"Did you ask the Colonel where he disposed of the body?"

Rosemond's crinkly eyelids popped open, and she snarled. "Of course not, you dolt. He said he took care of our problem and that I should focus on keeping Myles from ruining his future. And that was what I did, and I've been doing it for nearly fifty years."

Some private eyes would claim victory and tell their clients their loved one had been murdered, the perpetrator was dead, and the corpse was irretrievably lost. But not Nic Knuckles. Not when he didn't trust anything Rosemond Bethard said.

"You have no doubt that your husband, Jeremy Bethard, also known as the Colonel, murdered Gloria Butterfield?"

"He confessed as much, so yes. Unfortunately, it was sad that she had to die, but it was not surprising, considering that woman's impertinent nature."

Murmurs flooded through the chapel, but someone clearly said, "That's cold, man."

Rosemond flashed a self-satisfied smile at me. "I'm sorry to disappoint you, Mister Knuckles, but it looks like the only witness to the murder of that American woman was the man who did it, and he's beyond questioning."

The old gal made an excellent point. My best evidence only proved that Gloria Butterfield died a dastardly death at the hands of someone associated with Rockingham Manor, but not who did it. I only had one witness who claimed the Colonel was the killer, and she had everything to gain by pinning the crime on him, especially since he'd suffer no consequences. I also didn't have a body. I needed an intervention by a higher power to salvage my case, and if God weren't going to help me, then one of his earthly minions would.

Reverend Amethyst pulled everyone's attention back to the pulpit by announcing. "I feel strongly that Jeremy Bethard did not murder Gloria Butterfield."

This time, the gathered multitude almost blew the roof off the chapel with their gasps and screams. I even squeaked in surprise.

"As my father-in-law's health declined," she said, "he felt a need for spiritual counseling."

Rosemond groaned. "He didn't tell me anything about getting spiritual counseling, the bugger."

Reverend Amethyst ignored her mother-in-law and continued. "As time went on and thoughts of dying dominated the Colonel's waking hours, we grew closer, and I became his confessor." She explained that while being prohibited from discussing the confessed sins of her father-in-law, she was exempted from maintaining his confidence if a murder could be solved.

"While Jeremy admitted to multiple extra-marital affairs, several significant corrupt business dealings, and kicking the family dog, Gumdrop, he was most ashamed of facilitating the disappearance of a young woman decades ago."

"I thought you believed the Colonel didn't kill Gloria," I said.

Reverend Amethyst shook her head. "The Colonel never confessed to murder. He only said he once convinced someone to rid an unmanageable woman from his life. He shared no details, and I didn't ask, but he was deeply troubled. After hearing all that has been said today, I've no doubt the young woman he was talking about was Gloria Butterfield."

"Who do you think he hired to kill her?" I asked.

"I don't know. He never said."

And that was all The Rev had to say about the Colonel's end-of-life confessions.

Chapter Thirty-Seven

To the average resident of Village-In-Thistles in attendance, it looked like Nic Knuckles was back at page one. I'd already proclaimed Myles innocent of murder, excused Bristol, dismissed any of the Bethard women, and now Reverend Amethyst argued the Colonel, while sponsoring Gloria's disappearance, was not the hands-on killer.

But I wasn't worried. Nic Knuckles knew who did it and, in a few minutes, everyone in the chapel would as well.

"Ladies and gentlemen of Village-In-Thistles, give me your undivided attention. We will know who killed Gloria Butterfield before the first punters arrive at the Pissin' Pints. I must follow Nic Knuckles's investigative protocols to reveal the murderer, so please be patient."

The people grumbled as they settled in their pews, unhappy about my dithering. I wasn't too happy either because while I knew who the murderer was, I still wasn't sure how to expose the culprit. I figured the still living participants in the crime might help me out, so I assumed a position at the corner of the first row to ask my questions.

"Rosemond Bethard," I said. "Who was in the kitchen when you and the Colonel came upon Myles choking Gloria Butterfield?"

The woman plucked her chin before answering, "Melba. Melba, my housekeeper, cook, and longest-serving and most loyal downstairs staff member, was there."

"Thank you."

I stepped to my right and stood in front of Myles. "Myles, my hapless friend, who was in the kitchen when you attacked Gloria Butterfield in a rage?"

Myles's bony shoulders crept up his skinny neck. "I don't recall. I tend to black out when I throw a wobbly."

"Before you reached that state of craziness," I said, "Did you not have a cuppa as you tried to reason with Miss Butterfield?"

"Yes, of course."

"And who in the kitchen would have made that fine cup of Earl Grey?"

Myles drew in a loud breath. "Well, it would have to have been Melba. I don't know how to operate a kettle, and Gloria preferred to be served. So, yes, it was Melba."

"Thank you, Mister Bethard."

I looked behind the first row of Bethard family members at Bristol.

"Mr. Warford, proprietor of Warford's What Nots, which is now open six days a week and offers trainers at fifteen percent off."

I hoped that by giving Bristol and Pauline's shop some publicity, Bristol would cooperate in a way that could close this case. He did not disappoint me.

"You need not ask the question," Bristol said. "Melba was in the kitchen from when I first arrived until I drove away from the Manor with Miss Gloria's belongings."

I thanked Bristol yet pushed on him for one more answer, and the question was a doozy.

"Was Melba in the kitchen when the Colonel offered you a lifetime of business and housing in exchange for snuffing out what remained of Gloria Butterfield's life?"

Multiple variations of the phrase "Bloody Hell!" swirled in the air. Bristol also seemed bewildered and needed a minute to process his memory of that night. "Why yes," he said softly. "Of course, she heard the Colonel make the offer."

I thanked the shopkeeper and turned to Melba, who chilled me with her stare.

"Melba ... honestly, I don't know your last name," I said.

"The Housekeeper, you wanker. I'm known as Melba, the loyal housekeeper. You hear me, the loyal staff member of sixty bloody years."

"Good luck, mate, getting her to talk," Roland called out, wildly amusing the gathering.

I crossed my arms and waited for the laughter to stop. I hoped Roland and the chapel crowd enjoyed his humorous aside because now it was time to get the old cook and bottle washer to testify, and there'd be nothing funny about it.

"Melba, you wily rascal, what did you see in your kitchen early New Year's morning after Myles assaulted Miss Butterfield?"

"I seen the Colonel and Miss Rosemond and Master Myles and that American girl."

"And what did each person do while you were watching them?"

"The Colonel pulled Master Myles off of that woman as other folks have said."

"And what did Myles do after his father stopped his assault?"

"He got all 'Arry Nash with his mum and dad, and when they shut him down, he crawled back to the party."

I nodded. "Okay, what was Rosemond doing?"

"She fretted and waved her hands, which was too much for the Colonel, and he told her to return to her guests."

"What was Gloria Butterfield's condition at that time?"

Melba dropped her chunky head to one side and grumbled. "That scrubber was on the floor. That was her condition."

"Was she dead?"

"Not at first, but not for long."

The chapel's ceiling echoed with the sound of a dozen voices operating at their highest decibel level. It required a solid minute before people quieted, and I could challenge Melba's testimony.

"You were the only one in that kitchen throughout the night. Did Gloria die from Myles's attack, or did Bristol lie and he committed murder? Or is Rosemond truthful and the Colonel finished the job, and The Rev is mistaken?"

"Bit of a conundrum, innit, Knuckles?" she said, folding her arms across her bosom and pressing herself hard against the back of the pew. Her locked-lip expression convinced me that I'd get no more honest words from her. And since I had zero legal authority to force a confession, I turned to what I thought would be my second-best source for all things Melba.

"Roland, my friend and likely future Uber driver, could you please shed some light on your life as the chauffeur of Rockingham Manor?"

I was unsure who said it, but I swore Gram Edwards whispered. "Oh boy, that'll be a snore."

The man stood and shared a story that wasn't tabloid-worthy, but it had enough scandal to keep everyone on the edge of their seats. He'd come to work at Rockingham Manor when he was twenty-two, enticed by the prospect of driving a fabulous automobile. He saw the job as a lifetime opportunity for a poor, uneducated lad like him.

"The Colonel and Miss Rosemond were always cordial but maintained a proper distance," he said. "Mister Myles and Miss Cissy were usually away at boarding school, so most of my time was spent tending to the car, or driving the Colonel and Miss Rosemond."

"You are a man of approachable facial features," I said. "Living and working for the Bethards up at The Rock must have been isolating for a young man."

Roland fingered his cap, indicating to me he was uncomfortable talking about his early awkward years. I understood what it was like to be a lonely young man living in an unfriendly environment filled with cold and indifferent people. That was Nic Knuckle's home life until I escaped at eighteen. But I couldn't focus on my past. I had an important witness about to help me solve a murder.

"Did you have any social life that led to emotional relationships?"

"I would spend my free time visiting the pubs in the village," he said. "I might flirt with a woman or so, but I never had the time to treat her to a meal or a motion picture."

"Wasn't there a woman with whom you shared daily meals in the Manor kitchen? A woman who might today be an artist's model for garden gnomes but was attractive back then."

Roland lowered his eyes and muttered. "I suppose you're asking about

Melba."

Indeed, I was, and Roland slowly spun a classic late-sixties tale of sex, drugs, and rock and roll, without the music and other than an occasional bump of weed, no drugs. The audience went wild, however, when Roland admitted too much 'rumpy-pumpy' got Melba in a family way.

"At most estates, Melba would've been put out on the street, and me sent off without a letter of reference. But we both knew too much about the Colonel's indiscretions that Miss Rosemond kept us on."

A voice splintering with emotion rose from the middle of the chapel. "I knew you were me, daddy. I always knew you were." Rufford dropped his face into his hands and sobbed, which made me smile. Not because I enjoyed Rufford's sorrow, oh lord no. I had father issues of my own to behave in that way. Instead, as a private eye, I enjoyed solving the mystery of Rufford's paternity. I wasn't getting paid, but Nic Knuckles can't turn my interests off when I'm built to solve mysteries.

I continued questioning Roland by asking, "Why didn't you and Melba marry after she got pregnant?"

The cap in Roland's hand took a beating as the man pondered the question. "Well, we realized we were better off as manor staff with a torrid past than a married couple with a kid and no work."

Roland added they fought over his role as Rufford's father.

"She didn't like me trying to be a daddy to the boy, which made me less inclined to do so." He cast a pair of damp eyes at Rufford and said, "Sorry, lad. You still turned out all right, didn't you? I mean, besides the farm animals and you talking to each other."

Rufford lifted his eyes to Roland, a smile breaking across a face spotted with tears. "Yeah, Daddy, I guess so."

Roland said he and Melba maintained a cordial relationship after the pregnancy snuffed out the fire in their loins.

"We knew we didn't have a normal family at the Manor, but we still cared about each other."

"How did Melba feel about Miss Butterfield?"

"I think I've told you how I felt about her, you pillock," Melba screamed.

"I thought she was all tits and teeth, and it was crazy how Mister Myles indulged her."

"A man in the back shouted, "Don't hold back, Melba" and the chapel boomed with laughter. Reverend Amethyst raised her voice above the din and demanded decorum worthy of a house of worship. The chapel went silent, other than the sound of Rufford's sniffling.

Roland continued. "As she just said, Melba hated the woman—maybe even more so than Miss Rosemond."

"Did Melba talk about what went on in the kitchen that night when Myles attacked Gloria Butterfield?"

"No, she didn't say anything other than the American would never annoy her again. Otherwise, she told me nothin'?"

"You weren't the least bit curious? Didn't you wonder what was behind the mysterious commute with Cissy to London and the airport?"

Roland shrugged. "Not so much. It was never my way to ask questions about the family."

"You saw Bristol at the university emptying Gloria's dorm room, and you didn't think to ask Melba if she knew what was happening?"

Roland lifted his cap to his mouth and shook his head.

"The Manor must've been in turmoil the next day or two after the disappearance," I said, my voice rising. "Are you telling me you and Melba didn't discuss it?"

The chauffeur's cap was now between Roland's teeth.

"Be truthful here, my friend. Did Melba ever mention an offer from the Colonel, an offer that ensured lifetime employment and a cozy apartment for her and your boy?"

Roland studied the floor as if he were looking for a trapdoor he could use to escape.

"Is that why Melba was never let go as the Colonel, and then Rosemond sold off family heirlooms, including the Swizlelback necklace? Even when Myles borrowed recklessly and sacrificed his family's comfort, she was kept around, serving cabbage soup and caustic commentary."

Roland jerked the cap from his teeth and yelled. "She said she'd done the

Colonel a big favor, and if I treated her right, I could stop worrying about whether I had a bed to lay my head on when I was old and useless."

Every pair of eyes in the chapel turned and looked at Melba. The woman's lower lip was rolled like a fat grub, white and slimy. "I made the Colonel a batch of his favorite soup," she said, "even though it was nearly three in the morning. He said my soup was his only pleasure that night and that he'd keep me and my boy in his will."

I jumped at the woman, waving my index finger at her like Merlin the Wizard, casting a spell on a troll. "Are you saying that the Colonel guaranteed your lifetime employment and shelter for a bowl of soup?"

"Yup, I am. That man loved my potage."

"Even though, as the years went on and the Manor was threatened with insolvency, you're claiming the Bethards kept the Colonel's promise?"

"Again, Knuckles, a bit of a conundrum, right?" she said. "That man had singular tastes, and cabbage soup was one of 'em."

An angry voice exploded in the middle of the chapel, shouting one word. "Enough!" Everyone twisted in their seats to stare at Rufford, slowly standing, looking fearsome like a cornered honey badger.

"Stop it, Mum. Stop with your bloody lies."

"You watch yourself, lad," Melba said in a firm voice that barely contained a cold fury.

Rufford wasn't in the mood to watch himself. A fury of his own had taken hold, and he roared. "How could you have kept Roland from being my daddy? I could've used a decent bloke in me life to teach me things that a father teaches a son."

"I didn't need no bloke to raise my boy," she said. "I'd gotten through life just fine without some man makin' me work twice as hard to think I'm happy."

"Maybe if Roland had been more involved with me, maybe I'd been somebody instead of a farmhand living with me mum?"

"You didn't need him, and I didn't want him."

"Maybe if you let Roland be part of your life, Mum, you wouldn't have had to do those terrible things to keep us in the Manor."

"Don't be such a plonker, sunshine, or I'll knock you into next week."

The Reverend Amethyst pounded the pulpit's banister. "Let the man speak," she said. "He's obviously in great spiritual agony and needs to make confession to bring him peace."

"No, he don't need you tellin' him how he feels," Melba cracked back as she balled up her right fist. "I'll give him eternal peace if he don't keep his trap shut."

Like a tag team of wrestlers, I jumped in the ring and took over from The Rev. "What terrible things did your mother do to keep her place at Rockingham Manor, Rufford?"

"I saw, I saw what me mum did to Miss Gloria."

"No, you didn't, you tosser," Melba shouted. "You told us you scurried back to your bedroom when I saw you peeking through the hole in the vent. You never saw nothin' after that you said."

"I did see more, Mum. I couldn't stop worrying about Miss Gloria, so I snuck back to me hidey hole and saw you and her."

Melba rose out of her pew, her face the color of an eggplant. "You little rat, you ungrateful swine."

"What did you see your mom do, Rufford?" I asked. "What did she do to Gloria Butterfield?"

The man sputtered his reply. "She, she, she pried open Miss Gloria's mouth and, and, and pounded ice cubes down her throat."

Myles Bethard screamed and fell against his mother, who struggled to keep him from ending up on the chapel floor. Tongues were clucking, and heads were shaking throughout the chapel. Even Nic Knuckles, who had seen some pretty gruesome criminal behavior, felt weak in my knees. Melba was as nasty and evil as I always suspected.

"You can't prove that me and the Colonel had a bargain," Melba said, painting the chapel with an evil eye worthy of a witch. "We all know me boy is mental. And ask yourself, where's the body? I'll bet you a tenner Gloria Butterfield is livin' back in America in some old folk's home, not thinkin' about us."

"Not so fast, Mum. I know what you did with Miss Gloria's body."

All eyes and ears turned to Rufford, including mine. Having Gloria's remains could once and for all prove she'd been murdered.

Rufford went bug-eyed when he realized everyone was staring at him. Most of his life, people ignored him, and now being the focus of such intensity seemingly scared him.

"Go on, Rufford," I said. "You can do this."

The man gulped some air and spoke. "Among the Rockingham Manor hogs, there's a story about a long-ago New Year's morning when their ancestors were fed a feast of unusual succulence."

That was it for any decorum. The chapel fell into utter and complete bedlam. Myles collapsed onto the floor, dry heaving as he rolled back and forth. Bristol clutched his head, moaning. Cissy emptied the contents of her stomach onto Rosemond's lap. Reverend Amethyst's eyes rolled back in their sockets, and she spoke in tongues. Doc Johnson popped pills, Pauline pounded her fists against Bristol's chest, and the Pissin' Pints barmaid howled. Gram Edwards seemed to be the only one enjoying herself, as I saw her slapping her thigh as she doubled over in laughter. "I always said the sassenach's were numpties."

Chapter Thirty-Eight

The chapel emptied to the courtyard after Rufford shared his knowledge of what became of Gloria Butterfield's corpse. I had to admit that my head was spinning as well. Having grown up with a mother who served me breakfast with unidentifiable protein gave me the fortitude to carry on while the others struggled with feeling nauseous. It was one of the few times I could say, "Good old mom's home cooking," and mean it.

The barmaid and her fellow pub rats rushed off to the Pissin' Pints with their curiosity either settled, or their stomachs unable to handle any more revelations. Doc Johnson and Gram Edwards wandered toward the village, and I heard Gram offering a special, once-in-a-lifetime price to steam clean the doctor's cottage. Johnson picked up his pace to escape Gram, but the old lassie more than kept up with him. The farm hands and their spouses must've had their fill of watching rich people behaving badly, because they disappeared in the late morning rising heat.

The Bethard family, and those related by marriage or employment, wandered among the trees in search of shade. They settled under a large birch tree with Rosemond, Cissy, and Myles sitting on a wrought iron bench, and everyone else standing off in family pairs. Everyone, except for Melba, who scooted into the manor. Whether it was to plan her escape, or prepare the family's Sunday breakfast, I didn't care. Roland and Turquoise were the only people living at The Rock with driver's licenses, and I didn't see either of them helping her leave.

I was a little surprised to see Lizabeth West creeping from behind the chapel. Judging from the grin on her face, it was apparent that she'd eavesdropped on the whole carnival of confessions, threats, and craziness that had just occurred. I felt a tingle of alarm, wondering why she was still around.

"Hello, Nic," she said, "I must say your ability to whip up the folks from both Village-In-Thistles *and* Rockingham Manor was impressive. My Aunt Jane never came close to creating such a pig's ear."

"I've no time for compliments, Lizabeth. Are you here to lie to me and further disrupt my investigation? Or, since I'm no longer paying you, do you plan to just observe and hope I mess up on my own?"

Lizabeth gave me one of those thin, untrustworthy types of smiles. "Oh no, Nic, I did what I could to stop you, and failed. I must say you've done a fine job of exposing all the secrets of Rockingham Manor and the Village-of-Thistles."

"Why are you still here then?" I asked. "I thought even if you had only a little shame for double-dealing me, you'd stay away."

Lizabeth's grin spread further across her face. "You'd think so, wouldn't you?"

"I don't have time for you. I have to get Melba arrested for murder, bring assault charges against Myles, and have Rosemond, Cissy, and Bristol arraigned as accomplices. I'll also need a police van and enough officers to handle the transfer to the nearest hoosegow."

"The what?"

"Hoosegow, you know, a jail."

Lizabeth rolled her eyes. "You mean a nick, the slammer, a prison."

"Whatever, I don't have time for you and your strange vocabulary."

"Oh, I think you might need to make time. Keep in mind you're still a stranger in England and don't know how things are done here."

I laughed. "Nice try, Lizzy, but justice is pretty universal, and I know from watching too many imported PBS crime series that you Brits love to see a wrong being righted."

Lizabeth laughed, and unfortunately, her laughter was longer and heartier than mine. "The Bethard family has been here for decades, and Rockingham

Manor is essential to the local economy. The money Rosemond and Myles spend on their unique medical needs keeps Doc Johnson's office open, and that benefits everyone in the village. Bristol and Pauline would be on the dole without Rosemond's business. Roland, Melba, and Rufford would be homeless, and the farmhands who burn their meager wages at the Pissin' Pints would have to sober up. Reverend Amy's chapel would be closed, Turquoise and Dinwiddie would be booted to the cobblestone, and even I would lose out on the occasional quid Rosemond sends my way."

"I can't believe you easily sold your integrity as a private investigator for a few dollars. Agatha Christie must be spinning in her grave."

Lizabeth tilted her head and giggled. "Oi Nic, how do you think a single woman survives in a tiny village? My only talents are gardening and snooping. One of them had to pay."

I turned to Reverend Amethyst. "You're a local and can call the authorities," I said. "I don't need Lizabeth West's help, right?"

The face on the woman of the cloth paled. "Did Lizabeth say I'd lose my chapel?"

Well, call me Bozo and stick me in a clown car. Was The Rev seriously sacrificing justice for a stone building that sat empty six days a week?

"Come on, Rev, this is the time to stand strong. I'm counting on you."

"You don't know what sacrifices I made to build my chapel," she said as she glanced at Myles and Rosemond. "I earned it, Nic, I *earned* it, and I can't give it up now."

Holy Provolone, usually at this point in a Nic Knuckles murder investigation, I'm approaching the runway of a resolution. Today, however, any grand wrap-up was slipping from my grasp as human weakness triumphed over doing the right thing. Just when I needed that famous stiff-upper lip, my Brits go soft on me.

I was in a tight spot, but when in a tight spot, Nic Knuckles used the lubricant of knowledge to escape. I knew from my reading of Shakespeare that the English were big into ghosts, so I tried a new approach to get my crowd to behave responsibly. "Come on, people. Gloria Butterfield's spirit has wandered the grounds of Rockingham Manor for nearly fifty years.

Maybe that's why Myles is so sickly and can't make a buck. Perhaps Cissy would still be married to her first husband if this place wasn't haunted. Gloria's spirit must rest before anyone living here can find peace. Who of you will do the right thing?"

I scanned the blank faces of the folks in front of me.

"Seriously, people? Did your ancestors shrink from fighting the Germans when the Luftwaffe bombed the mortar from the bricks of their homes? Did the ancient English mariners never sail beyond coastal waters for fear of sea monsters? Did Ringo give up music when the Beatles broke up? No, they did not. Tell me, who'll stand up and help me bring justice to Gloria Butterfield?"

"I'll do the proper thing."

The voice of Turquoise Blix-Vixen rang through the courtyard, sending pigeons flying and Bethard's jaws dropping. "I'll ensure justice is done for Gloria and all the people harmed by Melba and my family."

It sounded like an out-of-tune steel calypso band had descended upon the churchyard, but it was Cissy, her flailing arms rattling her many bracelets. "Turquoise, you ungrateful scally. Why are you taking sides on this?"

Turquoise folded her arms, narrowed her eyes, and fired back. "I always suspected Melba poisoned my father and that the Colonel and you had a hand in it. I may have only been seven when Poppa died, but I saw you take that bowl of Melba's cabbage soup up to him the evening before he got ill."

"How can you accuse me of such horrible behavior?"

"It's easy, mother. You and the Colonel believed I was too consumed with the Back Street Boys to listen to your dinner-time conversations. But I heard the frequent references to replenishing the family treasury and the value of my father's life insurance."

"I loved your father, the Baron."

Turquoise bared her teeth. "He was the Count, you self-indulgent pillock. The Baron was your first husband."

Cissy shrugged. "Oh my, I believe you're right, dear. But still, you'll turn on your mother over a mental lapse?"

Turquoise continued her rant, describing how she'd grown close to Brice

Johnson, Cissy's third husband. "It'd taken me years to warm up to my stepfather, but he was kindly patient until I did. But when his real estate investment soured, and he lost his wealth, he was taken from me."

"I had nothing to do with him falling off the roof, Turquoise. You're being quite unfair to me."

Alexander Wilton Dinwiddie raised his hand. "Hello, may I speak?"

I gave him a thumbs-up. "Go for it."

"Over the past four Sunday family suppers, I've noticed that Melba always serves me last. The following day, I'm feeling lethargic and unwell. Should I be concerned?"

"What's the status of your financial investments?" I asked.

Dinwiddie's eyebrows rose, and he mumbled his answer. "I do have a rather sizeable stake in Houdini Crypto, I'm afraid."

"Going forward, you might want to pack a sandwich when you eat at the Manor."

My advice to Dinwiddie drew a hot rebuke from Rosemond. "That's outrageous, Mister Knuckles. You've turned my only grandchild against me, and now you're poisoning my relationship with my favorite son-in-law."

"That was a poor choice of words, Rosemond."

The woman didn't care. "Haven't you caused enough trouble for us, you nasty American?"

"Not yet," I said, "I'll keep dropping red, white, and blue trouble on this family until I see some of you in prison."

Rosemond turned to Elizabeth West. "Do something. I'm paying you to keep the family out of trouble."

"Turquoise is guessing how her father died," Lizabeth said. "She was seven years old, and no one will give her recollections any weight. It's time to end this circus, and all go to the local and get wankered."

Lizabeth's self-satisfied grin fell apart immediately as Pauline Warford stepped forward. "I'll testify against the Bethards," Pauline said, and although she stood shaking, her voice was strong. "My husband will also share what he saw and heard."

I wasn't sure Bristol becoming the prosecutor's star witness would earn him less prison time, but it was worth trying. Rosemond must have thought it was a legitimate threat because she raged at the couple.

"I found you, Pauline, when you were alone and in desperate straits. My husband and I arranged a marriage and supported that silly shop for years. How could you treat me so poorly?"

Pauline tightly held onto Bristol's arm. "You did not take me in out of charity, Rosemond. You did so because you felt guilty for seducing my father and destroying our happy home."

Rosemond dismissively flicked her right hand. "Oh, pish, dearie. Your mother drove your father into my arms because she was much like you. A viperous little mouse."

"Don't talk to my wife like that, Rosemond." It was Bristol Warford, face flushed and fists clenched, shouting. "Or, I'll…"

"Or, what, Bristol? What are you going to do? Quit the softest job you'll ever have in your life. If you'd done what my husband asked of you, we wouldn't have had to include Melba. You let down the family that night, Bristol."

Pauline jumped to her husband's defense. "He doesn't regret doing the proper thing. Do you, dear?" Bristol swallowed hard and shook his head. "No, Paulie darlin', I don't. I lost too much of me character telling all those porkies. I never want to make you ashamed being married to me."

Lizabeth attacked the Warfords. "Bristol can't prove the conversation between the Colonel and him ever happened. Pauline's misguided vindictiveness toward Miss Rosemond is a small example of what she'll do to ruin the Bethard family. The constable will quickly see this is nothing more than an ugly family squabble."

"I'll talk to the coppers," Rufford said. "I can tell 'em what the Colonel said to Mister Bristol."

Rosemond snarled and yelled, "If you do, you little tosser, you'll live with your chickens and pigs because I'll never let you set foot in Rockingham Manor."

Rosemond's threats were rendered worthless when Roland loudly announced that Rufford could live with him. The two men started crying and embraced.

"Forgive me, son, for being a terrible father."

"I do, Daddy, I do."

That sweet interlude ended when Rosemond screamed that neither of them would have access to Rockingham Manor ever again.

"You're both sleeping on the streets of Village-In-Thistles if you report us to the authorities."

Turquoise came to the rescue, bouncing Rosemond's threat back into the older woman's face.

"When this is all said and done, Grandmama, I will be the only family member not in prison, or on probation. Therefore, the courts will surely award me stewardship of Rockingham Manor."

Turquoise informed Roland that he'd retain his position as chauffeur, although the Bentley would most likely have to be replaced by a Ford Transit Connect. Roland swore he'd adjust. Pauline was told the Manor would continue to solely purchase all its whatnots from her store. Miss Blix-Vixen also promised to testify to Bristol's good character with the hope of getting him probation.

"Reverend Amy, you can preach in the chapel twenty-four hours a day, seven days a week if you wish," Turquoise said. "God knows this family needs a bloody lot of forgiveness from the Almighty."

Chapter Thirty-Nine

Two days after the great unmasking at Reverend Amethyst's chapel, Turquoise, Pauline, Bristol, and Rufford joined me at an empty Pissin' Pints back room. We were waiting for the Home Beat Officer responsible for administering the policing needs of Village-In-Thistles. Miss Blix-Vixen had educated me on how rural communities are assigned a dedicated police officer who shows up a few times a week for two hours to check in with the locals. Village-In-Thistles' man, Police Sergeant Stuart "Crusty" Packwood, only came once a month.

"Crusty can be a lazy bugger," Bristol said. "He assumes Lizabeth West would place a call if anything serious was happenin', so we get him irregularly."

No wonder Lizzy got away with so much double-dealing. She'd co-opted the law enforcement authorities as well as the Bethards.

"Why are we waiting here at the Pissin' Pints?" I asked.

Rufford explained the village was too small to have a dedicated police station, so Crusty Packwood held his meetings at the pub, where he could quench both his thirst for justice and a desire for an excellent ale.

I hesitated to ask, knowing the Brit's compulsive use of obscure and often profane slang to communicate anything, before I did. "Why do you call him Crusty?"

Turquoise and Pauline shared glances while Rufford looked away.

"I've heard multiple stories behind the nickname," Bristol finally offered, "and the most proper one has to do with his personal hygiene."

Whatever the source of the man's moniker, I'd soon be able to form my own theory as a large bulk of humanity filled the door to the room we were sitting in.

"Good mornin', ladies and gents, your favorite constable is here to mete out justice."

"Yullo, Police Sargent Packwood," Turquoise said.

Packwood looked at me, his bottlebrush eyebrow dipping toward a bulbous nose. "Who's this bloke?"

I stood and greeted PS Crusty, giving him my standard introduction. He queried my purpose for being in England, specifically, Village-In-Thistles. The mention of Gloria Butterfield and her unexplained disappearance didn't register with him.

"Before my time."

What impressed him was the presence of Turquoise, granddaughter of the Colonel and Rosemond Bethard, niece of Myles, and daughter of Cissy.

"I heard from my sources, Miss Blix-Vixen, that there's been a bit of a mish-mash up there at Rockingham Manor."

"Yes, Police Sargent Packwood, we might need more than two hours today to sort it all out."

I handed PS Crusty a written synopsis of the investigation and subsequent charges. I proposed first-degree murder for Melba, first-degree assault for Myles, and various levels of assisting the commission of a felony for Rosemond, Cissy, and Bristol. Since we didn't have a corpse, I couldn't accuse Melba of desecration. Besides, Rufford's testimony was based on hearsay of farm animals that were no longer alive.

"Well, bloody hell, I'll need to see some signed written statements from your witnesses, Mister Knuckles. And they better be ready to make an appearance in a court of law, what with the crimes you're accusing the folks up at Rockingham Manor of doing."

Turquoise, Bristol, Pauline, and Rufford stepped forward and handed the law enforcement officer their signed statements. The eyes on PS Crusty's face bulged, and his head vibrated as he read each document. He kept mumbling, bloody hell.

"I think you'll find our evidence more than reasonable and justifies arrests of the named perps," I said. "I might suggest you call in reinforcements, since the folks up at The Rock are a devious and treacherous gang of miscreants."

Packwood looked up at me, his right eyelid pinched shut. "Oi, mate. These are my people, and I don't need your help getting them down to The Nick. Now kindly sod off and let me do my job." I didn't sod off like he asked, rather, I rode with Turquoise to the Manor and arrived as PS Crusty knocked on the big wooden front door. My heart was all a-twitter, anticipating the look on Melba's face when Packwood slapped the iron on her wrists.

Melba went quietly, but the heat from her face could've roasted a pig if it had been on a spit and within ten feet of her. I approached the handcuffed woman as she sat in the backseat of Packwood's police car. Standing eleven feet from the open backseat window, I shouted. "Why'd you do it, Melba?"

The woman turned to me, her eyes sunk deep into their sockets. "Someone had to cover for those weak little boys."

Then the sky opened, the dam broke, and the herd stampeded.

"I came from nothin', and after a lifetime of workin' me fingers to nubs, I still was gonna have nothin.'"

With an unhurried cadence, she described watching the Colonel, and then Myles mismanage the estate. "Those two fools acted like makin' a profit would blind them. Between me, Miss Rosemond, and Cissy, we kept the Manor from the banks and the courts."

"I suspected as much," I said. "But how'd the Colonel convince you to kill Gloria?"

"He didn't."

I felt a grin sprout on my face and then spread like out-of-control kudzu across my puss. "Of course, the Colonel didn't. It was Rosemond, right?"

"Yeah, Mister Genius," Melba said, and then filled in the details. After Bristol turned down the Colonel and left the kitchen, the older man stood over the unconscious Gloria Butterfield, fretting about what to do.

"He got on me last nerve, so I told him to get his arse out of me kitchen and send in his wife. He did as he was told and once again, me and Miss Rosemond took care of a mess made by a Bethard man."

"Killing someone is above and beyond your typical kitchen tasks," I said.

"Why the extreme loyalty to Rosemond?"

Melba rolled her bottom lip as she thought. She then looked at me, and spoke as matter-of-factly as if she were describing a dinner menu. "Miss Rosemond fought for me when I got in the family way. The Colonel wanted to toss me to the cobblestone, but she wouldn't let him. I owed her me life."

"It probably helped your cause that Rosemond had done the old little dittle herself."

I wasn't sure little dittle was British slang for pre-marital sex, but it sure sounded like it.

Melba stretched her body into the open window so her face was closer to mine and whispered. "I'll deny what I told you if you try and squeeze me in front of that copper."

I chuckled. "Not to worry. I don't see Rosemond or you bonding over crumpets and tea much before mid-century, so I don't care. But I do have one last question."

Melba threw her head back against the headrest. "Lock me up now, please, Lord."

"You said Cissy was part of the Rockingham Manor all-female rescue squad. Tell me. Did you use cabbage soup to poison the Count?"

Melba smiled. Her grin looked so out of place on her face that it startled me. "Sorry, Knuckles. You get to solve only one murder mystery this week."

The other arrests at Rockingham Manor weren't as dramatic. Myles Bethard flopped, Miss Rosemond fainted, and PS Crusty Packwood deemed each too frail to survive a prison cell. They were confined to Rockingham Manor and placed under the supervision of Reverend Amethyst.

The Home Beat Officer ordered Cissy to stay on her side of the Manor and report to the Brighton Police Station every Wednesday. He arrested Bristol, however. Apparently, being related to the Bethards only by marriage didn't afford him the same leniency as Myles, Rosemond, and Cissy.

PS Crusty was quite proud that he'd read the statements, executed the arrests, and set the parameters to ensure a fair trial for all accused within his two-hour allocation for Village-In-Thistles. He said he even had time to return to the Pissin' Pints for a pint before hauling Melba and Bristol back to Brighton.

"This is how policin' is done here in the UK," he said to me right before turning the ignition of his patrol car. "We don't need no bloody American playin' Columbo."

Chapter Forty

I ignored PS Crusty's dissin' my role in solving the Butterfield disappearance. I wasn't surprised he said something critical and dismissive. Whether here or back in America, cops generally hated private eyes, disliking our lack of a badge and lone wolf nature. I felt bad about the arrest of Bristol, however, since he came clean and helped further the cause of justice. Rufford surprised me when he came up with a quick way of making Bristol's bail. He swore he could raise the money by selling one of the Manor's Berkshire sows. Turquoise was all in favor of the sale, and it appeared Bristol's pre-trial imprisonment would be short.

Rufford pulled me aside and whispered that a particularly nasty sow who loved to bully him would be shipped to the butcher in the morning. But he said I couldn't say anything so as not to alert the others. "Them Berkshires can be as dangerous as football rowdies on a bender; they can."

I was happy to see Turquoise step up so quickly to take charge of the Manor's business operations. "It looks like you're ready to take over from Grannie Rosemond and Uncle Dipstick," I said to her. "And I think you have the smarts to make a go of it."

The young woman's complexion pinked up. "I must admit I'm actually excited. I want to think my father, the Count, would be cheering for me."

Since my old man left when I was an infant, I couldn't relate to the idea of a supportive father cheering on your success. But I refused to let bad childhood memories sour my sense of accomplishment. After solving a British murder mystery, Nic Knuckles was more than America's premier private investigator. He was now the best criminal investigator in the

English-speaking world.

"What are you going to do now, Mister Knuckles?" Turquoise asked.

"There's only one thing a rugged private eye can do after solving a big case. I'll move on to the next mystery and bring justice to those who'd been deprived of their lives, or in some cases, expose a cheating husband. Maybe I might help close down the illegal gerbil trade. You never know in this private eye business, kid."

Turquoise wished me luck, and we said goodbye to each other. She entered the big stone house, and I headed down the woodland path toward Village-In-Thistles. I wouldn't miss the wild creatures of unknown viciousness hiding in the woods or the stink of the sheep dip, but I'd miss the quiet. You can't find that silence in Queens. The tranquility ended almost as soon as I stepped on the village's cobblestone, when the Bethard Bentley suddenly pulled up next to me, and the open driver-side window revealed a smiling Roland.

"Hey mate, you got a minute?" he asked.

I'd need more than a minute. Inside the Bentley were two women.

"Well, look whose riding in the big car?" I said. "Hello, Rev Amy."

Reverend Amethyst invited me to slide my tuchus into the Bentley and join her. The other woman sitting with her was less excited to see me.

"Hello, Lizabeth," I said.

"Hello, Nic."

I asked the Reverend what was happening, and she admitted she indulged in some corporeal delights by taking a ride in the Bentley before Turquoise sold it. Lizabeth was there for another reason, she explained.

"I saw Miss West working in her garden and had Roland stop so I could chat with her. Our conversation took an unexpected confessional turn, and we agreed that finding you before you departed England was important."

I looked at Lizabeth. "Here I am, Lizzy. What do you have to say?"

Lizabeth folded her hands in her lap, her eyes analyzing her bootlaces. "Having several days and restless nights to consider my behavior during these past two weeks, I wanted to apologize."

Apologies were rare in Nic Knuckle's world, so I tuned my ears exclusively to Lizabeth's wavelength. "Okay. I'm listening."

"While my dire financial position often forced me to behave duplicitously, I regret it came at your expense. I'm sorry."

I thought about asking the woman if she was sorry enough to return my money, but I didn't. Lizabeth looked a hundred percent remorseful, and I didn't need an extra one percent. I also knew that calling her Lizzy greatly irritated her, so I was already ahead on points.

"Okay, Lizzy, I forgive you."

Lizabeth raised her eyes to me. "I did want you to know that my motivation in facilitating the cover-up of Miss Butterfield's murder was not only because of the money. You might recall that prior to Myles marrying the Reverend Amethyst, he had recovered enough from the Butterfield trauma to romantically approach another woman."

I nodded to convey that I recalled her reference, although my notebook was a more trustworthy source than my memory.

"Well, Nic, that woman was twenty-year-old Lizabeth West, newly arrived to the village to care for her aunt."

"Holy Provolone, Lizzy, you say you've been carrying a torch for Myles all these years? If Nic Knuckles carried a torch for every woman that dropped him, Smokey the Bear would've choked on the soot from all the fires."

Lizabeth ignored my admission of romantic failure and continued her story, describing how Rosemond wouldn't have another broke commoner distract her son and demanded Aunt Jane keep her niece away. Lizabeth admitted that she still resents her aunt's failure to support her need for love and affection.

"Although my love for Myles was short-lived, I could never stop wondering, what if? Would we have been happy? Could I have been the woman to help Myles grow a pair? Or, would I've been terribly disappointed and have the Bethard clan crush my self-respect like his current wife?"

I didn't say anything because Nic Knuckles understood how a broken heart can make you do and say stupid things.

"Alright, Lizabeth. I understand your motivation."

"And, Nic, I have one more thing to say."

"Yeah."

"You're a bloody good investigator."

Oh no. Her kindness was unexpected. My mouth went crooked, and my emotions tried to flood my eyes, but I held it all in check. It's a well-known fact that a crying private eye is an unemployed private eye.

"Thanks." I burbled and then quickly turned to Reverend Amethyst. "Now you, Rev, I can't figure out."

She tittered that adorable titter. "Really, me?"

"Yeah, really. Most of the village heard what you always suspected; your husband still was in love with Gloria Butterfield. Now you learn that another woman willingly committed a multitude of sins to protect that bony, decrepit man. How do you not just hide away from the embarrassment of being Myles Bethard's wife?"

I suspected The Rev had pondered that question many times in the past because the answer was ready on her tongue. "How could I preach about the joy of confessing one's sins if I judged those who sought absolution? If I taught my flock that marriage was sacred, especially when times were difficult, how could I not stay true to my own marital vows? And, didn't the Lord instruct us to find the good in everyone, even a weaselly, insipid mama's boy like my husband? If I walked away from Myles, I'd be walking away from my faith and vocation."

I shook my head, impressed with her reasoning. "Being in the God business isn't for sissies, Rev. It's nice you can find some happiness in your misery."

Reverend Amethyst gave up a sad little smile, like the one you see on the faces of Catholic saints right before they get martyred. It was true. Every key did have a keyhole.

"Ladies, I appreciate this conversation," I said. "But we need to wrap it up. Lizzy, I wish you luck in finding a new line of work that doesn't involve skullduggery. And maybe try spending some time at the Pissin' Pints. You never know which pub punter might be looking for a serious woman to make a home."

Lizabeth gave me her patented sneer masquerading as a smile. Boy, oh boy, I wasn't going to miss *that* woman.

"Reverend Amethyst," I said, "I wish you happiness in whatever form you can find it."

"Bless you, Nic Knuckles."

I reached up and tapped Roland on the shoulder. "Take me to the launderette, Roland. I have to prepare for tomorrow night's departure from Heathrow."

An hour and a half later, I was thinking about how fortunate it had been to live above a launderette. After more than two weeks in Village-In-Thistles, my supply of clean underwear had dwindled to the pair covering my tush, and I now sat observing the dryer as it warmed some fresh replacements.

Gram Edwards came down from her kitchen with a plate of cheddar cheese and biscuits to augment the tea I was enjoying. She said she'd miss me, considering I brought so much entertainment into her life with my humbling of the Bethard clan. But she swore my cheese intake cut deeply into her profits.

"Thanks, Gram. You've been an outstanding host. When I get home, I'll definitely five-star you and your fine establishment."

Gram grumbled her gratitude and asked me to verify the gossip she'd heard around the village.

"Is it true Pauline was sellin' her store to pay a bondsman to get Bristol out of the Knick?"

"No, Gram. Rufford and Turquoise are selling one of the hogs."

"I heard Cissy's husband, Dinwiddie, plans to remain at the Manor to assist Turquoise as she manages the estate."

I nodded my head. "I feel confident that Turquoise will rise to the occasion, whether Mister Dinwiddie helps or not. Besides, he should have his hands full keeping Cissy out of further trouble."

Gram swallowed a mouthful of tea. "I understand Roland moved upstairs in Melba's apartment, and he and that nutter, Rufford, are both pretty cuffed being together."

"I can't confirm that rumor, but I hope it's true. Roland and Rufford getting together is the only happy part of this story."

Gram's eyes narrowed, and she hummed a low note. "I wonder who'll be doin' their cookin' now that Melba's gone?"

"Maybe that's another line of business for you, Gram, catering haggis to the wealthy."

"I hated cookin' haggis when me Jimmy was alive, so I don't think so. But with Melba not workin' at the Manor, maybe I can get the folks up there to send me their laundry."

The smile on Gram Edwards' face stretched the wrinkles so tight she looked twenty years younger. "That's a whole boatload of changes for the toff living at the Manor," she said. "I might be greatly increasin' me wealth goin' forward."

"I'm happy for you, Gram."

The woman looked at me, her head cocked to one side. "You must feel good yourself, tying up all the loose ends so neat and tidy like you did."

"I wish that were true," I said. "I still haven't figured out how I'm telling my client that her big sister was brutally murdered."

"That's a hard one, dearie. No one wants to hear that bit of news."

"That's not as difficult as explaining why there aren't remains to bring home to bury."

Gram snickered. "Oh my, that was dead sick, that was."

I felt my stomach pinch. "You Brits have a way of doing things, don't you?"

Gram raised her hands to her face. "I'm a wee lass from the Highlands, Nic. Even after all the years living here, I'm still an outsider to these villagers."

I bit off a piece of cheese but didn't let chewing it interfere with my talking. "That's one thing I love about New York City. Once you develop the proper cynical attitude, no matter if you just arrived a year before, you're a New Yorker."

Gram and I swapped opinions on living in the big city versus the wee village, concluding that both had advantages. I liked the anonymity, while Gram preferred knowing what was happening in the village because it gave her a competitive business edge.

"What about you, Nic? What's your plan?"

"I don't know what will happen next for me," I said. "Being America's premier private investigator means I'll probably be on a new case within hours after I get home."

Gram looked at me and chuckled. "Hours, you say? Blimey, Nic, don't go tellin' tales now."

Dang, I could never lie to an older woman. That was why I seldom visited my mother. I'd cough up the truth about my life as soon as I entered the room, and she'd belittle me, and I'd run off in tears. Five minutes was the longest visit I had with her in the last year.

"Okay, it might be weeks or months before my next case, but I have plans to use my vast knowledge as a private eye to earn a steadier living."

"What you gonna do, dearie?"

I cleared my mouth of food and announced that I intended to become an educator. "I plan to open a school where I'll teach the youth of America the fine art of criminal investigation."

Gram snickered. "So, you're gonna be one of those internet influencers, singin' and dancin'?"

"No, Gram, I'm going to be an educator, a professor, a molder of young minds."

"My my, Nic, you have a high opinion of yourself, you do."

I had to admit Gram's doubts were starting to hurt my feelings. Why shouldn't I be confident about my new endeavor? By finding the person who killed Gloria Butterfield, I solved a decades-old murder without relying on DNA magic, tracking cell towers, or even fingerprints.

"I think I have much to offer the next generation of investigators," I said. "Who knows, maybe I can pass on my knowledge to the next Nic Knuckles."

"Why don't you try clonin' yourself, laddie? You know, it'd be cheaper and faster than you giving out caps and gowns to teenagers," Gram said, barely keeping from spitting her tea; she was enjoying her mockery so much.

I placed my teacup on the table, my irritation at its peak. "In America, when some blond girl disappears, and she has either a dodgy boyfriend, or a blank-eyed mother, or a mouth-breathing stepfather, hundreds of untrained sleuths on the internet start working the case. They don't know what they're doing and create problems for the professionals. It's a potential gold mine, teaching all those ignorant but earnest crimefighters."

Gram still missed the brilliance of my idea, and I think she did it purposely. "Will you field a sports team with cheerleaders at Nic Knuckles U?" she asked. "What will you have as a mascot, a dancin' magnifying glass?"

I felt more heat coming off my face than the dryer in front of me, and my response was equally heated. "I'd be satisfied teaching the eager law-abiding citizen-sleuths' good basic investigative techniques," I said. "That is all I want to do."

Gram must've finally noticed the brittleness in my voice because she stopped her nonsense and skittered back to her kitchen, returning with a small plate in hand. "It's the last of me cheese, Nic, I thought you might enjoy it."

I stared at Gram and her peace offering, still frosted at her goofing on my future plans. It got suddenly quiet when the dryer in front of me shut off, and my clean undies slowed and tumbled to the bottom of the drum. I guess it was my move.

"I will miss your cheese," I mumbled, as I took the plate from her. "And you were a good friend to me."

Gram smiled and switched up topics to move us further along the road to reconciliation.

"Are you ready for your flight home?" Gram asked. "You need me to press a shirt or block your fedora?"

"I'm good, Gram. I'm almost packed, I have my transportation to the airport plotted out, and I just need to print off my boarding pass."

"That's a long day and night of travelin', Nic. How you gonna keep that squirrel-like mind of yours entertained for all those hours?"

"Good point. I do need to pick up something to read on the train and the flight."

Gram said she had a collection of paperback books left by previous travelers. I could find one there that'd hold my attention for all those hours.

"Do you have a copy of Jane Eyre?"

Gram laughed. "You must be psychic, lad, because I got a pile of them. Almost every American female English Lit major has left a copy here. You want one?"

I smiled. "That'd be wicked, Gram, just bloody wicked."

Acknowledgments

Steven Packwood

Also by William Ade

PREVIOUSLY PUBLISHED WORKS (as William Ade):
   The Man Who Fixed Things (2023)
   The Inevitable Failure of Jonathan Golding (2022)
   Do It for Daisy (2021)
   No Time for His Nonsense (2019)
   Art of Absolution (2019)

PREVIOUSLY PUBLISHED WORKS (as Nic Knuckles):
   Big Scream in a Small Town (2023)

About the Author

William Ade was born and raised in a large family in small town Indiana during the fifties and sixties; an experience that strongly influences his writing. While attending graduate school at the University of Illinois, he met and married his wife, Cindy and following graduation, they headed to the East Coast. After settling in Northern Virginia, they raised two children into adulthood. Those years of love and life also influences many of his stories.

Ade's latest novel, written as Nic Knuckles, is *Big Scream in a Wee Village* and is the second in the Nic Knuckles Collection published by Level Best Books (LBB). LBB also published *Big Scream in a Small Town* (2023), and, *Do It for Daisy* in 2021. Other novels by the author includes, *The Man Who Fixed Things* (2023), *Art of Absolution* (2019), and the serialized *The Inevitable Failure of Jonathan Golding* (2022). His short story collection, *No Time for His Nonsense* was released in 2019. His short story, *Punch Drunk*, was part of the 2024 *Chesapeake Crimes: Three Strikes – You're Dead* anthology, and his story, *Maggie and Rick* will appear in the *Malice Domestic Presents: Murder Most Humorous* anthology in April 2025. Other short stories have appeared in *Mysteries Unimagined*, the *Rind Literary Magazine*, *The Broken Plate*, *Black Fox*

Literary, Mindscapes Unimagined, and the 2018 and 2019 *Best New England Crime Stories.*

AUTHOR WEBSITE:
  Writing as Nic Knuckles
  https://nicknucklespi.com/
  Eclectic Stories for the Humans at billade.com

SOCIAL MEDIA HANDLES:
  TikTok: WmAdeAuthor@williamade945
  Instagram: williamade87
  Facebook: william87
  As Nic Knuckles:
  Website at https://nicknucklespi.com/
  Tiktok.com/@ nic.knuckles